"Shh! Stop!"

He pressed a finger gently to her lips, making her heart race and her mouth instantly desperate for his kiss. "You have no need to apologize for anything, so I do not wish to hear it, Lady Cecily." His hand fell away. "Whatever you may have done, responsibility for it rests with me, for I was the one who—"

"Shh!" Now it was her turn to silence him. Greatly daring, she lifted her finger and touched it to his warm lips.

Instantly, and seemingly without forethought, he pursed his lips and kissed her finger. She snatched it away, blushing, yet knew that both her finger and her own lips were tingling from his touch, and that every nerve in her body was suddenly alive and begging for more.

There was a breathless silence, during which they looked at each other, both seemingly frozen. She was acutely aware that they were in the gallery, where fellow guests and servants might appear at any instant. If not for that...

Author Note

Welcome to the third in my series featuring ladies from Ledbury House. Each book can be read separately. In book one, *The Earl's Runaway Governess*, Marianne arrives as the new governess to Lady Cecily Thornhill, then aged just twelve. Book two, *Rags-to-Riches Wife*, features Marianne's personal maid, Jane, who is called to visit wealthy relatives in the north. This book, *Captivating the Cynical Earl*, focuses on Lady Cecily herself, who is now aged twenty and has recently returned from visiting her friend Nell at Christmas—as those of you who have read "A Midnight Mistletoe Kiss" (part of the *Christmas Cinderellas* collection) will know.

CATHERINE TINLEY

—

Captivating the Cynical Earl

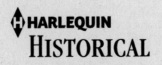

HARLEQUIN®
HISTORICAL™

Recycling programs
for this product may
not exist in your area.

ISBN-13: 978-1-335-40728-3

Captivating the Cynical Earl

Copyright © 2021 by Catherine Tinley

This edition published by arrangement with Harlequin Books S.A.

For questions and comments about the quality of this book,
please contact us at CustomerService@Harlequin.com.

Harlequin Enterprises ULC
22 Adelaide St. West, 40th Floor
Toronto, Ontario M5H 4E3, Canada
www.Harlequin.com

Printed in U.S.A.

Catherine Tinley has loved reading and writing since childhood, and has a particular fondness for love, romance and happy endings. She lives in Ireland with her husband, children, dog and kitten, and can be reached at catherinetinley.com, as well as through Facebook and on Twitter, @catherinetinley.

Books by Catherine Tinley

Harlequin Historical

A Waltz with the Outspoken Governess

The Ladies of Ledbury House

The Earl's Runaway Governess
Rags-to-Riches Wife
Christmas Cinderellas
"A Midnight Mistletoe Kiss"
Captivating the Cynical Earl

The Chadcombe Marriages

Waltzing with the Earl
The Captain's Disgraced Lady
The Makings of a Lady

This is my lockdown book, and as I was writing,
I was continually aware of the everyday heroes
keeping us all going during the pandemic.
Those in health care, essential retail, social care,
education, public services, and science
and research, and the other unsung and
unrecognized heroes. Thank you all.

Chapter One

'People of our class do not marry for *love*.'

Augustus Henry John (Jack) Beresford, Eighth Earl of Hawkenden set down his wine and glared at his younger brother, who made no reply. Outrage and shock warred within him. *Tom is married, and thinks himself 'in love'? Lord, what a fix!*

'Tell me this is a jest, Tom, designed to make me laugh.'

Tom shook his head, his hesitant smile fading. 'It is true. I am lately married. I did write to inform you of it, Jack. Indeed, I have not as yet made any public announcement as I wished to ensure you were the first to know in London.'

The two men were shut away in Jack's library in the London townhouse, seated facing one another in matching armchairs. Outside, darkness was falling, and the servants had closed the shutters against the chill of early spring. Tom had accepted Jack's offer of wine but had seemed unusually nervous. Jack now understood why.

'You know I am just returned from France,' he declared bluntly. 'I have not yet opened my correspondence.' Jack's hands tightened on the arms of the chair as disbelief gave way to anger. 'How could you marry like that, without as much as discussing it with me beforehand?'

Tom's eyes flashed. 'Because,' he rejoined haughtily, 'I need no man's permission to marry. Our parents are long dead, and I am eight-and-twenty years old. I reached my majority many years ago, brother!'

Jack blinked. This was most unlike Tom, who would normally consult him on anything of importance. 'As head of the family, I would expect—'

'Head of the family, is it? We both forswore that nonsense after Papa's death!' Tom's face had reddened a little, and he sat straighter in his chair. 'You may be the Earl, but we both know that Papa—the *former* head of the family— had quite ruined your inheritance. People of our *class*,' Tom added pointedly, 'do not take such an active role in matters of business as we do.'

'That is different.'

'How? How is it different?'

At that moment, Jack, strangely, could not find the words. 'It just is.'

'Pah!' Tom's dismissive gesture was one that would have led to a fist fight when he was eight and Jack ten. Now that they were twenty-eight and thirty, that would be entirely inappropriate. Still, bile rising within him, Jack considered for a moment how satisfying it would be to draw his brother's cork. Manfully, he resisted the impulse.

Why could Tom not see how important this was? Marriage was the single biggest decision a man could make. A lifelong commitment, with implications for the entire family. Why had he gone ahead without even telling Jack? He looked Tom in the eye. 'So who is she?'

'Who is who?' Tom's dander was definitely up.

'Your dear lady wife.' Jack's lip curled. 'And, more to

the point, how much has it cost me—cost *us*—in marriage settlements?'

Tom gritted his teeth. 'You will speak of Nell with respect, or we shall not speak of her at all!'

'Let us not speak of her at all, then!' Jack flashed back.

'As you wish.' There was a silence. The clock ticked, and the fire spat. Between the brothers the air was tight with unspoken words.

After a long moment Tom rose, set down his glass and adjusted his cuffs. 'I shall wish you goodday, brother.' With the shallowest of bows, he turned on his heel and marched out, vexation writ clearly in the tense lines of his figure.

The door closed behind him with a loud click, and the Earl stared at it for a long moment, scarcely able to take in what had just occurred. His hands gripped the arms of his chair. *Tom, married? Never!*

He could barely take it in. He and Tom were close—much closer than many of their friends were to their own families. Or, at least, so Jack had thought.

Lady Cecily Thornhill was in a fix. Having carefully counted out what remained of this month's allowance, she now knew it would not be enough. Leaning both elbows on the fine mahogany table, she cradled her head in her hands.

Lord, how are we to manage this time?

Once again, Cecily had had to use her own precious funds to settle her mama's accounts, leaving her purse almost empty. Under usual circumstances—had they been staying at Ledbury House, where she had been born, for example—she might have managed until next month's allowance arrived. But they were in London and were expected to attend routs and balls and Almack's, suitably attired, as well as paying for their hotel. All of that required money. Money that was now in short supply.

She lifted her head and addressed her mama, who was currently sipping tea from a fine china cup. 'Mama, why did you order that new bonnet?' Her tone was low, and she tried hard to keep the frustration from showing. Mama had just returned from visiting with one of her friends and had sunk into a satin-covered chair with some relief, declaring that her feet ached.

'Because I liked it, of course! Lord, what a foolish question! Why does any lady order new clothes?' She laughed for a long moment at her own wit then, realising her daughter had remained stony-faced, her eyes narrowed suspiciously. 'Cecily, never say you have *paid* for it!'

'Well, of course I have! I was never so mortified as when Mrs Newcomb the milliner came to see you today to ask for payment.'

'Oh, for goodness' sake, child! I declare you have the soul of a cit! People like us do not *need* to settle our bills on time, because the likes of Mrs Newcomb knows that to have the patronage of *me*, Lady Fanny Thornhill, Dowager Countess of Kingswood, does much more for her business than a trivial bill for a bonnet that, on reflection, was not as pretty as I had believed it to be.'

'But, Mama, you cannot afford another bonnet.' Cecily spoke quietly but firmly. She had never won this particular argument but refused to concede defeat.

'Of course I can! For eight years—since the very day your father died—people have been telling me that I cannot afford things, that I must practise economy and be sensible with my allowance. And I have continued to live in *exactly* the way I want to, and yet none of these dire predictions, such as bankruptcy, have come to pass.'

'But that is because other people have helped you. Your friends, and Ash—'

'Ash evicted us from our home. The least he can do is to pay my bills now and again.'

'Mama, please. That is unfair, and you know it. As the new Earl, Ash was perfectly entitled to move into Ledbury House, as you are well aware. He and Marianne have made it clear that we can stay there any time we wish, and the dower house remains at your disposal.'

Marianne, who had first come to Ledbury House as governess to the then twelve-year-old Cecily, became Lady Kingswood soon afterwards. She and Ash had provided a refuge for Cecily and her mother over the years, on the occasions when Lady Fanny's financial difficulties became too pressing.

Lady Fanny dismissed this with a wave of her hand. 'Pah! I have no wish to visit the wilds of tedious Bedfordshire. I should much rather be here in London now the season is almost upon us.'

'The season will not properly begin for nearly a month. We really had no need to arrive so soon. And, besides, how shall we pay for it all?' One hand to her brow, Cecily indicated the luxurious suite they were currently renting. 'How much will it cost to stay here, in one of the most expensive hotels in London? We have been here only a week, and already I cannot sleep easily at night for worrying about the cost.' She bit back the harsher words she wished to say to her mama.

Oh, if only I had the freedom to manage our money!

Over the years, with Ash's support, she had engaged in learning as much as she could about matters of finance and had occasionally even advised Ash on dilemmas to do with business. She had, she knew, an aptitude for such matters, although it meant little in the face of her mama's spending habits.

Lady Fanny tilted her head to one side. 'You know, Cecily, if I could not distinctly remember the agonies of birthing you, I would wonder if you were my child at all. I simply do not understand why you should worry about such trivialities.'

Since Fanny and Cecily looked quite alike—both fair-haired and rosy-cheeked, although Cecily's eyes were amber while her mama's were blue—this required no comment from Cecily. She did, however, object to her mama's characterisation of their eternally perilous finances.

'Trivialities! Why—'

'Enough.' Lady Fanny's tone brooked no further disagreement. 'This very day I have managed to secure an invitation for us to stay with one of my friends.'

Cecily's shoulders sagged in relief. 'Who is it?'

'You should have more faith in me, child. I always contrive in the end.'

'Whom are we to stay with?'

Lord, please let it be with someone sensible!

'With Beatrice—Mrs Godwin. It seems she enjoyed our company so much at Christmastide that she wishes to invite us to stay with her while she searches for a townhouse to buy. She has rented a delightful place in Piccadilly—she received a generous settlement when Mr Beresford married her stepdaughter, you know. Young Nell and her husband are also in Town.'

Cecily did know. Her dear friend Nell Godwin, Beatrice's stepdaughter, had fallen hopelessly in love with Mr Beresford over Christmas. To Cecily's great surprise, they had been married within weeks of meeting each other. At the time, Cecily could not feel easy about it, and had worried that Nell's haste would turn out to be a mistake.

The Hon. Thomas Beresford, while appearing entirely gentlemanlike, had managed to upset Nell on more than one occasion during the Yuletide festivities. Nell had become ill with distress, and only her reconciliation with Mr Beresford had made Nell contented again. Nell's letters indicated that she and her Tom were now perfectly happy together and had no regrets about their swift marriage.

'We shall move to Mrs Godwin's house on the morrow,' Lady Fanny declared. 'I know you will supervise the maids and ensure all is packed and ready, Cecily.'

'Yes, Mama.' Cecily's mind was already focusing on their move, other considerations being put to one side for now. 'I shall send for them this instant.' She tried not to sigh. Another move. Another temporary home. Still, her money worries were lessened. For the present, anyway.

Jack released a breath. Rising from his chair, he crossed the room and poured himself another generous measure of wine. His mind was still reeling from his brother's unexpected—and entirely unwelcome—news. Rummaging through the correspondence on his desk, he found two letters in Tom's familiar hand. Without bothering to sit down again, he broke the seals and read them both.

Her name was Godwin. Miss Eleanor Godwin, of Chiddingstone, Kent. *Nell*, Tom had called her. The name conjured up an image of a buxom farmer's daughter, with dimples and a fetching apron. Godwin…the surname was vaguely familiar, yet at this moment, Jack could not think why. Miss Eleanor Godwin was not, however, one of the known heiresses on the marriage mart. Those names he half-knew, as he would probably have to select one for his Countess. This being his thirtieth year, he had decided recently that he would begin his own search for a suitable wife this very season.

It was inconceivable that Tom had married, and not, it seemed, for riches. Unless—could this Godwin woman be wealthy, but *not* of a good family? Despite their agreed need to increase the family fortune, that would almost be worse. Would Tom really do such a disservice to the family name?

So why, then? Why had Tom done this? The worst possibility was that Tom had not been jesting when he had said he had married for love. *Love?* The very notion was nonsensical. It was madness, pure and simple, and Jack had never taken Tom to be a madman. Or a fool. Jack simply could not countenance it. Tom, believing himself to be 'in love', like the cloth-heads he had derided in Almack's last season, and the season before? How could his brother have succumbed to the same madness, even though he had seen it afflict others? *Impossible.*

Tom, like Jack, *knew*—understood completely—that love was not real. Oh, their mama had probably loved them before her death. Jack was willing to accept that warm maternal instincts probably existed. He had only the haziest memories of her—memories that were, to be fair, vaguely positive. However, the fact that she had deserted them by dying at an irresponsibly young age meant that Jack could not in all honesty attest to her having loved them. Somewhere deep inside Jack, the absence from Mama's abandonment still ached.

Papa, on the other hand, had offered his sons the courtesy of dying fairly recently—the year Jack had achieved his coming of age, in fact. By that stage Papa had enjoyed many years of punishing—and ignoring—both his sons. Much as Jack had hated school, he had always felt a sense of escaping from home at the start of each new term. At least at school the tormentors had not been family members.

The sense of relief when his father had finally had the grace to die—overturning his carriage while taking a bend much too fast—had quickly been replaced by shock at the mass of debts Papa had accumulated. Jack and Tom had vowed to restore the family fortunes by entering the world of commerce and had worked closely together to build what was rapidly becoming a substantial network of businesses.

No, 'love' was not something that existed. Tom knew this as well as Jack did. So why the sorry tale of marrying some wench 'for love'?

Could Miss Godwin truly be a simple country miss with little to recommend her beyond a pretty face and a good figure? If so, Tom would not have shown her more than a passing interest, surely? Such women were ten-a-penny in London each season. Even now, matchmaking mamas would be dragging unpromising virgins to dressmakers and milliners to try and disguise the girls' limitations and falsely advertise them to potential suitors during the upcoming season. Jack had seen it every year since his coming of age, and it never ceased to amaze him how the most limited of young ladies sometimes managed to find a spouse. A winning smile and a neat ankle was enough, it seemed, to turn previously rational men into idiots.

He and Tom had used to laugh about it, and even on occasion to wager on the progress of some or other Incomparable, trying to predict which enamoured fool would be unlucky enough to win her hand. Being a logical creature, Jack had no time for such nonsense and neither, he had believed, had Tom. Indeed, they had spoken of it, many times. Their pact had been to devote their energies to restoring the family fortunes and they had agreed to not allow themselves to be distracted by ladies—beyond, of course, the fleeting *affaires* that were commonplace among the *ton*. Marriage could wait.

Yet here was his brother, with the appearance of sincerity, informing Jack that not only had he married but he had married for *love*. It simply could not be true. Therefore, there had to be some other reason why Tom had spouted such nonsense.

Throwing the letters down in disgust, Jack paced the floor, his long legs eating up the space. Five strides. Turn. Five more. When Jack had left for France three months ago, Tom had given him no hint of this. So what reason could there be for Tom to have married this Godwin wench, and so quickly?

The anger he was feeling towards his brother was laced with confusion, as he considered again the seeming sincerity with which Tom had declared himself to be enamoured of his wife. Jack's brow creased. Tom was not as heedless as to throw all away on the basis of a sudden *tendre*. It was not in his character. Jack pondered this, running a hand through his thick, dark hair. Tom had never before, to his knowledge, thought himself 'in love'. Like Jack, he was a rational man who had no room for such nonsense. There must be more to this.

He frowned. Might this girl—this Eleanor Godwin— have some hold over him? At this moment he could not think what would induce Tom to marry in haste, hide it from his only relative, then spout nonsense about 'love' to justify it. Yet the alternative—that his hitherto sensible brother actually believed himself enamoured of this unknown girl—did not bear thinking about.

He refilled his glass and drank long and deeply. Staring into the fire, his fingers drumming on the desk, all at once inspiration came to him. Perhaps Tom had compromised the chit. Like Jack, Tom had had his fair share of amorous adventures, but they normally focused on women who understood that marriage would not be an option. Could Tom have been so foolish as to have pursued a girl he ought to have avoided? He groaned at the thought of Tom caught seducing some willing wench, and an outraged father forcing them both to the altar. Or, indeed, forcing Tom only, for such cases were, he understood, generally deliberately engineered by the enterprising young lady and her avaricious parents.

Ah, Tom, why did you not come to me?

The answer came to him immediately. Tom would have been mortified to find himself trapped in such a way, and his pride would probably have prevented him from confiding even in his own brother. Besides, Jack had been out of the country, and for an unusually long period. Generally, Tom and Jack had been inseparable these many years, ever since Tom had joined Jack in Herald's Hall Boarding School—or Hell's Hall, as the scholars had dubbed it.

Entrapment. The notion sent a shiver down Jack's spine. If it were true, then the person or persons responsible would pay. His fingers tightened into a fist. Noticing, he slowly unlocked it, reminding himself to be cautious. If this Godwin family had indeed successfully trapped the Hon. Thomas Beresford into marriage, then they had to have been clever, for Tom was no fool. Not usually, at least.

Searching his memory for any signs of coercion in Tom's account, he was disturbed to find that there had been none. Tom had had every appearance of sincerity. He toyed again with the possibility that Tom genuinely thought himself to be 'in love', then dismissed it almost instantly. He and Tom were of one mind on such matters. So whatever rationale had been behind Tom's hasty decision to become leg-shackled, Tom was determined to conceal it from his own brother.

Very well. Now, how to remedy the situation? His brow creased. Marriage was so…so *permanent*. Even if it had been simply a betrothal, Jack would have contrived a way for the girl to cry off—yes, even at considerable expense. If the greedy Godwins had planned to milk him for life, he would have found a way to make the betrothal so intolerable that they would have changed their minds. Paying off a disgruntled betrothed lady would still have been cheaper in the long run than Tom burdening himself with a wife!

Marriage, Jack knew, was a business transaction. It involved the transfer of money, land and property in exchange for security and a good position in society. Jack himself would have to marry—to a well-behaved girl of impeccable bloodlines and substantial wealth. As Earl of Hawkenden, with a good fortune and an appearance that many ladies found pleasing, he understood that once he decided to wed, he would have the pick of that season's tiresome virgins. The earldom must be passed on to a son, so he would in time require an heir for the considerable wealth he and Tom had been assiduously building.

Tom's unexpected tidings might alter the case. Jack frowned. Marry he must—but perhaps not yet. If this season had to be spent addressing Tom's encumbrances, then so be it. Something inside, he recognised, was relieved at the notion that perhaps he could delay playing empty games of courtship for another season, yet the expectation of securing an heir still weighed heavily upon him.

His dalliances to date had been with willing widows and courtesans, and he found the Almack's virgins to be insipid and uninspiring. *Hmm…* Never one to shirk his responsibilities, Jack recognised the selfish wish to avoid the parson's mousetrap for a while longer, although thirty, he had always believed, was the right age for an earl to choose a wife.

He could not hold back a bark of bitter laughter. Here he was, avoiding the notion of matrimony, yet Tom had hastened to the altar without as much as a by-your-leave. The irony was clear. As Earl, he *had* to wed, but Tom had no need to marry at all.

If Tom's marriage was real, and unalterable, then some of their carefully earned wealth could be wasted, thrown away on an undeserving chit who would likely cost a small fortune on her upkeep—not to mention the considerable expense of any children that came along.

Unnecessary children. A nephew could, of course, become Jack's heir, but the notion did not sit comfortably with him. *Marry he must, and he would damn well sire his own heir!*

Wishing his as yet unborn nieces and nephews to perdition, Jack considered the problem, his quick mind continuing to puzzle over this unexpected turn of events. He and Tom had always been of one mind on serious matters. Marriage, he mused, had certainly not been on Tom's horizon the last time they had met. Tom had been preparing to travel to a Christmas party—somewhere in Kent, Jack now recalled.

Jack's three-month journey to visit their various holdings and business interests in France had been fruitful—although it had lasted longer than he had originally anticipated. He had enjoyed a quiet Paris Christmas, far removed from any disturbing reminders of how Christmas 'should be'. He had no time for such nonsense.

Merton, his man of business, had kept all of the London-based financial threads from tangling, but Tom and Jack now needed to pick up those threads and make decisions on a wide range of matters. In the coming days Jack had intended to spend a great deal of his time with Tom and Merton, working through all of the various strands of the business empire. Tom's marriage and the resulting quarrel interfered with those plans and necessitated a change in Jack's priorities.

'Damnation!' Setting down his glass, he rang the bell for his valet. Now that he and Tom had disagreed so vigorously, it even made it temporarily more difficult for him to gain an introduction to his unwelcome sister-in-law. Nevertheless, he would manage it. Somehow.

Chapter Two

'It is such a joy to see you!' Nell's hug was just as warm and genuine as ever, and Cecily was delighted to sense the happiness radiating from her friend.

'When we arrived in London,' Nell continued, 'I knew you would be the first person I should like to call upon—and the fact that you are now staying with Beatrice makes it much easier. I shall visit both of you at the same time and mean to do so regularly.'

'I am glad to hear it!' Cecily smiled at her friend. 'When did you arrive in the city?'

'The day before yesterday. We have been busy—er, settling into our house. Like Beatrice, we have rented a place for the season, although eventually Tom wishes to buy a townhouse for us. We are in Duke Street, a little further out, but it will suit us very well.'

Cecily glanced across the room at Mama and Beatrice. Mrs Godwin was ringing the bell to ask for tea. 'Is it strange to be your stepmama's guest? Instead of being simply her stepdaughter, I mean.'

Nell laughed. 'Being a married lady has brought me many new experiences.' She looked a little mysterious for an instant, then giggled. 'Some of them are rather disconcerting.'

'Strangely, you look exactly the same,' Cecily declared. 'I am unsure why, but I thought that being married would make you look different somehow.'

Nell smiled. 'I do feel different, it is true.'

There was the smallest of pauses, and Cecily could not think what to say. While being around Mama meant that she was more aware than most young ladies of the goings-on of the *ton*, some of the mysteries of marriage were still unknown to her. 'What a pretty dress!' she offered. 'But have you no new clothes that are more suited to your status as a married lady?'

Nell smoothed her printed muslin morning gown, sighing. 'It is true that as a young matron I can now wear more colours and different styles—yet I am still wearing my missish dresses. It is one of the many consequences of having married so quickly.' Her face brightened. 'Now that I am in London, I shall have such fun ordering new clothes! Do come with me to visit the dressmakers!'

'Of course I shall. What an adventure!' They chatted on, eventually agreeing to meet the next day to visit various London dressmakers. Cecily, naturally, had no intention of making any purchases. Mama had bought her a few new dresses, but much of her wardrobe was from last year. She felt no envy towards Nell, who could now, it seemed, afford the best of everything. Last season's dresses would do her very well.

'I do have an evening gown that will be suitable for tonight, although it may be the last time I get to wear it. Wearing grown-up clothes also means saying farewell to some of my favourite young-lady gowns. Are you going to Lady Jersey's soirée tonight, Cecily?'

'Eh? What's that?' Mama, her hearing acute when something of relevance was under discussion, interrupted.

Nell opened her mouth to reply, but her stepmama intervened. 'Lady Jersey has invited a select few to her house tonight for the first soirée of the season. Although the season will begin properly at the end of the month, Town is already surprisingly busy.' Beatrice preened a little, smoothing her fair hair. 'I shall, naturally, be attending. I have secured invitations for both myself and my stepdaughter, but I have not yet told Lady Jersey of Nell's marriage.' She giggled. 'I cannot wait to reveal to everyone that she has managed to catch the brother of an earl!'

Oh, dear.

Ignoring Nell's flushed reaction to her stepmother's vulgarity, Cecily focused on more pressing concerns. They had not been invited, yet Beatrice had. Her mama would be displeased.

'Hmm,' mused Mama, 'I must pay an afternoon visit to her ladyship later.'

Cecily, with some determination, refused to allow a pained expression to cross her face. Mama could be rather…*direct* at times.

'I do hope you will be invited,' said Nell softly. 'My husband is already committed to meeting some of his own friends tonight, so I shall be with Beatrice at the soirée.' Her mouth turned down a little at the corners. 'Now that we are in London, he and I shall have less time together than before, I think. Tom has many matters of business to attend to, and friends he must not neglect. As do I!' She smiled. 'I am so happy that we are in London together!'

Cecily nodded. 'London is always more tolerable when we are both here at the same time.' They hugged spontaneously, Cecily's heart warming at being with her dear friend again.

'Now then, girls,' Beatrice called briskly from her settee, frowning at their unseemly display of affection. 'Come and join us, for I need your advice about what to wear tonight.'

With a quick shared glance, they crossed the room to the older ladies, and had no further opportunity for private conversation. A little later, Nell departed. She had arranged to meet her husband for tea, as they would not be together in the evening, and she did not wish to be late.

'Well!' Beatrice was all smiles after her stepdaughter's departure. 'Nell is in high spirits, I think. I am glad of it.'

'And why should she not be, with such a fine-looking young gentleman as her husband?' Cecily's mama adopted a knowing air. 'I do hope he is entertaining her well these nights.'

Beatrice laughed, a hand over her mouth. 'My dear Fanny, you are positively shocking!'

Mama grinned. 'I know. But have you seen those Beresford boys? Those thighs! That bottom!' She sighed. 'If I were but ten years younger…' They both laughed raucously.

Cecily, as she often did when Mama's conversation became too warm, kept her head down and pretended not to understand them. The meaning was clear, however. They were referring to Nell and her husband's marital activities. Was that what Nell had meant when she had referred to many new experiences?

'Cecily!' Mama's tone was sharp. 'You are daydreaming again, child! We shall go to Lady Jersey's in a quarter of an hour, so go and make yourself ready. And remember, your behaviour and appearance reflects on *me*, so make sure you do not disappoint me!'

Cecily suppressed a sigh.

Am I never to be a person in my own right?
'Yes, Mama.'

Jack, having submitted to his valet's ministrations for what felt like the longest half-hour of his life, sighed with relief when the man finally helped him into his plain black evening jacket. It was new, commissioned for the season, and was uncomfortably tight. With an unvoiced curse towards the absent tailor, Jack dismissed his valet. 'You may go.'

As soon as the valet had departed, Jack crossed to the side table in his spacious bedroom and picked up the letters from Tom. He had brought them upstairs when he had left the library, knowing he would read and reread them, searching for clues as to Tom's state of mind. Quickly selecting the earlier letter, his long fingers deftly unfolded the paper. This was the communication where Tom had talked of his wedding, and Jack wished to again check the date.

What he read made his blood turn cold. They had married at the end of January, yet to his knowledge Tom had only met the girl when he'd travelled to Kent for Christmas. He had married the creature after knowing her for only one month. *A single month?* He frowned. Not enough time for him to have got her with child and her family knowing of it.

Leaving the bedroom, he strode along the landing then down the ornate staircase, his eyes sliding over the enormous paintings adorning the walls. In the hallway, the footman was waiting, and Jack donned his cloak, hat and top boots without a word. Outside, the carriage awaited.

'Where to tonight, sir?' The coachman holding open the carriage door, clad in a multi-caped greatcoat and a neat hat, looked appropriately neat and well turned-out, as befitted the Earl's status.

Jack climbed neatly into the carriage and settled himself on the silk damask-covered seat before replying. 'First, my club, then to Lady Jersey's.'

Chapter Three

For the second time in just a few hours, Cecily followed her mama out of the carriage and up the shallow stone steps to Lady Jersey's well-appointed townhouse in Berkeley Square. She and Mama had paid an afternoon call and come away having secured gracious invitations to tonight's party. Cecily had to admit that her mama's charm had not lost its potency. Lady Fanny was received everywhere and knew just how to make friends with the most influential people in society.

As they had been driving away in the rumbling carriage earlier, sunset had gleamed red-gold on the mottled trunks of the plane trees in the beautiful gardens. The trees were already in bud, their knobbly branches swelling with green shoots and hopefulness.

It is springtime, Cecily reminded herself now. *A time of new beginnings and fresh starts.* She was looking forward to an evening in Nell's company.

An hour later, and Cecily declared herself content. The company and entertainment were good, the ratafia and wine plentiful, and both Cecily and Nell were enjoying the pre-season gathering of those members of the *ton* who had decided to return to London early.

Although she would never say so, Cecily was secretly rather glad that Mr Beresford was at his club tonight, for it gave her the chance to spend some pleasant time with Nell.

Word had not yet circulated about Nell's marriage, for which she seemed grateful, preferring the anonymity of a place among the debutantes. Mr Beresford was informing his brother of the marriage, and until he did so there was to be no London announcement. Even Mrs Godwin had agreed to be silent on the matter—for now.

Cecily and Nell, at twenty and nineteen, would be considered almost beyond redemption in the Marriage Mart— young ladies who had failed to secure a husband in either of their previous seasons. This was despite the fact that Nell's papa had died—rather inconveniently, it had to be said—just as Nell had turned seventeen, and so she had missed out on making her debut. From next week Nell would wear an elegant matron's gown and a lace cap at evenings such as these, marking her as a married lady, but for now the gathering throng in Lady Jersey's elegant drawing rooms would assume them both to be unwed.

Tonight, Cecily was wearing an evening gown of pale blue crape, trimmed with rich lace and embroidery, and finished with an overdress of celestial blue gauze. Her fair hair was piled upon her head, with ringleted side curls framing her face, and her evening gloves, satin slippers, silk stockings and delicate fan were all unexceptional. What was not apparent to the other guests was that the stockings had been procured for just five shillings at a stall in the bazaar, and the slippers had been re-dyed and re-soled since last season. The dress was new, as Mama had insisted Cecily should have at least three new evening gowns. Despite her worries about funds, Cecily could not but acknowledge a thrill of pleasure at her new finery.

Nell, too, looked delightful in a gown of palest green, which perfectly complemented her auburn hair, pale skin and green-flecked hazel eyes. Together, the two ladies had attracted a fair share of interest and attention, despite, Cecily thought wryly, having reached such an advanced age. They had been feted and complimented tonight by no fewer than four gentlemen already—two of whom known lechers and the other two married.

Cecily was no longer surprised by this. Her own mama enjoyed all the freedoms of her widowhood, which had included numerous *affaires* over the years—mainly with gentlemen who were themselves married. At first, young Cecily had been shocked by the casual disregard for wedding vows of many gentlemen of the *ton*, though she had soon learned to endure. Society wilfully turned a blind eye, it seemed, as long as couples were reasonably discreet.

Apart from Ash and Marianne, Cecily knew no married couple among the *ton* who shared the felicity of a long-lasting loving marriage. Most society couples, once an heir had been secured, lived separate lives. They maintained a veneer of respectability in public, but *affaires* were common. Nell and Tom's marriage was also a love match, but Cecily understood how rare such arrangements were. It was one of the reasons why she had so far not accepted any offers of marriage herself.

Scanning around the room, Cecily reflected on her own cynicism. There were different groups among society men, she knew, and they were all represented here tonight, in Lady Jersey's elegant mansion. Some men seemed not to be interested in women at all, preferring to spend their time in the company of other men. Many of these were addicted to sport—to fencing and boxing, as well as gambling and drinking until they fell down. Others were rumoured, shockingly, to prefer *affaires* with other men.

The men who were interested in women generally had numerous flaws. There were the married ones, eternally seeking a new widow or married lady with whom to dally, and some of these were fond of leering at or touching young women in ways that left one feeling decidedly uncomfortable. Cecily was by now adept at avoiding situations where she might be vulnerable to such unwanted advances.

Her eyes moved on, picking out examples of another group. Unmarried gentlemen.

These, Cecily thought wryly, *fall into two categories*.

The first, men on the hunt for a wife. These specimens were generally recognisable by their advanced years, portly figures and predatory smiles. There were one or two exceptions, she supposed—Mr Harting, Mr Gillespie— but, generally, marriageable gentlemen were distinguishable by the feelings of aversion they generated in Cecily's stomach.

And then there was the second category of bachelors— the men who wished to avoid marriage at all costs. This latter group, who were generally youngish, often handsome and frequently drunk, refused to engage with debutantes except in the most light-hearted way. They flirted, and complimented, yet Cecily knew instinctively that there was nothing of meaning in it.

At only twenty years old, Cecily understood very well how it all worked. She grimaced, aware that her thoughts reflected experience that had made her older than her years. Sometimes she felt positively ancient.

Perhaps I am too gloomy, she thought now. *No*, she corrected herself. *I am simply rational and unsentimental*.

She saw the world for what it was, and knew that her own chance of a felicitous marriage, while possible, was small.

There was a sudden murmur of female interest, drawing Cecily out of her thoughts. At the same time she heard Nell gasp beside her. All eyes were drawn to the door, where a new arrival had just been announced.

He stood just inside the room, a head taller than almost everyone there. His figure was strong, lean and imposing, his face starkly handsome. Or at least it would be, Cecily thought, if there had been any kindness in it. He wore the full evening dress required for events such as these, but had chosen a black jacket, giving him a faintly sinister air. It was moulded to his form, drawing the eye to the breadth of his shoulders, the narrowing of his back, the smoothness of his hips.

I'll wager he needed two valets to get into that, thought Cecily dryly. *And men accuse us women of vanity!*

All around the room ladies were sitting up a little straighter, smiling a little more broadly, and chattering just a little more loudly than they had been. Cecily sighed. Sometimes she quite despaired of her sex.

The man in the doorway remained impassive, as if he had not noticed the reaction to his arrival. Lady Jersey hurried forward to greet him, pressing a kiss to his cheek and drawing him into the room.

Is there something between them? Cecily wondered idly, her mind as ever going to details of the latest chatter.

But, no, it was rumoured that Lady Jersey was currently engaged with Viscount Palmerston, right under her husband's nose. Still, she was fairly discreet, and was an acknowledged leader of society. There would be no consequences.

The footman's announcement sank in. 'Lord Hawken-den!' echoed Nell. 'Tom's brother. My, how alike they look!'

'Indeed!' Cecily had seen the Earl at numerous events and had even spoken to him on a couple of occasions over the past couple of years, since she had made her debut. They had been introduced two years ago, but he had no memory of her, she knew. He was spoken of as a man with a passion for wealth, and he reputedly only came alive when discussing matters of business with his friends and acquaintances. A debutante like Lady Cecily would simply be of no *use* to him. Cecily, who watched, and considered, and really *noticed* people, knew this without ever having thought much about it.

During both brief conversations with him, Lord Hawk-enden's gaze had gone through her without really seeing her. She shivered. He had seemed to her to be soulless, empty in some way. The Empty Earl, she remembered calling him inwardly. He had always moved on after the briefest of interactions.

Mama, who had long admired his handsome face, dark eyes and strong form, had nevertheless dismissed him as a possible lover on the grounds of his being too young for her, although, Cecily recalled dryly, it was also true that Lord Hawkenden had never shown any interest in flirting with Lady Fanny. For this, Cecily was profoundly grateful. The thought of Mama bedding the Empty Earl left a sick feeling in her stomach. Not that she should care who her mama took as a lover. Normally she had no opinions about such matters. But there was something about Lord Hawkenden…

When Mr Beresford, the Earl's younger brother, had arrived at Beatrice's Christmas house party a few months ago, Cecily had been careful not to encourage any connection. Watching from a safe distance, she had noticed that he was rather more engaging than the Earl, yet she had maintained a cool reserve that usually worked well in deterring friendships or attention she did not seek. Despite her notions about him, she had seen a warmer side to Tom emerge as he had come to love Nell. She eyed the Earl speculatively. Might he, too, have a heart beneath that cold exterior?

She shook herself. They were two of a kind, the Beresford brothers. Similar in looks, similar in terms of priorities. They had a reputation for being driven by the acquisition of wealth, and neither of them had ever engaged in a serious way with any lady, until Tom had fallen in love with Nell. His brother, though, had had no such redemption.

Her doubts about Lord Hawkenden were out of step with society, she knew. The Earl was welcomed everywhere, with men admiring his business acumen and women his broad chest, dark eyes and fine teeth.

Cannot they see? she had often wondered. *Or do people simply not care? Probably the latter*, she realised. Balls and parties were not commonly seen as opportunities to delve beneath the social surface and uncover people's true characters.

Nell was now looking decidedly uneasy—as well she might be. 'Have you met Lord Hawkenden before?' asked Cecily.

Her friend shook her head. 'I had never met Tom either, until he came to us for Christmas.'

Cecily frowned. 'It is a pity you could not have met the Earl before this. It is not right that you will meet your brother-in-law for the first time in public.'

'He has only just returned from France. Tom went to see him earlier today but…' Nell looked directly at Cecily '... I do not think that the Earl has welcomed our marriage.'

'Why do you think that?'

'Something was troubling Tom earlier. And he would not speak to me of what passed between him and his brother. He says only that it will come right in the end, and that we must wait a little time before announcing anything.'

Oh, dear.

'I see. Well, Mrs Beresford, all you can do is to play your part.'

'You are right.' Nell, her courage clearly strengthened at this pointed reminder of her new name, lifted her chin.

For the next half-hour they waited for him to approach, yet he did not.

Is he deliberately slighting his sister-in-law, or does he also not know who she is?

Cecily, while conversing easily with Nell and with the people who flitted by, was nevertheless entirely conscious at all times of his location. Despite herself, she felt strangely drawn to him—probably because of her anxiety for Nell.

She enjoyed a comfortable ten minutes with Mr Harting, who spoke sensibly and warmly with both ladies, and showed some signs of a particular interest in Cecily. Yet, throughout, her attention remained on the Earl. Awareness pricked at her, tingling along her skin. Now her right side, now the back of her neck. It was a most unwelcome sensation.

Finally, he was in her direct view. Nell, who was half-facing her, could not get a clear observation, but Cecily could. He was conversing with Mr Hollamby, leaning a little to minimise the difference in height. She saw him ask a question, and Mr Hollamby scanned the room, then pointed towards her and Nell.

Here it is, then. Now he must come and speak to us.

As she watched, he looked their way. His gaze travelled over Nell then rested on her, his dark eyes penetrating right through her, it seemed. For the first time he really *saw* her.

It seemed to Cecily that the moment between two heartbeats lasted an eternity. There was a whooshing sound in her ears as a wave of shuddering emotion rushed through her. Their eyes locked for a brief, endless moment before she broke her gaze, pretending to scan the room. A wave of heat flushed her cheeks, and she took refuge behind her fan.

My goodness, what a strange sensation!

She, who had rarely felt anything so powerful, was profoundly disturbed by what had just passed between them. It had not felt like anything she had ever experienced before. It was as though a hitherto unknown storm had blasted through her, confounding her with its force.

And for it to centre on the Earl of Hawkenden, of all people! Why, she barely knew him, and she probably would not even *like* him! Confusion clouded her brain momentarily, but she could find no answer, no meaning to the unexpected feelings.

It must have been nervousness, she told herself. *Be calm. Any moment now, he will approach us.*

Yet he did not. He remained with Mr Hollamby, the pair then being joined by Lady Jersey again. The gong sounded for supper, and they all filed through to the large dining room to fill their plates. Nell began a conversation with Miss Kelton, whom Cecily knew a little, and she let them chatter, still trying to understand the continuing tumult within her. Was it fear? Or simple nervousness? Possibly, although there were shades of something else there, too. Something novel, unexpected, overwhelming. The whole thing was quite disconcerting.

Abruptly, Cecily made a murmured excuse to Nell and made for the doors to the garden. She needed solitude, and quiet, and cool night air.

Thankfully the terrace was deserted, although flambeaux had been erected at both ends for the convenience of any guests seeking respite from the heat and crush inside. The moon had risen, a half-circle of white light. Cecily turned her back on the house and stared up at it, drinking in its stillness. Here, her pulse would calm. Here she would find peace. Her eyes fluttered closed.

A deep voice broke her reverie.

'So here you are. I have found you.' She whirled around, somehow knowing as she did so who was standing there.

Chapter Four

Jack had hoped to find his brother at Lady Jersey's soirée, but his hostess informed him that she had not seen Tom since before Christmas and was unaware he was back in Town.

'Like myself, he is only lately returned,' Jack replied coolly. 'He may not yet be up to the social whirl.'

Lady Jersey laughed and proceeded to regale him with a long list of engagements already planned for the coming weeks. 'It is nearly a full month until the season officially begins, but tonight, here in Berkeley Square, we are making a good start,' she announced with satisfaction. 'And my little soirée is quite the crush, is it not?'

'As always,' murmured Jack, noting her glow of pride. It never did any harm to cultivate good relationships with people such as Lady Jersey. One never knew when they might come in useful.

He made his way to a group of acquaintances, listening with half an ear to their accounts of prize-fights, duels and horseflesh. Unlike Tom, he had little interest in sport, though he frequented some of the major gatherings if he needed to engage certain individuals in a social setting.

Tonight, he hoped to find out more about the witch who

had beguiled Tom to such an extent that he had forgotten the work of years, throwing away his freedom and his wealth on, it seemed, little more than a whim. It did not take long for him to single out his target—Mr Hollamby, a dapper, middle-aged gentleman who was blessed with an unusual interest in people. He was a veritable walking Debrett's, knowing not only who the people were but every branch of their relations and history. He could be rather prosy but was both useful and eager to please.

'Hollamby,' he said baldly. 'The Godwins of Kent. What do you know about them?'

'Good evening, my lord. The Chiddingstone Godwins?'

'The very same.'

Hollamby tilted his head to one side, considering. 'Let me see. Yes, Mr Godwin died about three years ago, soon after marrying Miss Chester. You will remember Beatrice Chester? She is here tonight, somewhere.'

Jack's eyes narrowed.

Miss Chester—of course!

Tom had asked him for an introduction late last year. He had forgotten her married name, but now it came back to him. He had vaguely known Miss Chester—now Mrs Godwin—for a number of years. A spinster in her thirties, he recalled. Fair hair. Society had long since given up on her ever marrying when she had met and married a country gentleman within months and had disappeared to a rural existence. *To Kent.* Her husband had died not long after, and she had returned to society when her mourning period had ended last year.

Tom had expressed an interest in buying the Godwin house as a base for his business parties, Jack recalled—a perfectly rational decision. He frowned. Had Tom, then, married the widow? From what he remembered of Miss Chester, she was vain, silly, bird-witted, and had little to recommend her. If she was now Tom's wife, this would be disastrous indeed! *But, no*, he reassured himself. Tom's letters had referred to a *Miss* Godwin. And her given name was Nell, not Beatrice.

'Who, then, is *Miss* Godwin?'

'She is Mr Godwin's only child. The mother was one of the Wyatts—the last of that branch, in fact. Perfectly respectable, I assure you. Miss Godwin is actually here tonight, along with her stepmother and the Thornhill ladies—you know, Lord Kingswood's relatives.'

She is here? Jack was unsure what to make of this. Tom was not here, yet his new wife was. Perhaps, then, he was not so enamoured of her. A few weeks wed and 'in love'? Surely Tom, if he were truly devoted to this unknown lady, would have accompanied her to the soirée?

Maybe he does not mean to acknowledge her yet.

The thought gave Jack hope. If all was not well between the newlyweds, perhaps Tom and his bride might be persuaded to annul this unwelcome marriage before society was even aware of its existence. Annulments were rare, he knew, and not easily obtained, but an annulment would be so much more convenient than the scandal of a divorce.

And if they remained married? Jack gritted his teeth. *Then she will have to be managed so as to limit her drain on the Beresford funds.*

He sighed. Such a foolish, unnecessary act on his brother's part.

His thoughts returned to Hollamby's description of Miss Godwin and her family. *Perfectly respectable, eh?* He shrugged inwardly. It mattered not. Respectability was not enough to make this marriage acceptable to him. This unknown woman might have a fondness for spending, or for gambling. She might be as disastrous for the family as his own papa had been. He literally knew nothing about her.

He turned his attention back to Mr Hollamby. 'They are intimate with Lord Kingswood?' Ash, Lord Kingswood, was one of the few sensible men he counted among his acquaintances. Like himself, Ash had had to rebuild the family fortunes on inheriting an earldom. It had happened to many in these uncertain times. Thankfully, since Waterloo, things had settled down—in Europe at least. He counted Ash as a friend, and something of a guide. The Earl of Kingswood was only eight years his senior, and Jack often spoke to him on business matters. They had both taken their seats in the Palace of Westminster, and had a relaxed, easy acquaintance.

'Lady Fanny, the Dowager Countess, appears to have formed a friendship with Mrs Godwin.' Hollamby indicated the area near the long, shuttered windows, where Beatrice Chester—no, Mrs Godwin—was laughing with Lady Fanny, whom he recognised. Both fair-haired, both bird-witted. As Lady Fanny typified the silliest of the *ton* widows, he had taken pains to avoid deepening his acquaintance with her. Lady Fanny, like Mrs Godwin, had been a fixture in society for many years. While she was welcomed everywhere, she had held no particular power or position since the death of her husband, the previous Lord Kingswood. Her friendship conferred no special status on the Godwins, and so his opinion of the unknown Miss Godwin remained unchanged.

'Lady Fanny's daughter,' Mr Hollamby continued, 'is also friendly with Miss Godwin. Now, where are they?' Mr Hollamby searched the room with his eyes. 'Ah—there they are! Two beautiful young ladies, I dare say!' He indicated a settee at the far side of the room, where two vaguely familiar young ladies were indeed conversing.

Perhaps I have met them both previously.

He had no idea when or where, as he had no interest in debutantes. Or maybe it was simply that all young ladies looked remarkably alike. Lady Fanny's daughter was likely as silly and bird-witted as her mother, so this friendship conferred no added worth on the Godwin girl.

He eyed them closely. Neither wore matron's caps, and both were attired in the pale colours of the debutante. *Good.* This was a further indication that the marriage was unannounced. *Which one is Tom's wife?*

Jack assessed them both with a critical eye. The one he could see in profile seemed pretty enough, with auburn hair and very pale skin. The other—

He caught his breath. She was a vision of loveliness. Her fair hair gave her an angelic look, and her rosy cheeks, dark eyes, and perfect form seemed flawless.

Oh, Lord! He thought. *If that is Tom's wife, then it may be possible after all that he believes himself to be in love.*

Suddenly it began to make sense. An unwelcome sort of sense.

She was looking directly at him, he realised.

She must be the one. And someone must have told her who I am.

Her gaze was level, steady, assured—unusually bold for so young a person. Strangely, as their eyes met, he momentarily felt lost, as if standing on soft ground, the world tilting about him in the most alarming matter.

She broke their gaze, her attention wandering around the room. Jack brushed an imaginary speck from his sleeve, determined to regain his equilibrium. It had not been *she* who had affected him. Of course not. It was simply the realisation that, given her beauty, extricating his brother from her clutches might prove to be rather more challenging than he had anticipated.

When had they met before? He thought hazily that he must have been introduced to her at some point in the past. They had probably attended the same parties, yet she had clearly made no particular impression on him.

See? he thought. *She is not special in any way. Seeing her merely brought back my shock at Tom's folly.*

Mr Hollamby had moved on to a treatise on the Kingswood earldom and the Thornhill family. 'Lady Cecily,' he was saying, 'is the daughter of Lady Fanny and the Fourth Earl, and the *current* Lord Kingswood—that is, the *Fifth* Earl—is her guardian. He was cousin to the Fourth Earl. Unusual that the mother was not given guardianship but, then, Lady Fanny has never been the most, er...*reliable* matron, eh?'

'Quite.' Jack was barely listening. What to do?

I must speak with her.

He had no idea what he would say but trusted the instincts that had carried him through negotiations with hard-headed mandarins, stubborn French vineyard owners and people of dubious reputation here in London. A chit, an untried girl, would be no match for him.

The gong sounded for supper, and he followed the crowd into Lady Jersey's dining room. Keeping an eye on her was easy. Her fair head and blue gown were easily spotted in the throng. And so it was that he noticed her glance around furtively, checking that the people near her were focused on their plates. She murmured something to her auburn-haired friend, then left her side. His senses now wide awake, Jack watched as she walked towards the long, glazed doors that led to the terrace. With one final look around, she pushed one of the doors open a little and slipped outside.

It took a couple of minutes for him to work his way across the room and follow her. The dim light that met him on leaving the brightly lit house seemed inadequate. After only a moment his eyes began to adjust. There she was, on the edge of the terrace. Despite his aim of speaking to her directly, he could not help but be struck by how delightful she looked. The faint, warm light of the flambeaux lit her back, the blue gauze of her elegant gown seeming to shimmer in the orange glow. He could see part of her face, uplifted to the heavens, bathed in white moonlight. Her eyes were closed.

Aphrodite, he thought idly. *Or perhaps Athene.*

Did she know how beautiful she was? Did she have any idea that he was there? Pushing away the distraction of her beauty, which was making him feel decidedly uncomfortable, he reached into his heart to find the anger banked within him, and the knowledge that she was married to his brother.

Is this marriage due only to Tom's foolishness, or has this woman deliberately tricked him into such a hasty decision?

He allowed his indignation to rise, then spoke. 'So here you are. I have found you.'

Chapter Five

Cecily whirled around, somehow knowing as she did so who was standing there.

Do not let him intimidate you.

'You were searching for me, my lord? To what end?'

He strode towards her, tension visible in the rigid lines of his tall frame. Something in his demeanour was alarming.

Oh, I should not be out here alone, Cecily thought. *If something untoward were to happen, no-one would even hear me if I were to call out.*

She was glad that her voice had sounded reasonably steady. Now, how could she escape to the safety of the dining room?

'My lord? Then you know who I am?' His tone dripped with arrogance. A man clearly sure of his place in the world.

'We have been introduced,' she returned calmly, adding, 'Indeed, we have spoken on two occasions.'

There! Was that a flicker of uncertainty in his expression? It was hard to tell in the dim light. Perhaps he disliked her exposing the fact that he had not remembered her.

'Of course. Yes.' He paused. 'At this moment I cannot exactly recall…'

Ha! He clearly had no notion where and when he had met her before. *Well*, she thought, suddenly angry, *I have no intention of enlightening him.*

'Nor I,' she declared blithely. 'After all, one meets so many people during the season. It is difficult to keep them all clear in one's head, do you not think? I arrived before you tonight and had the advantage of hearing the footman announce you.'

He blinked, clearly unused to such disinterested anonymity. 'I see. Yes. I see.'

Cecily was beginning to enjoy this. 'For what purpose did you wish to speak to me, my lord?'

'Ah, yes. My purpose…' He seemed to gather himself. 'My *purpose* is to ask you what on earth you have done to my brother!'

She recoiled in shock. 'What I have *done* to him?' Her brow creased. 'I am unaware of having done anything to him at all!' She thought back to her hostile encounter with Tom Beresford the night at Christmas when Nell had gone missing. 'I was angry with him, for good reason. Is that what you are referring to?'

He waved this away. 'I care nothing for whatever games you play with him. It is this foolish marriage that concerns me.'

Oh, dear.

So Nell was correct—the Earl *was* unhappy about Tom and Nell's marriage. She eyed him helplessly. It was not her business to comment on what should be a private matter between Tom, Nell and Tom's brother. 'My lord, I do not think it helpful for us to discuss this.'

'Not helpful? Not *helpful*?' He glared at Cecily. 'What I wish to know is, why did you do it, and what will it cost me to remove you from Tom's life?'

Cecily gaped at him. *He is quite mad!* She began to

edge sideways so that he did not stand between her and the doors. She knew, of course, that there were people who experienced bouts of madness—why, the King himself was known to be seriously unwell. She herself had never been in the presence of a lunatic, until now. Although there had been no rumours of his insanity. Biting her lip, she glanced at the moon. It was only half-full, thank goodness.

I must keep him talking.

'What it will cost you?' she replied smoothly. 'Why, nothing at all! I am quite happy never to see you or your brother again.' She took another small step to the right.

He laughed harshly. 'And I am expected to believe this?'

Strangely, anger now replaced Cecily's fear. How dared he address her so? Summoning all her self-restraint, she replied silkily, 'I refuse to discuss this with you, my lord, and you should know better than to accost a young lady on a deserted terrace and speak to her in such a way! I am unused to such vulgarity. Good evening!'

Her head held regally high, she swept past him towards the doors. Sweeping inside, she closed the door behind her with a firm click.

Jack watched her go, unable at that moment to think what he should do. Never had he felt such rage. It boiled within him, white-hot and ravenous. Oh, he had known how evil men could be. How selfish. How shallow. And he had known that women, despite their reputation for warmth and softness, could be just as ruthless as any man. But never in his adult years had he faced a situation where he had felt so lost.

Her calmness and serenity in the face of his approaching her had been frustrating, but the fact that she, a slip of a girl, had had the temerity to admonish him—well, that was not to be accepted in any way! *Vulgarity?* How dared she? A country miss of 'respectable' background and no title.

Does she not know I am the Earl of Hawkenden?

He stopped short. She had known exactly who he was. That, after all, was why she had somehow persuaded Tom into marriage.

She had not, he noted, engaged with his accusation of entrapment at all. Indeed, she had lied to his face, pretending she would be happy to never see Tom again. Naturally she would not engage properly, for she believed herself the victor. Aligning herself with an earl. Marrying an honourable gentleman. Self-advancement, at Tom's expense.

And mine.

And she looked so angelic! Her skin, so pure and clear. Her eyes, wide with feigned innocence. Her beauty a disguise for the vanity and self-interest that drove her.

She cannot be more than one-and-twenty, he thought, *and already she has persuaded my brother into marriage in quite the most pitiless manner.*

Stepping down from the terrace, he paced Lady Jersey's gardens by moonlight, barely able to contain the rage within. He recalled his brother's face, soft with hope as he had spoken of his marriage. In contrast, he recalled Tom's wife's demeanour as she had serenely chastised him—a peer of the realm! She had showed no proper respect for him as head of the Beresford family, no understanding that he had the perfect right to question her. If she was now Mrs Beresford, then she would soon need to learn how to go on.

If Tom truly believes he loves this creature, then it is my moral duty to rescue him.

Until Tom's defiance in the library earlier, Jack had rarely had cause to consider his obligations as head of the family. And yet, somewhere within, the responsibility had eaten into his bones, his gut, become part of him. It could not be ignored.

For the first time in a very, very long time Jack was at a loss. Anger and frustration consumed him. To return indoors was impossible—he would simply be unable to disguise his disdain for the hussy. In the end he made his way to the kitchen door and bribed a surprised and grateful footman into fetching his cloak, hat, cane and boots, and calling for his carriage. 'Tell your mistress I am unwell and send my apologies for not taking my leave of her properly. Tell her I shall call on her on the morrow.'

'Yes, my lord,' replied the footman, opening the front door.

Jack had never been so relieved to reach the refuge of his well-sprung carriage. Although part of him recognised that his enemy was causing him to run away, still he knew it was the right moment to retreat. A public incident would not help his cause. As long as the marriage was not widely known about, he still had the slightest chance of ridding his brother of the heartless chit who had entrapped him.

'Lady Cecily!' It was Lady Jersey, her hostess. 'Have you been out to take some of the night air?'

Cecily managed a half-smile. 'Indeed. I became too warm, and feared a headache might come on, so I stepped outside for a moment.'

'Oh, how vexing!' Lady Jersey looked at her closely. 'You do look rather pale, my dear girl—and you are trembling!'

'Oh! I— Actually, it was colder outside than I had anticipated.'

'But you might have caught a chill!' She patted Cecily's hand. 'I shall order a tisane, and your mama shall take you home directly.'

'Oh, no!' Cecily protested weakly. 'I am sure I shall be quite well again shortly.'

Lady Jersey would not be denied, her kind heart leading her to insist—in much too public a manner—that Cecily should withdraw to a quiet parlour at the back of the house, while a tisane was prepared and Lady Fanny found. Cecily, glancing around, could not see Nell, Beatrice or Fanny.

They must be in the other room.

Conscious of too many eyes upon her, she agreed with alacrity, following her endlessly chattering hostess to a delightful parlour hung with red satin stripes. Once alone, she paced the floor, reflecting in quite unladylike language about the character, behaviour and general wickedness of arrogant earls who had no business judging young ladies, or speaking to them harshly on deserted terraces. 'Oh!' she fumed, hands bunched into fists. 'How I should love to call him out to a duel! I should like nothing better than to put a bullet through his empty, frozen heart, or stab him with a sharp sword!'

A maid arrived then, with a hot tisane. Cecily smiled crookedly, drank it slowly, and tried to calm her mind. A few minutes later the door opened again, admitting Nell. 'Here you are! Lady Jersey has said that you are unwell.' She hurried to Cecily's side, her face creased with concern. 'What has happened?'

Cecily opened her mouth to reply, then shut it again.

What could she say to Nell? Lord Hawkenden was either mad or was so implacably opposed to Nell's marriage to his brother that he even wished for Nell's friend to be removed from Tom's life.

She gripped her cup a little tighter. Of course she could not add to Nell's distress. 'I have the headache, my dear

Nell. It was such a crush in there and, truly, the thought of supper made me feel ill.' That part was true, at least.

'Oh, my poor Cecily!' Nell pressed a hand to Cecily's forehead. 'I see you have a tisane. Is it helping at all?'

'It is.'

'I shall find Lady Fanny. You must go home this instant!'

'Oh, no. I think Lady Jersey will already have spoken to Mama. Mama may be displeased if she is asked to take me away—you know how she hates to leave a party before she herself wishes to.' They exchanged a wry glance. Both Fanny and Beatrice tended to put their own wishes first.

'Very well.' Nell pulled a chair close to Cecily's. 'Then I shall stay here with you.'

'Would you not prefer to remain at the party? I am perfectly comfortable here, I assure you.'

Nell grimaced. 'I am too uneasy to enjoy the soirée now that I have seen Lord Hawkenden.'

Cecily sat up straighter. 'Has he spoken to you?'

She shook her head. 'He has left, I think. At least, I have not seen him since supper.'

Cecily let out the breath she had been holding. 'Good. I do not think I would like to face him.'

'Why not?' Nell's forehead creased. 'I mean, I know why *I* am nervous, but you? You have ten times my courage.'

'I—er—encountered him briefly on the terrace earlier.'

'You did? What happened?'

'I have met him before, as I mentioned earlier,' Cecily replied carefully. 'We spoke briefly tonight.'

'Oh, Lord!' Nell put her head in her hands. 'Did he speak of me and Tom?'

Cecily bit her lip. 'I do not mean to repeat what he said, but it would be well if you and your husband give him time to come round to the notion of your marriage.' She could not be completely open with Nell about what had just happened. Or that Lord Hawkenden's tirade towards her had had nothing of logic in it.

Now that she had had time to reflect, she regretted not encouraging Lord Hawkenden to speak more plainly. Why would he try to remove Nell's friend from their lives? It made no sense.

In all of this, Nell was her primary concern. Nell had already entered into this marriage, and Cecily saw—reluctantly—that she would have to counsel her friend through this trouble.

'You mentioned earlier that you believe Lord Hawkenden to be opposed to your marriage. I fear you may be right.'

Lord, what a muddle!

'I am happy to discuss all of this with your husband too, if he would be willing to engage in such a conversation.' Perhaps Tom could explain what ailed his brother.

Nell embraced her briefly. 'Thank you, my dear friend. I truly appreciate this.'

Cecily, already feeling rather guilty about her own part in the situation, could only refuse to be thanked and repeat her willingness to be of assistance.

She pressed a hand to her temple, where a pounding headache had indeed made itself known.

This headache is not unexpected, she thought, *for the situation is much, much worse than Nell understands.*

Chapter Six

The unforgiving sunshine of an early spring day pierced through Cecily's aching eyes and made her head hurt in rhythm with her pulse. The headache that had begun last night remained with her. She had not slept well, her dreams troubled by notions of wolves and a menacing half-moon. Three times she had awoken, her heart pounding, and had struggled to find sleep again. And now it was almost midday, and the maid was doing her hair, and everything hurt.

Emotions warred within her yet—rage and an unlooked-for attraction fighting for supremacy. At present, rage was in the ascendancy. It was unfair that only men were allowed to duel, for she would love nothing more than to put a sword through the Earl of Hawkenden. Each time she recalled his arrogant disdain, his hurtful tone, her blood felt as though it were boiling within her.

How I should love to hit him!

Her own vehemence was surprising. She could not recall ever feeling such an impulse before—she, who was usually so practical and known for her good sense.

It seems I am my mother's daughter in some respects, after all.

In the mirror she saw raw emotion on her own face and smoothed it out for fear of terrifying the poor maid.

'All done, my lady, if you please.'

'Thank you.' She swallowed, managing to maintain a reasonably normal expression.

The maid departed, and Cecily, exhaling loudly, took a swift turn about her airy, light-filled bedroom. Each time she thought of the sneering tone in his voice, the curled lip that she had been unable to see properly in the half-light but had known for certain had been there, she became angry all over again. What contempt! What disdain! What presumption, to speak in such a way to *any* young lady, never mind one he knew to now be close to his family!

And why did it hurt so? She barely knew the man. Had she, following that earth-shattering look between them, been foolishly tempted to hope there had been some meaning in it?

Oh, Lord! Sinking onto a delicate-looking chair, Cecily hid her head in her hands. Whatever foolishness had led Cecily to briefly wonder if she, like Nell, might melt the cold heart of a Beresford, the illusion had been totally shattered. Not only did Lord Hawkenden, head of the Beresford family, disapprove of Nell and Tom's marriage, he disliked Cecily so much that he wished her to perdition! Injustice and hurt battled each other inside her head, making her temples pound and her eyes sting.

And Cecily, Nell's best friend, had been too angry to manage the situation in a sensible way. There had been an opportunity to let Lord Hawkenden speak of his concerns, perhaps even to influence him, to give him a sense of darling Nell's true character. But she had been so overcome with rage—and shock, she allowed—that she had simply walked away. In doing so, she had failed Nell.

Lord, what madness came over me last night?

A lifetime with Mama had given Cecily the skill of self-control. Or so she had believed. Last night had been a serious lapse, a loss of self-restraint on a scale that she probably had not experienced since childhood. It had been a very long time since she had felt anything as deeply as she had last night. Briefly, she closed her eyes, remembering that first moment when she and the Earl had locked glances. His anger towards her on the terrace. How her heart had pounded and her stomach had twisted at the realisation that he was opposed to her future involvement in Nell's life. But *why*?

Her inner cry was much more intense than it should have been. In all the years by her mother's side, she had seen both good and bad in people. She had encountered anger, had been on the receiving end of frustration and ire from Mama's spurned lovers, from tradespeople demanding settlement of bills, once from a wife angry at Mama's pursuit of her husband. Yet never had words cut as deeply as they had last night.

She allowed her mind to go further back, to the dark days after Papa had died. Ash, the new Earl, arriving for the reading of the will. Mama's distress. The announcement that this stranger was to be her guardian, rather than her own mama. Meeting Marianne, her new governess. At twelve, it had all been frightening, and distressing, and she had felt a duty to protect Mama as well as herself.

Yet, she reminded herself, all had turned out well. Ash had been an excellent influence on her as she had moved from childhood to adulthood, as had Marianne, his darling wife. The former governess felt as though she were a second mother to Cecily, and she was as unlike Mama as it was possible to be.

Where Mama was flighty, Marianne was safe. Mama lived for thrills and adventure, while Marianne lived quietly, gaining joy from a simple life with her husband, her children and her household. Marianne loved to read: Mama had not the patience.

I am fortunate to have had Ash and Marianne.

Cecily squirmed a little at what felt like disloyalty to her mama.

Yet such thoughts were as nothing to the way in which she had failed Nell last night. She had clearly felt the Earl's anger and frustration—had sensed how his rage had become white-hot by the time she had taken her leave of him. Instead of calming the situation, she, Cecily, had simply allowed it. She closed her eyes again and shook her head slowly. *Because I could not think clearly. Because I expected something different from him. Because this unaccountable attraction prevented me from speaking up for my friend.*

There was a scratching at the door, distracting her from her ruminations. 'Yes?'

'Pardon, my lady. Mrs Beresford has arrived.'

'Thank you.' Squaring her shoulders, she rose, smoothed her gown, and prepared to be sociable.

Jack dismounted, handing the reins to the waiting groom. Not bothering to wait while the man led his stallion to the stable mews, he stalked up the steps and through the front door of his townhouse. As he did so, the sense of relief he had felt while out riding began to fade. Riding in London parks could not compare with the countryside, but for now it would have to suffice.

Although he had never understood the point of the hunt—for his steward was well able to deal with troublesome foxes—he nevertheless enjoyed the freedom he felt while flying through familiar fields and over hedges on horseback. He and Tom often made progress on matters

of business during hunting breaks, and for Jack they represented the perfect blend of business and pleasure.

Tom. A stab of something remarkably like anxiety
pierced him. Never before had he and Tom been estranged
like this. They had weathered together the storms of separation, boarding school cruelties, Papa's coldness and
their near-ruin after Papa's death. Over the years, they
had had plenty of disagreements, too. Fallings-out, even.
They were too alike in many ways, both tending to dig
their heels in stubbornly over matters that later proved
to be trivial.

But something about this felt different. At this moment
it was difficult to see how they would manage to overcome
the harm done by this nonsensical marriage. Having now
met his brother's determined wife, Jack continued to be
horrified by Tom's hasty decision, yet he had to admit to
a certain level of understanding. It was now patently clear
that the Godwin girl was no innocent victim in this. Her
demeanour last night had been serene, displaying supreme
confidence in her unassailable position. She had refused
to even engage in conversation with him. She had clearly
ensnared Tom using her wiles, and his brother was hopelessly entangled, like an exhausted fox at the end of a hunt.

'Is my bath ready?' He was not normally so brusque
with servants, since it cost him nothing to be polite. Today,
however, he felt drained, and there was simply nothing
inside from whence to pull the niceties of everyday life.

'Yes, my lord.' At least that. Much as he had needed
to ride in the park, he could not carry on with his day—a
planned mix of meetings and social engagements—while
smelling of the stable. Once divested of his hat, coat and
boots, he mounted the stairs with determination, only the
frown he knew currently marked his forehead betraying
anything of the tumult within.

* * *

'Let us take a turn in the Green Park, perhaps?'

Nell made the suggestion with a smile. She and Cecily had spent hours visiting dressmakers and milliners' shops, and Nell's footmen had been given a number of small packages to carry. Nell had been measured and pulled at, and, as a newly married lady buying multiple items, heavily complimented. She had ordered the beginnings of her bride-clothes—dresses more suited to a married lady than to a debutante, along with hats, shoes, gloves and spencers. Enough was enough, however, and both she and Cecily had had their fill of the delights of shopping.

'The very thing!' agreed Cecily. Gradually, as the time had passed and Nell continued to behave normally, Cecily realised that her friend still knew nothing of what had occurred last night.

I should tell her...but will that make everything yet worse again?

Wrestling with the dilemma, she desperately tried to decide on the best course of action.

The Earl's prejudice against Nell had been clear. 'This foolish marriage,' he had said. The nerve of the man! The scornful assumption that he knew anything about Nell! Nell, who was the sweetest, kindest girl Cecily knew. The cold, arrogant Earl knew nothing of Nell, but had revealed much of himself in his hasty judgement of Tom's chosen wife.

Still, Cecily's refusal to engage in debate with him had, she felt, inflamed the situation further. While she was a little sorry for it, part of her could not regret giving the presumptuous Lord Hawkenden a check. He had clearly expected Cecily to tremble, and grovel, and apologise that her friend had had the temerity to marry a Beresford. Instead, Cecily, drawing upon her own strength, had simply left him to his rage.

Nell might not be of the aristocracy, but she was much more a lady than the Earl had been a gentleman last night! On those grounds alone, Cecily reasoned, he had deserved her defiance, and if there had been no consequences for others, she would have been fiercely glad and almost looking forward to a further bout with him. Almost.

But consequences there were, and potentially serious ones. Resolving to try to put the matter out of her head, she hoped Nell would not be too upset when she finally realised just how angry Lord Hawkenden was, and that they would all somehow work through their differences.

Jack stepped outside the door of White's, breathing in the spring air with a sense of relief. Today, nothing was right. He could not settle into his usual conversations, could not engage in business chatter, could not even enjoy the—normally delicious—food in his club. A walk in the fresh air might clear his mind.

His mind, however, had other ideas. His mind had one focus, and one only: the beautiful, calm chit who was now married to Tom. Quite why he had moved on from ruminating over solutions, or focusing on Tom's motives, he was not sure. Walking down the steep hill towards the palace, all he could think about was how impressive she was. That determination! That fierceness! Her downright refusal to even discuss her marriage with him!

Despite himself, he had already realised she was no ordinary lady. He groaned, causing a gentleman emerging from Lock's, the hatters, to glance at him in curiosity. Turning the groan into a belated cough, he urged himself to be rational. Something had to be done. Something must be possible. Never in his life had he encountered a challenge that bested him in the end.

Reminding himself of this helped. Gradually, his rational mind strengthened again. Despite his undoubted privilege, all through his life he had faced difficulties. Some problems had seemed initially intractable, some situations untenable, yet he had survived them. Mama's death. The loss of his old nurse. Papa's punishments. Briefly, his thoughts went to a dark chamber at school, shadowy figures looming over him, but he pushed the memories away. School cruelties had not broken him. A determined young lady certainly would not.

Later, his father's near-bankruptcy had seemed impossible to overcome, yet they had done so. They had. He and Tom, together. The Beresford brothers. A team, always. The two of them against a cruel world. Today, the thought made him strangely sad.

Cecily and Nell meandered down Piccadilly, then into the park, carefully avoiding St James's. It would not do to walk anywhere near the gentlemen's clubs there. One of the footmen had been sent back to Nell's house with her purchases, while the second continued to accompany them, following at an appropriate distance. The two young ladies linked arms, enjoying the mildness of the early March day. The trees were in bud, crocuses in bloom, and there were definite signs of nest-building among the avian population.

'I have just had a delicious thought.' Nell looked excited. 'Now that I am a married lady I can be your chaperone, Cecily!'

They stopped and looked at each other, similar grins growing on both faces. 'Mama will be delighted,' declared Cecily. 'You know she finds chaperoning me tiresome.

Such fun we could have, without Mama and Beatrice watching us all the time!'

'Perhaps,' Nell offered shyly, 'you might visit the Beresford hunting-box with us next week? It is in the South Downs, and Tom tells me it is an idyllic place. We plan to stay for a fortnight, or possibly three weeks, then return for the season proper.'

Time away from Mama, and the silliness of London in the early season?

The thought was wonderful, yet Cecily could not forget last night's events, and the knowledge that the trouble she had sown had yet to bear fruit. 'But do you and your husband not prefer to travel alone, Nell? I do not wish to be in the way.'

'Oh, well, the hunting season is nearing its end, but Tom wishes me to see Hazledene before Easter. Once the hunting season is done, the house will be shut until the harvest is in, you see. Tom will be busy riding during the day, so I should welcome the company. And—' her eyes blazed with excitement '—we shall be there without Beatrice *or* your mama!'

Cecily could only gape at her. Such freedom was unknown to either of them. Since her papa had died eight years ago, Cecily had always had Mama, Ash or Marianne by her side, apart from brief walks out—and even then servants were always near. It did not matter how well-loved she was, the feeling of being watched, and guarded, and controlled, was always with her. To be under Nell's guidance would be the most liberation she had ever experienced. At twenty, she was more than ready for it. *So marry, then.* That would give her similar freedoms, and yet…

'Oh, I should love it!' She frowned. 'But Mama may not permit me to be away for weeks on end.'

'We cannot know unless we ask her,' Nell replied, practicality in her tone. 'Besides, we shall be there for three weeks at most, in the middle of the countryside, and only a handful of people present. Your mama cannot object, surely?'

Cecily was only half-listening. There, walking towards them, was an elegant gentleman. His tall beaver hat, well-cut jacket, and smart cane proclaimed him a man of fashion, yet there was nothing of the macaroni in his strong shoulders and long, muscular legs. Her mouth suddenly dry and her heart racing, Cecily could only walk slowly in horror towards her doom.

It was the Earl of Hawkenden.

Chapter Seven

Jack recognised her instantly. Well, how could he not, when she seemed to haunt his every thought? Her friend was with her, he vaguely realised—the same young lady that had been beside her at Lady Jersey's. The light that night had been fairly dim—candles in the drawing room and flambeaux and moonlight on the terrace. This was his first opportunity to see her in the clear light of day.

She was altogether too beautiful. He noted with both appreciation and resentment her perfectly proportioned figure, elegant walking gown and pelisse and charming bonnet, its ribbon tied saucily under one ear. He marched on helplessly, his feet taking him inexorably towards her. Now he could make out her features, his brain committing them to memory, despite his better judgement. Fair curls peeping out beneath the bonnet. A perfect, innocent complexion. Delicate features. Amber eyes, he noted with some surprise, having expected blue to complement the flaxen hair. As his brain idly tried to decide if her eyes were the exact shade of champagne, or rather leaned more towards brandy, his entire body, all of his senses, were focused on her.

A few steps more, and he would be forced to speak.

She was looking at him, he noted, a strange expression on her face.

He was entirely devoid of a plan.

Never, not once, in all of his thirty years on God's earth, had Jack Beresford felt this way. All of the social niceties were urging him to behave normally. Somewhere inside remained banked rage. Yet, at this instant, he was entirely overwhelmed with what felt strangely like be-wilderment.

The moment was here. Jack paused briefly, tipped his hat to both ladies, murmured a cold, 'Good day,' then continued on. As though they were casual acquaintances. As though she had not trapped his brother into wedlock.

As though he was not rapidly becoming obsessed with her.

'Oh, my goodness, Cecily! That was *him*!' Nell was as pale as her white, white gown, and her hands were trembling.

Cecily, who herself felt decidedly overwhelmed and shaken, took Nell's gloved hands in hers. 'At least he ac-knowledged us.'

Nell shook her head. 'He acknowledged *you*. He barely glanced in my direction and did not take the opportunity to introduce himself. Oh, Cecily! He has given me the cut direct and will not even try to make my acquaintance. Oh, poor Tom!'

'Poor Tom? Poor Nell, more like!'

'But Tom cares so much for his opinion. You cannot know what they have endured together.'

Cecily snorted. 'Indeed, I care not! My concern is for you, my dear friend, not for your abominable brother-in-law.'

They stopped, and Cecily took a furtive glance behind

them, noting with relief that the Earl had turned up a side path and was even now walking towards the nearest exit from the park. 'He is gone, thank goodness.'

Nell turned too, and they both stayed like that for a moment, neither speaking. Overhead the sun shone, and birds tweeted, and small clouds scudded busily across the sky. It was the strangest thing, that the world should continue so prosaically when Cecily's senses were so disordered. Strangely, along with everything else, her foolish eyes had focused on noting just how handsome the Earl was. The current flutterings in her heart held unlooked-for attraction as well as everything else.

How inconvenient!

Why, she had yet to find anything likeable about him. And yet her foolish senses were severely disordered, and in a way that had little to do with their previous difficult encounter and everything to do with the Earl's fine form and handsome face.

Footsteps sounded behind them. 'Ladies!'

They turned back towards the palace to see Mr Beresford hurrying towards them. At least he had approached from the opposite direction from that his brother had just taken. They would not have seen each other.

'I did wonder if I might find you still here! The footman has returned to the house and informed me it was your intention to walk in the park. I understand you have spent a small fortune on trinkets, for he was struggling with all the parcels!' He was a little out of breath, and his face lit up as he took his wife's hand. Nell was beaming with happiness.

He kissed Nell's gloved hand, and held it, seemingly reluctant to let go. 'My love, it was bad enough that I could not accompany you last night to Lady Jersey's, but now today it is *you* who have abandoned *me*!' His tone was playful, and there was genuine amity between them, Cecily noted.

Turning to Cecily, he gave a bow. 'Good day, Lady Cecily. It is delightful to see you again. Are you well?'

'I am indeed well.' Her tone was guardedly polite. Did he know how his brother had accosted her? 'Felicitations on your marriage.'

'Thank you.' He grinned, seemingly delighted with himself.

'Oh, Tom,' Nell was saying, excited hope in her tone. 'May I invite Lady Cecily when we travel to Hazledene next week? She will be company for me while you are out hunting.'

'Of course!' He smiled at her indulgently. 'You may have anything you wish, my love.'

Cecily could not help a slight pang of envy. She eyed the happy couple, noting this warm, indulgent Tom looking at Nell as though she were the most precious creature on earth. Nell, too, was glowing with happiness, her eyes shining, as she sent her husband a sideways glance. In sharp contrast, last night the Earl had shown his true self—arrogant, entitled and domineering. It was interesting to note how different he was from his younger brother.

They walked all the way to the Queen's Basin and back. Their conversation was not unpleasant, Mr Beresford seemingly in a jovial mood and Nell glowing with happiness. The ladies' recent encounter with the Earl was not mentioned.

Mr Beresford bade them farewell at the gates, hurrying to his next engagement—an engagement on some business matters. Cecily was all politeness, but underneath she was still vexed by the Earl's opposition to the marriage and confused and hurt in equal measure by his involving her in it.

* * *

'Well, Merton, where shall we begin?' Jack, with some effort, focused his mind on the matters at hand. His man of business, Merton, indicated the papers he had been preparing. They were laid out on Jack's desk in neat piles and represented a significant amount of work. Normally, Jack would have been eager to discover the tasks before him, to enjoy the stimulation and excitement matters of business always gave him. Today, however, he remained distracted and sombre.

'I have separated them into three, my lord. These are documents needing your signature alone, this pile is for both you and your brother to sign, and here is new information on the prospects you asked me to look into.' He glanced at the clock on the library mantel. 'Mr Beresford should be here shortly.'

Jack looked up, keeping his tone casual. 'My brother has confirmed he is coming?' There was a risk that Tom's stubbornness would cause him to miss this important meeting. He never had before—not even during their previous disagreements. It was a sad reflection on the depth of the breach this time that Jack had to even consider the possibility.

Merton's brow creased. 'Why, yes, sir. As is my usual practice, I informed him of the time we agreed to meet.' He hesitated. 'Is there some reason why he may not be here?'

Jack dropped his gaze back to the papers in front of him. 'I believe he may be busy with other engagements. I am not sure he will be able to join us as usual.' Inwardly, his stomach was churning in quite an inconvenient manner. Never had there been dissent such as this between him and Tom. Their disagreements were less frequent these days and tended to focus on business matters.

Occasionally they irritated each other over trivial concerns too, as most brothers did, but never before had Jack felt such a distance between them. He did not like it one bit. And since he had met Tom's headstrong wife, Jack's path had become even less clear.

Voices in the hall indicated that Tom had, in fact, arrived. Jack ignored the leap of joyful relief within, instead focusing on the challenges the next half-hour would bring. His brow creased.

Can I convince Tom to put aside his wife, before an annulment becomes completely impossible?

He glanced at Merton. Nothing could be discussed in front of a servant.

'Good day, Jack. Good day, Merton.' Tom's stiffness seemed immediately apparent to Merton, who returned the greeting then glanced quickly at Jack, a frown marring his forehead.

'Good day, Tom.' Even Jack could hear the strain in his own voice.

'Ah, yes. Very good.' Merton pulled at his right ear, suddenly busy. 'There are a number of papers for you to sign, Mr Beresford, for the shared holdings.' He drew the middle pile across the desk and pulled up a chair for Tom's use.

Without a word Tom picked up a pen and began scanning the first document. Jack, recognising instantly the sullen stubbornness on his brother's face, could not help but be irritated by it. Here he was, trying to understand the most monstrous folly on his brother's part, and Tom did not even appreciate his efforts. Worse, he clearly had set himself against Jack's common-sense questioning of this reckless marriage.

Jack gripped the pen tightly. He dared not think about *her.* Not right now.

Merton, his face blank and expressionless, stepped back as the silence grew and thickened. The air in the room crackled with unspoken divisions as Tom worked methodically through the pile of papers assigned to him, read each one and signed it as if he had not a care in the world. At one point he even whistled a tuneful air, as if attacking Jack with his own cheerfulness.

Jack, realising he had now read the first document four times without taking it in, signed it anyway—thereby breaking one of the earliest rules he had set himself since his passion for matters of business had begun.

Ignoring his inner reservations, he picked up a document from Merton's third pile. It related to a field he wished to purchase, which ran along the eastern edge of his estate. Mr Harting, the current owner, who had not yet been approached about the sale, was apparently building new cottages on the far side of his own estate, but, Merton reported, was woefully short of labourers. Jack, relieved to finally have something to pique his curiosity, glanced up.

'Interesting, Merton. I wonder if Harting would appreciate some assistance with his building work from some of my own labourers? As a neighbourly kindness, of course.'

Merton smiled slightly. 'The possibility, my lord, did occur to me. Has Mr Harting agreed to hunt with you this month, as you had discussed before Christmas?'

Jack nodded. 'I saw him at my club yesterday. Both he and Carmichael will come with me to Hazledene on Tuesday.'

Tom, who had been studiously ignoring their conversation, looked up at this. 'But I am already engaged to use Hazledene this month. It was all arranged with the staff ten days since.'

Jack, manfully hiding his true feelings, shrugged. 'You will have to change your plans.' Although the brothers shared use of Hazledene, Tom knew full well that it belonged to Jack.

Tom eyed him defiantly. 'You are the one who must give way. I had already set my plans in motion. Your trip with Harting and Carmichael can wait. I have always been able to use Hazledene at this time of year.'

'It does not suit me to delay.' All wisdom lost, and consumed by intense irritation at Tom, Jack was vaguely aware that he and his brother were locked into a meaningless battle—such as they had used to do when they had been children. Yet, just as he had felt back then, Jack knew that winning this battle of wills was, at this moment, the most important thing in the world. Vaguely, Jack was aware that Merton had dropped his gaze and was pretending to not hear their conversation.

'Neither does it suit me to delay. I shall arrive in Hazledene on Monday next, and intend to remain there for most of March.' Tom gave an arrogant flick of the hand. 'You may invite your friends to stay any time after that.'

'You know as well as I do that this month will be the last of the hunting.'

'I also know you have no passion for hunting, as I do.'

'My *passion*—' Jack's voice was a little louder '—is for business. I believed you to be of the same mind. We have worked together for eight years to build a secure future. We both know how important it is.'

'Of course! But you may ride with Harting on the downs a month later, nevertheless!' With a flourish, Tom signed the last of his papers and rose. 'Good day.' His bow was insultingly shallow. For the second time in a row he stalked out.

Jack, deprived of a target for his anger, resorted to swearing vociferously at the closed door, causing Merton to raise his eyebrows in shock.

'I shall travel to Hazledene on Tuesday, Merton,' he stated firmly, 'along with Mr Carmichael and Mr Harting. Please inform the staff there.'

'Yes, my lord.' Gathering up the papers, both signed and unsigned, Merton fled.

Chapter Eight

Hazledene was an elegant, solid house, with multiple chimneys and neat, symmetrical windows. Its half-timbered design and mullioned panes proclaimed it to have been built in the time of Good Queen Bess, and Cecily and Nell could not help but exclaim with delight when they turned up the short driveway towards the front door.

Mr Beresford, who had accompanied the carriage on horseback, grinned at their reaction. 'I thought you might like it,' he murmured, reining in alongside them as the carriage slowed to a halt.

Cecily stepped down onto the gravel path, grateful to be able to stretch and stand after hours in the rolling carriage. She and Nell had spent the journey sometimes chattering, sometimes resting, and generally at ease with each other.

They had been able to see each other almost every day in the past week, and had enjoyed shopping trips, ices at Gunter's and walks in the park, usually alone. Nell seemed to be accepting of her new husband's habit of spending some time each day engaged with friends. 'We both agreed it was important not to simply disregard friends who have been important to us for a long time,' she had said, linking her arm in Cecily's. 'Like me, he has not got many friends, but those we have we wish to keep.'

Nell remained anxious about meeting Lord Hawkenden again, to the extent that she had avoided soirées and early season parties since the terrible night at Lady Jersey's. Thankfully, the encounter in the Green Park had not been repeated. Nell confessed to having developed a quaking terror of the man, and his avoidance of her at Lady Jersey's soirée, followed by what she saw as a direct insult in the park, had, in her mind, confirmed that he did not approve of his brother's new wife.

Cecily, who knew full well that he was implacably opposed to Nell—and even to Nell's friends—could only be relieved, and both young ladies were happy to wave Beatrice and Lady Fanny off in the evenings, while pleading tiredness, or a headache, or a desire for solitude. 'You will never get a husband like that,' Mama had scolded, wagging a finger in Cecily's face. 'It is all very well for Nell, who has bagged herself an earl's brother, but you cannot afford to let this season's debutantes have first pick of the bachelors!'

'But, Mama,' Cecily declared, flinching a little at her mother's direct language, 'I do not want a husband. At least, not yet.'

'Fustian! It is your duty to wed, and once you have given your husband an heir, then you may begin to live a little!'

Cecily had replied in a placating manner, hinting she would go out in society more after her trip to Hazledene once the season was properly underway, and Mama had, thankfully, let it go. She was relieved to avoid yet more conversation about her own future, as she experienced confusion and anxiety every time she thought of it. The problem was she wished for a marriage such as that of

Ash and Marianne, or Nell and Tom, and *not* like most of society. Yet she saw no way to ensure such an outcome.

She still felt deeply uncomfortable about her conversation with Lord Hawkenden, and had resolved to tell Nell the truth at Hazledene. Nell could hardly be more distressed about the situation, anyway. At the house they would be together much more than in London, and so there would be more chance of having time to discuss it properly. Guiltily, she wondered what Lord Hawkenden would say if he knew she was to visit one of the Beresford family properties, after he had made his dislike of her friendship with Nell so plain.

No other guests were to be present during their stay, and Cecily anticipated leisurely days spent walking, reading and conversing with Nell, and evenings full of cosy contemplation. While she enjoyed London and all its delights just as much as any young lady, Cecily often had a secret hankering for peace and solitude. Mama's life was a whirlwind of engagements and parties, routs and soirées. Cecily found that too many such events drained her, whereas Mama seemed to thrive on them.

As they greeted the Hazledene staff, who had lined up to welcome Mr Beresford's new wife, Cecily was conscious of a familiar feeling—and one that she had not expected to experience here. It was that old notion that she did not belong. At home with Ash and Marianne, she felt secure and comfortable, but spending most of the past eight years moving from house to house, hotel to inn, had taken its toll.

Knowing that Mama's visits to her friends were as much about their limited means than simply friendship, Cecily had become accustomed to a certain wariness. Sometimes their hosts betrayed through an unguarded grimace or throwaway remark that they knew quite well that Lady Fanny was hanging on their coat-tails via convenient friendships. If Mama were less personable, Cecily reflected, they would probably spend much more time with Ash and Marianne, and would likely be happier for it.

The irony, of course, was that both Cecily and Lady Fanny had perfectly adequate allowances. Ash was not in any way miserly and had ensured a good dowry for Cecily as well as a respectable allowance for both ladies. Indeed, he had done more than had been required of him in Papa's will. Cecily's financial constraints in the quarter had little to do with her true financial stability, for she knew herself to be well-dowried.

The difficulty was that Ash's definition of 'a respectable allowance' did not match Mama's spending habits. Lady Fanny had a habit of gleefully disposing of her allowance as quickly as she wished—normally on clothes, expensive food and wine, and gifts for her friends, trusting that others would cover her bills towards the end of each accounting period. Most of Cecily's own allowance was frequently taken up paying Mama's bills. There was no point in asking for a larger allowance either, as Mama would simply spend that, too.

Visiting Hazledene should have felt different. Cecily knew that Nell truly valued their friendship, and that she genuinely welcomed her company. But the disquiet she was feeling about her encounter with the Earl meant that she could not feel easy about it.

Thoughts of the Earl were never far away. Just ten minutes ago Nell had repeated how much she was looking forward to nigh on a month in Hazledene, free from the vexation of wondering when she might see her disapproving brother-in-law again. 'Tom will still not speak of him,' she had confided to Cecily. 'I fear they are at odds over our marriage.'

'I believe you are right,' Cecily had agreed cautiously. 'But hopefully he will accept in time the fact that you are wed.' Since the arrogant Earl had expressed his clear opposition to his brother's marriage, Cecily now found herself even more determined to support it. And why should she be forced to give up her friendship with Nell just because Nell's brother-in-law disapproved of her for some unknown reason?

Greetings done, all of their worries were temporarily forgotten as they explored the house together—the grand hall with its huge fireplace and double height ceiling, the various smaller rooms downstairs, the spacious parlours upstairs on either side—one done up in red, one yellow—and the Long Gallery and five sumptuous bedchambers on the top floor, just below the attics. As footmen hauled their trunks upstairs, Cecily and Nell dashed about like girls, exclaiming with wonder at the clever way in which such an old house had been preserved.

Mr Beresford informed them that he and his brother had had to complete substantial work to the place in the past few years, as it had fallen into disrepair.

His trunks and that of his wife had been moved into the grand chamber—in fact, two bedchambers linked by a connecting door. Cecily was offered the choice of the other three rooms, and she eventually settled on the Blue Chamber, which was at the far end of the Long Gallery. All the bedchambers had views to the front, with the hills and pastures of Sussex unfolding before them as far as the eye could see. She and Nell gazed at the view alone for a few moments; Tom had returned downstairs to consult with the staff.

'This is simply delightful!' Cecily sighed. 'Oh, Nell, I do hope you will be happy here with your Mr Beresford.'

Nell was smiling. 'I do believe I shall! Indeed, Cecily,' she added shyly, 'I had never known such happiness was possible!'

The following hours gave Cecily her first opportunity to observe Nell and her husband at close quarters. It did her heart good to see that Tom seemed as besotted with his wife as she was with him. Neither did anything to make Cecily feel uncomfortable—indeed, she knew that Nell was genuinely delighted to have her company—but it was noticeable that, after the ladies retired to the yellow parlour following a delightful dinner, Tom did not wait long before joining them. Some awareness told her that Nell and her husband were eager to retire and so, feigning tiredness, she wished them a good night.

Climbing into bed, and thanking the housemaid who had assisted her, Cecily fleetingly wondered what might be occurring in the marital bedchamber at the other end of the house. She had heard enough of her mother's frank conversations with her friends to understand that marital duties were not always the painful, awkward necessities that young ladies were sometimes led to believe. Indeed, her mama and the other widows seemed to positively enjoy sharing a bed with a man. They did, she recalled, sometimes hint that not all men were the same—that some were more to be welcomed in the bedchamber than others.

Cecily was woman enough to have felt her heart flutter at a smile from a handsome man, or to notice with interest a young man's strong physique. She was also girl enough to be still confused about exactly what occurred between men and women. Mama had been little help, merely laughingly telling her to enjoy it when the time came or reminding Cecily of occasions when they had observed animals mating.

Marianne had been a little more helpful, explaining the essence of the physical act with the context of how wonderful it could be when the two people had developed trust between them. This had made sense to Cecily, as she simply could not imagine any maiden *enjoying* something that seemed as strange and comical as the farmyard matings she had seen.

For a moment, she allowed herself to imagine what it might feel like to go beyond the chaste kisses she had so far experienced as a debutante. A man's hands on her body. Her hands exploring, touching his skin. His body on hers. Desire sprang to life within her. Her breathing quickening, she allowed herself to become lost in imaginings. Her eyes fluttered closed—only to open wide again as she abruptly realised that her foolish mind was picturing intimacies with none other than Lord Hawkenden!

'Never!' she declared aloud, rolling onto her side. For an instant she again allowed herself to remember the feeling she had had when they had looked at each other in Lady Jersey's drawing room then, dismissing it, she settled down to sleep.

Chapter Nine

'Good morning, Cecily.' It was Nell, scurrying into the breakfast room, a sunlit chamber on the eastern side of the ground floor. 'I have terrible news!'

Cecily looked up from her breakfast plate, fork paused in the air. 'What has happened? My dear Nell, are you unwell?' Nell looked and sounded agitated, and her blunt greeting left Cecily struggling to understand why.

Her friend shook her head. 'Oh, Cecily!' She slumped into a chair. 'Lord Hawkenden is to arrive today!'

Cecily's blood ran cold. *What?* But I understood he was not to be here?' She laid down her fork, her appetite abruptly vanishing.

Nell nodded miserably. 'The staff have just told Tom that he is coming. He is to arrive later today, with two gentlemen. They assumed Tom knew.'

'But—but this is impossible! We thought we could avoid him here!'

'I know. Tom says he and his brother disagreed about it, and because he had already made arrangements for us to be here, he never dreamed that Lord Hawkenden's stubbornness would lead him to come anyway. He also admits it is all his own fault, for Hazledene belongs to the Earl.' She put her head in her hands. 'Oh, Lord, what a fix!'

Cecily's brain was struggling to function. Desperately, her mind sought a solution—one that would allow her to escape the upcoming confrontation. Nothing came to her.

He does not want me here!

She glanced at Nell, seeing real distress in her expression. 'Oh, Nell!' Rising from the table, she crossed to Nell and hugged her fiercely. 'You are married, and there is nothing *that man* can do about it.' Her tone dripped with loathing towards him, partly fuelled by her own anxiety. 'Your husband and his brother will have to work out their differences, so my advice is to keep away from their quarrel and simply allow them to debate in whatever style they choose. If we are to return to London, then we shall do so.'

And if I am forced to return by myself, as if in disgrace, then I shall.

She put a soothing hand on her friend's arm. 'Think! The Earl is bringing some friends. That means *everyone* will have to behave in a sensible way.'

Nell's shoulders dropped a little. 'That is true! Oh, Cecily, you must think me a poor creature! I, who have been used to managing Wyatt House since Papa's death, should be able to meet challenges with fortitude. It is just that…' She took a breath. 'I wanted Tom's brother to be happy for him. And he is not.'

Cecily nodded sympathetically, before returning to her friend's previous statement. 'I have no doubt that you will manage, Nell. And I am here to stand with you.' *At least for the present.*

Nell gave a weak smile, then visibly gathered herself. 'My first problem is to work out where they are all to sleep!' She laughed. 'I had a similar challenge during Ma-

ma's Christmas house party. That ended with me sleeping
in the servants' quarters!'

'Oh, I remember that!' Cecily frowned. 'And you are
right—there are not many bedrooms.'

The door opened, admitting Mr Beresford. He was followed by a footman bringing more hot food. Mr Beresford
wished Cecily a good morning, flashed a reassuring smile
towards his wife, then went to the sideboard to help himself to breakfast. Nell poured herself some tea.

*I must tell them what occurred between me and Lord
Hawkenden.*

They needed to know that the Earl was unaccountably
opposed to friendship between Cecily and Nell. Cecily
glanced at the footman, who was now standing impas-
sively by the sideboard.

Not exactly now, though.

'At what time will your brother arrive?' Nell asked
the question as soon as Mr Beresford had joined them at
the table.

'Around sundown.' There was a slight frown creas-
ing his forehead. All were supremely conscious that they
could not be fully open in front of servants.

Nell set down her cup. 'You mentioned that he will
bring some of his friends, I think? Where is everyone
to sleep?'

Tom grinned. 'I shall arrange everything, my love. You
cannot be expected to take on such responsibilities in your
first day in Hazledene.'

'Thank you, Tom, that is quite a relief! Do you know
who the Earl's friends are?'

'Mr Carmichael and Mr Harting will accompany him.'

'Oh!' said Nell. 'We are acquainted with both gentlemen.' She sent Cecily a speaking glance.

Mr Harting! That friendly gentleman had shown signs

of being interested in Cecily when they had last met at Lady Jersey's party. Cecily sighed inwardly. *Not now!* Someday, despite her objections to Mama, she would probably end by marrying *someone*, and if so, then she would prefer someone young, healthy and attractive in face and form. Someone she could tolerate in terms of his demeanour. Someone with warmth.

Despite her recent conversation with Mama, Cecily now reflected briefly on the security that a judicious marriage might bring. No more worries about how to pay for a hotel, or which friend they might stay with next. No more anxiety over allowances that were much, much smaller than the time allocated to them. Companionship. Security. Freedom.

Her mind wandered further, away from the practical considerations. Someone who held her hand and looked at her as though she were precious… *No.* She pushed the thought away, her customary cynicism reasserting itself. Marriage was too big a decision to be taken lightly. Seeing how Nell's hasty marriage had caused discomfort and concern gave her even more reason to be cautious.

Returning to the sensible considerations of a wise marriage, there was also, she reflected, a further blessing. A married lady could dispense with the need to be chaperoned. As they had discussed in the park only a few days ago, Nell and Cecily had long chafed against the restrictions of their lives as marriageable virgins. Unable to go where they wished. One's every utterance watched and judged… As a married lady, Nell was already tasting the delights of increased freedom. Cecily, sitting in her friend's shadow, could not help but be a little envious.

This month in Sussex should have been an opportunity for Cecily to stretch her wings a little, away from her mama's eye. Instead, she sat in increasing anxiety, knowing that today *he* would be here, and she would have to face him, *and* admit to her friend how she had unwittingly inflamed the conflict over Nell's marriage. She could delay no longer. Today was the day.

Her opportunity came immediately after breakfast. Mr Beresford offered them both a tour of the Long Gallery, where paintings of various Beresford ancestors were hung, and where, he said, he and his brother had used to play as children. 'Our old nurse was very tolerant and used to take us up here on rainy days,' Mr Beresford said, 'for she knew we had a need for havoc!'

As they climbed the stairs, Cecily could not help but try to imagine Lord Hawkenden as a playful child. *Impossible.* It was beyond her meagre powers. Even as a child she pictured him as glowering, cold…unhappy. She squirmed a little at the thought, reminding herself that she barely knew the man. Besides, imagining the child he had been was not helpful to her peace of mind, so she refused to linger on the thought.

Bracing herself, and checking that no servants were present, she tore her gaze away from the Gainsborough of the Beresford grandparents. 'There is something I should tell you.' Both turned to her, with similar enquiring expressions. 'About my conversation with Lord Hawkenden at Lady Jersey's soirée.'

Mr Beresford frowned slightly, while Nell put a hand on her arm. 'Did he upset you, dear Cecily?'

'Well, he did,' replied Cecily cautiously, 'but, then, I also upset him.'

'What do you mean?' She now had their full attention.

Briefly, she outlined how it had happened—that the Earl had followed her out on the terrace that night in order to speak to her. 'I am sorry to say, my dear Nell, that he does not approve of your marriage.'

Nell's eyes filled with tears. 'I knew it! I sensed it all along. Did I not say so?' She turned to her husband, who looked grimly tight-lipped.

Wordlessly, he took his wife's hand then turned to Cecily. 'Must we speak of this now, Lady Cecily?'

'I fear we must. I had not mentioned it before, but now that he is coming, I thought Nell ought to know.'

Mr Beresford shook his head, looking back at his wife. 'I had hoped to spare you from my brother's resistance. Unfortunately,' he added ruefully, 'as Lady Cecily has highlighted, his insistence on coming here means we cannot evade it.' He sent Cecily a glance. 'I still would have preferred to discuss this with Nell myself.'

Cecily nodded. 'I am sorry for raising it. But—there is more.' She bit her lip, then gathered her courage. 'Lord Hawkenden asked me…' she took a breath '…how much it would cost him to remove me from his brother's life.'

The words shattered like glass into the stillness of the Long Gallery. Mr Beresford was as rigid as a statue, while Nell's jaw had dropped in horror.

'But *why*?' Nell's forehead creased. 'Am I not permitted to choose my own friends? And why should he try to induce you with bribery?'

'I do not understand it either, Nell. I know that my mama…' she glanced briefly at Tom, whose face was rigid with what looked like shock '…is not always discreet about her *affaires*, but she is received everywhere. And I myself have never been involved in anything the least bit scandalous! Indeed, my greatest sin, according to Mama, is apparently that I do not flirt enough, and am likely to end an old maid!'

'Oh, Cecily! How awful for you! How on earth did you answer him? If it had been me, I believe I should have been instantly crushed!'

'I—er—that is to say, I…'

They waited.

'I'm afraid I quite lost my temper. I did not quiver and quake and agree with him. I simply refused to discuss the matter with him further, accused him of vulgarity, and left.'

Nell's eyes grew round. 'Oh, Cecily, you are so brave!'

'It was not in the least bit brave, for he should not have said such a thing to me, and I was determined he should know it!' Her face softened. 'I am sorry, though, that being my friend will cause trouble for you, my dear Nell. I should not have come here, for I think he will be severely displeased.'

Nell brushed this away. 'Pshaw! I shall choose my own friends, whatever he may say! He has no right to say who I shall spend time with, and there is no reason in the least for him to find you objectionable! But now I know why you were so ill that night. Oh, Cecily, once again you have become embroiled in my affairs, and have acted as my protector.'

'You are my best friend, Nell,' she replied gruffly. 'I should like to maintain our friendship, but I am prepared to give way if he makes life difficult for you.'

There was a silence. Summoning all her courage, Cecily glanced at Tom, who had remained silent throughout. Nell also looked his way.

'Let me be clear, Lady Cecily,' he managed, his jaw tight with some unexpressed emotion. 'My brother actually accosted you angrily, asking you to remove yourself from Nell's life?'

'Well…to be accurate, he wishes me to be removed from *your* life, which in the end is the same thing.'

'Outrageous.' He shook his head. 'And you declined

to agree to his abominable demand, and instead you walked away?'

'Er—I suppose I did. I was, in fact, rather rude to not engage with him. Oh, dear!'

'But you are astonishing! And it is not rude to walk away from someone who is being insulting towards you.'

Cecily was astounded to see laughter lurking in his eyes. As they watched, it spilled out into a hearty—and infectious—guffaw. Helplessly, and knowing it was vaguely inappropriate, they all ended up laughing together, Cecily's mirth strongly tinged with relief.

'Lady Cecily, you are a treasure!' he declared, when he had himself under control. 'I remember how cross you were with me at Christmas, when my foolishness ended up distressing my darling Nell. I must declare I was glad then that Nell had such a friend, and I am glad now that you challenged my stubborn brother so! Even now, he will be suffering the agonies of trying to plan how he can rescue us from whatever imagined objection he has to your friendship with Nell!'

'I hope you know that I did not intend to—'

'Oh, I understand *exactly* how it came about, never fear, and I applaud your ability to withstand him. My brother can be most ferocious!' He bowed. 'Brava, Lady Cecily!'

Cecily wiped away a tear, unclear if it originated in merriment or relief. 'Well,' she declared, 'he certainly was on that occasion. I do regret that my walking away, and my words, may have inflamed his anger, Mr Beresford. And I do not wish to be unkind by laughing at his discomfiture.'

'It is not in the least unkind, for he is the one being unreasonable here. Never fear, he will see what a good friend you are to Nell—and I hope that he will, like me, appreciate such a friendship.' He grinned again. 'You should call me Tom. After all, I do believe I have gained a sister this day!'

Nell clapped her hands at this, while Cecily smiled and gave a nod of the head. 'Very well. And you should call me Cecily. I have not had a brother before. It will be a novel experience.' Indeed, something within her warmed at the very idea. *A brother...*

He spoke again. 'There is something else. Ladies, I think you have both made my brother something of an ogre in your imaginations. Am I correct—particularly after his disgraceful attack on you, Cecily?'

They confessed that it was. Cecily certainly had a monstrous notion of him, interlaced with a dark pull of attraction.

'Then let me tell you that he is—despite the stubbornness, and the occasional arrogance, and his belief that everything, in the end, is about money—the best of brothers. I had hoped he would be more understanding about my marriage, and I am more than angry about how he has been behaving, but I believe he will come round in time. Nell, he cannot fail to love you! And, Cecily, there can be no objection to your friendship with me and Nell! Just let us allow him the chance to know you both better.'

'He may insist that I leave, which removes any such opportunity,' Cecily pointed out.

'Yes, and what of his bringing guests when he knew you were already planning to be here?' Nell's chin was raised, her eyes flashing.

'Ah.' Tom nodded grimly. 'He and I occasionally play out battles of stubbornness, I must admit. I am angry with him for many reasons today, and I must ask you both to excuse my part in this. Hazledene is his, so I should have given way.' Laughter twinkled in his eyes. 'But I cannot let him win, for he is behaving outrageously!'

The ladies glanced at each other, neither having anything to say to this. Despite being firmly on Tom's side on the matter, Cecily was interested to hear they had had similar fallings-out in the past, fuelled by obstinacy on both sides.

Perhaps both men are at fault, then. Why, they are no better than schoolboys!

'Now, let us forget about my brother for a few hours! Shall we perhaps go out in the carriage so that I can show you something of the surrounding area?'

'An excellent idea!' Nell clapped her hands. 'Why, we have *hours* yet before he comes!'

How quickly, Cecily thought, moments become minutes, and minutes turn into hours. She was in her new bedchamber, awaiting the dinner gong, when she heard the sounds outside that heralded the arrival of Lord Hawkenden and his guests. Swiftly crossing the room, she peeped down at the driveway below, where men, horses, trunks and chaos seemed to reign in the twilight. Her heart sank for a moment then she lifted her chin and reminded herself that, as Nell's friend, she had every right to be here, despite what the Earl might say.

They had agreed that Tom and Nell would, as was proper, go downstairs first to greet the new arrivals, and that Cecily herself should wait a few moments before descending. Those few moments felt like aeons. Finally, she judged enough time had passed. Checking her appearance for the final time, she nodded at her reflection. This evening she had chosen a pretty pale green silk with embroidered patterns of flowers and leaves along the hem, and with a matching green ribbon in her hair. Perfectly unexceptional.

She glanced around before leaving the chamber. Years

of being a guest in other people's houses had inured her to the challenges of unfamiliarity. She always slept well in a new place, and could not understand people who struggled to do so. Her nomadic seasons with Mama had also reinforced the feeling of being an outsider, the unwanted one—a feeling that was strongly impressing itself upon her at this moment.

Smoothing her dress one last time, she left the room and went downstairs.

Chapter Ten

Jack refused to regret his decision to travel to Hazledene. Well, why should he? The house was his, even if Tom used it more than he did. It was too small for true entertaining, having only five bedchambers, and so it tended to stay closed up outside the hunting season.

Jack did most of his own business entertaining at Springfield Hall, part of the lavish Hawkenden estate. The estate that had very nearly made him bankrupt after their father had died. The sensible course of action would have been to sell Springfield and begin again, particularly as the property was unentailed, but Jack and Tom had agreed to only do so if absolutely necessary.

With a determination borne of responsibility coupled, he now knew, with astounding naivety, he had resolved back then to learn the science and art of becoming wealthy. Luck had played a part, he conceded now, but his stubbornness and refusal to concede to the hand fate had played him had been at the heart of his success. He had not been forced to sell Springfield, or Hazledene, or the London townhouse. Somehow, despite the odds being against them, he and Tom had prevailed.

Such success had made up somewhat for the feelings

of worthlessness he had endured as a boy. A cruel father and a cruel school had followed the death of his mother and abandonment by his nurse, and had left a hole within him that had become filled with the need for continuous achievements in commerce. Each time he had successfully acquired a new company, or boosted his cash reserves, or succeeded in a venture, part of him inwardly crowed at those long-gone oppressors and deserters.

See? I am worthy. I can achieve things. I do not need your approval. Or your presence. Or your love.

The same obstinacy that had driven him after his father's death had also led Jack to follow through on his invitation to Harting and Carmichael this week. Knowing how things stood with his foolish brother, knowing too that Tom's beautiful, venal wife would also be present, Jack really could have given way and taken a different road. He had refused to do so. This visit would offer opportunities to assess the situation, to develop a strategy, to lay the foundations for his eventual victory.

As the carriage wheeled into the driveway of Hazledene and the candlelit windows came into view, he reminded himself that he had never lost a war he had truly focused on. Battles, yes. But keeping his mind focused on the ultimate prize had always led to success in the end.

This time his goal was still shifting somewhat. He had wanted to undo his brother's marriage. That was now unrealistic, given the fact that word of the wedding was now beginning to spread in London. Twice yesterday people had asked him to pass on their congratulations to Tom. Mrs Godwin had shared the good news, they said.

Of course she had.

Besides, Tom and his fair-haired beauty had, of course, consummated the marriage. Jack's hands formed into fists. Of all the aspects of this unlooked-for complication, that was the one that caused the most visceral response. Why should he care that Tom was bedding her? It was, after all, at the heart of how Tom had likely fallen into this trap. Tom was no doubt feeling like the cock of the walk these days.

I shall sleep in the Blue Bedchamber, as usual, he resolved, knowing Tom would have appropriated the double chamber for himself and his wife.

He wished to be as far away from their nuptial activities as he could manage. He wanted no reminders of their marital congress. Harting and Carmichael could take the other two chambers.

Public knowledge of the marriage did not, however, mean that he had accepted Tom's folly. He and Tom had invested too much in terms of time, effort and pain building up their wealth to throw some of it away on an unworthy woman. The fair-haired baggage might believe she could empty Tom's wallet, but she was soon to discover who was truly in control.

The carriage came to a halt, and the coachman jumped down to lower the steps and open the door. Jack stepped down, followed by his two guests. Responding mechanically to their compliments—people were always impressed by the Elizabethan house—Jack stretched and loosened his shoulders, determined to maintain an air of unruffled calm.

Inside, a queasy feeling was troubling him. Being at Hazledene was always difficult. Painful memories lurked in every room and behind every corner. Yet showing Tom he would not be dominated was currently more important than avoiding recollections of past hurts.

Jack's valet, along with those of Carmichael and Harting, were now emerging through the open door. They had travelled down earlier with the bulk of the luggage and had been awaiting their arrival. The servants busied themselves helping the coachman to unload the smaller trunks that had been attached to the Hawkenden travelling carriage. As Jack walked towards the open door, his brother came into view. Tom looked composed, while the woman by his side—

Jack stopped abruptly, almost causing Carmichael to bump into him. They automatically apologised to each other, then Jack walked on into the house, his eyes fixed on his new sister-in-law. She was of average height, pretty, with flaming auburn locks, pale skin and greenish coloured eyes. She was very clearly *not* the woman he had spoken to at Lady Jersey's soirée. Jack's mind was all disorder.

What the deuce...?

'I would like to introduce my wife,' Tom was saying. He looked at her. 'Nell, this is my brother, Hawkenden.'

She curtseyed. 'I am pleased to meet you, my lord.' She looked nervous, he noted distractedly.

Jack replied instinctively, before introducing Harting and Carmichael to her. It seemed they knew each other already, Harting in particular greeting Tom's wife with warmth and familiarity.

'And here is our other guest!' Tom declared, as a lady in green appeared through the door at the far end of the Great Hall—the one that led to the staircase.

Jack felt his jaw slacken. It was *her*. Dimly, he heard the greetings. Lady Cecily Thornhill.

Of course!

Ash's ward, and Miss Godwin's great friend. His mind reeling, he yet managed to play his part in the ritual of polite greeting and response. Afterwards, he could not have said exactly what was said, or by whom. His mind was wholly fixed on the beautiful woman before him, and the astounding knowledge that she was *not*, in fact, Tom's wife. Feelings of confusion and relief chased each other like swirling leaves.

Lady Cecily Thornhill. Not Tom's wife.

Tom was indicating that dinner was to be served soon, and so Jack and the two male guests were swiftly ushered upstairs to wash and change. Jack's valet was awaiting him in the gallery, wringing his hands. After ensuring that his two guests had entered their chambers, Jack turned to the man. 'Well?'

'My lord, where are you to sleep?'

Jack's jaw dropped. Of course! Tom and his wife would have taken the Earl and Countess's interconnecting rooms, leaving only the Blue Chamber.

'Is Lady Cecily using the Blue?'

'She is, my lord.'

And Tom, knowing what was to happen, had done nothing to resolve the situation. 'Then you must bring my trunks to the nursery. There is no other choice.'

The valet looked horrified. 'The *nursery*, my lord?'

'Do you have a better suggestion?' He waited. 'I thought not.

Twenty minutes later, as his valet fussed around him in his cramped, low-ceilinged bedchamber, Jack finally began to think rationally again.

A victory for Tom, he acknowledged.

Judging by the studied innocence in Tom's expression, his brother had clearly known about the difficulties with room allocation. Not only that but he had taken full advantage of it in order to maximise Jack's discomfort.

Now recalling the humour glinting in his brother's eyes downstairs, Jack's ire was reasserting itself, replacing the temporary disorientation he had felt just now. His brother had clearly conspired to humiliate him in front of his own friends, which could not be easily forgiven. That Jack had not realised immediately that he would of necessity be forced to sleep in the nursery—the *nursery*, for goodness' sake!—and had behaved with propriety in company did not excuse the fact that Tom must have known he might disgrace himself by losing his temper.

Bad form, Tom, he thought.

While he was, naturally, regretful of his error in addressing the wrong woman on the terrace that night, he could not regret the instincts that had led him to do so. It was unfortunate that Lady Cecily had been on the receiving end of his frustration that night—little wonder she had looked so confused. He pictured her, serenely refusing to engage in debate with him, but now her withdrawal took on new significance. He had been entirely wrong—not a feeling he was used to.

The valet was familiar enough with Lord Hawkenden's moods to read the signs. He worked in silence, while Jack frowned with concentration. As he washed and dressed, his mind was whirling. Lady Cecily's flashing eyes that night on the terrace had clearly revealed anger—justified anger. What on earth she had made of his rantings, he had no idea. Had she realised he had mistaken her for her friend?

Suddenly realising that all his attention was focused on Lady Cecily, he ruthlessly brought his mind elsewhere. She was now irrelevant, he reminded himself. His focus needed to be entirely on the redhead—Tom's actual wife. Dinner tonight would be his first opportunity to gain knowledge of the true Miss Nell Godwin—now Mrs Tom Beresford. He would not waste the opportunity.

Yet as the valet departed, Jack's thoughts again drifted back to Lady Cecily Thornhill. He fitted a diamond pin to his cravat and dropped his watch into its pocket.

She is not Tom's wife.

The thought repeated itself endlessly in his brain, and he was unsure why.

Three hours later, the ladies departed from the dining room, leaving the gentlemen to their port. Staring into his glass and allowing the gentlemen's conversation to wash over him, Jack considered what he had learned. He had naturally been placed at the head of the table, and Tom at the foot, as was their habit.

On his left, Tom's wife and Mr Carmichael had sat, politely discussing a range of topics in an amicable way. The conversation had been sensible to the point of dullness, leaving Jack wondering what on earth his brother had seen in Miss Godwin. Oh, she was a good-looking chit, there was no doubt. Had he himself not been blinded by a certain fair-haired lady, he might have looked long enough that night in Berkeley Square to see the undoubted attraction in his sister-in-law's pretty face and fine figure.

Having acknowledged that, he was yet to comprehend why Tom, having been hounded by matchmaking mamas these eight years and more, had finally succumbed to the wiles of a simple country miss, with little to recommend her beyond a pleasing smile and a neat ankle. Miss Godwin was not one of the most talked-about virgins of this season, neither was she a substantial heiress, nor was she a diamond of the first water in terms of her looks. Now, if it had been Lady Cecily… Dragging his thoughts away from Lady Cecily yet again, he focused on Tom's wife. *Respectable* was the word Hollamby had used to describe the Godwin family. Not particularly wealthy or well-connected. Country gentry. Nothing that should have tempted a Beresford, if Tom had had any respect for his name and lineage.

Tom, he had noted, had watched his wife constantly throughout dinner, and with the warmest of expressions in his eye. *Damnation!* Tom looked every bit as vacuous as the lovesick fools he had long despised. Never had Jack thought he would see a good man tumble so low. Quite why this angered him so much he could not fully articulate, even to himself. It had something to do with fear, and risk, and leaving oneself open to abandonment... Better that a man marry for money, or for an heir, than marry for love. In addition, now that Tom was so focused on making sheep's eyes at his lady, where did that leave his brother? Where did that leave the reliance they had on each other? Despite their regular arguments, Tom was his rock, and he was Tom's. Or he had been, until now.

The wife herself had seemed guileless, but Jack was old enough and clever enough to know how appearances could be deceiving. No, for now he must hold to the same view of her, unless proven otherwise. Either Tom's wife was herself a scheming vixen, or someone—Mrs Godwin perhaps—had engineered the marriage. Tom would surely not be so foolish as to fall for her inducements without conscious effort on the part of Miss Godwin and her stepmother.

His thoughts drifted back, as they had continually tonight, to Lady Cecily. Might she have been the manipulator in the background, securing a stellar match for her friend? Their conversation tonight had confirmed she had attended the same house party at Christmastide where Tom and Miss Godwin had met. He snorted inwardly. Lady Cecily was certainly cool enough. And clever enough, too. Cynical matchmaking was not just the preserve of hopeful mamas. Yes, Lady Cecily Thornhill might well be his true opponent.

Surely, his mind prompted fleetingly, *it is Tom himself that I am pitted against?*

Not liking the thought, he did not pursue it.

To his right, Lady Cecily and Mr Harting had engaged in an undeniable flirtation at the dinner table and enduring it had irritated him no end. He knew Harting fairly well, and quite liked him. Straight, reliable and pleasant, with a good mind and a decent fortune, he would undoubtedly make a good husband for someone. The knowledge that Harting's eye had fallen on the fair Lady Cecily was… unfortunate, although Jack of all people could not deny her beauty. Well, how could he, as she had been haunting him since the night at Berkeley Square?

Carmichael was currently teasing Tom on the felicity of Harting's having been seated with Lady Cecily at dinner, causing Jack's attention to sharpen again. 'Your wife is a delight, of course, Tom, but she is spoken for! Why did you not place me with the divine Lady Cecily?'

Jack's jaw tightened. They were flocking round Lady Cecily like bees around flowers. Normally he remained detached from such things, but seeing their attempts to gain the lady's favour was supremely irritating. He foresaw days of vexation ahead.

Tom laughed. 'We shall not stand on formality here, Carmichael. There will be plenty of opportunities in the coming days to better your acquaintance with her.'

Carmichael rubbed his hands together. 'Good, for I mean to give Harting a run for his money!'

Jack sighed inwardly. *Et tu, Carmichael?*

Harting was smiling at Carmichael's challenge. 'Now, my friend,' he replied mildly, 'you cannot think her to be remotely interested in you. Why, she had eyes only for me all evening!'

Carmichael disagreed, calling on Jack for support.

'Hawk, you must agree! Lady Cecily is much too well-bred to practise coquetry across the table at another gentleman. Why, her conversation with Harting was simply politeness, was it not?'

Jack shrugged, frowning. 'If you both mean to vex me with pointlessness, I shall begin to regret inviting you.'

They protested at this, being used to his way, and returned to baiting each other. After a few more minutes, and unable to withstand it any longer, Jack suggested joining the ladies.

As soon as the suggestion was made, he regretted it.

Now I must endure my brother making sheep's eyes at his lady, and feel uncomfortable with Lady Cecily.

Exasperation rose within him. He had spoken to both ladies briefly at dinner, in the interests of maintaining a facade of good manners. Tom's wife had reminded him of a frightened fawn, while her friend had irked him with an air of calm superiority. Being honest, he knew he was drawn to her, against his own wishes, and the struggle frustrated him. The sooner Lady Cecily returned to London, the better. Then perhaps he could wrestle with his real concerns—like Tom's marriage—without the continual distraction of her presence.

He led the gentlemen to the red parlour, maintaining a disinterested air as the others vied with each other to engage the two ladies in railery that was as lacking in wit as it was sense. Horrifyingly, he then heard them decide to walk out together to a local beauty spot on the morrow. Clearly, Tom had no notion of giving way and returning to London.

'But are we not here for hunting?' he asked. 'Indeed, when I invited you both you declared you could not wait to take to the saddle!'

Harting waved this away. 'Hunting must wait, for we

now have more important considerations. We may ride out on the next day—unless, that is, you have made a commitment on our behalf?'

Jack had to admit there was no such engagement, and could not help but bristle at the humour he saw in Lady Cecily's eyes.

'I should like nothing more,' she declared, 'than to walk in these woods with you all tomorrow. What a delight it is to be in the countryside, and in such a fine house!'

Normally, praise for Hazledene would have soothed Jack's pride. He had a secret affection for the house, which was entirely unbecoming in a man of business such as himself. Affection could have no place in his life, particularly if it risked poor decision-making. Hazledene, he reminded himself, was simply a useful place for persuading gentlemen to engage in business arrangements that would be to their mutual advantage. The fact that he had spent a near-fortune repairing and restoring the place had therefore been a sensible undertaking, and a wise use of his funds. Nothing to do with childhood memories, painful or otherwise. Of course not. That would be nonsensical.

Briefly, recollections of happy summers here flashed through his mind, setting off an old ache in the region of his chest. Mama, Jack, Tom and their nurse, Tilly, enjoying sunshine and freedom while Papa visited friends... Turning away from the memories, he instead listened with half-pleasure as the party discussed how beautiful and wonderful Hazledene was, before becoming embroiled in a conversation about how it had fallen into such disrepair, and the efforts it had taken to restore it.

'Lord, do you remember the time the chimney pot fell down, just when we were standing outside, Jack?' Tom asked, seemingly forgetting momentarily that he was at odds with his brother. 'Dashed near killed us both!'

'I remember how much that fellow charged us for the replacement,' Jack growled. 'Not to mention the roof repairs!'

'Well, I think it was work well done,' said Tom's wife softly. 'It is a beautiful house.'

Jack's eyes narrowed. Was she seeking to suggest it would do for her and Tom? Well, he wasn't going to let her have it. But, no, Hollamby had said she had a house of her own in Kent—the house that Tom had wished to purchase. He had got it anyway, through marriage. Meeting his brother's gaze, he realised that Tom had read his expression and was now glaring angrily at him.

He maintained a defiant stare, until Tom's wife broke the sudden silence by rising to ring the bell for tea.

Lady Cecily, he noted, was eyeing him evenly.

She is very bold, he thought. *Too bold. It is unbecoming.*

It did not occur to him to notice that he was judging her by standards different from those he normally demanded of anyone, man or woman. Indeed, confidence and clarity of thought were qualities he generally admired.

After tea, the card table was brought out, and they all played a couple of hands of Commerce. It was clear before long that everyone was rather fatigued, and so they said their goodnights. Jack had the misfortune to be following Lady Cecily up the stairs. A scent of delicious perfume reached his nostrils, and his ears were attuned to the rustle of her skirts. Every sense was focused on her and only her, while inside his head his mind was desperately fighting this unwelcome fixation. Unfortunately, the fine form of her hips and bottom was directly in his eyeline as he followed, three stairs behind.

Normally, such a sight would please him, as it would any red-blooded male, but his enmity with Lady Cecily meant that the more he desired her, the more frustrated he was about doing so. Harting and Carmichael were just behind him, and were no doubt making the most of the delightful sight of Lady Cecily's backside gliding up the staircase in front of them.

Further behind, Tom and his bride were strangely silent. Without thinking, Jack glanced back. They were stopped on the third stair, kissing. Jack rolled his eyes, gritted his teeth and stomped on.

Chapter Eleven

Well! Cecily reached the sanctuary of her room and exhaled in relief. Finally she could rest. Leaning against the door, she slipped her feet out of her satin evening slippers and began loosening her stays. She felt both exhausted and strangely invigorated, and her insides were churning with myriad feelings.

Lord Hawkenden, arriving at the house, had been forced to bite his tongue on realising that Nell's unwanted friend was already in residence. She had easily read his surprise at her appearance. Did he think her such a poor creature that his words on Lady Jersey's terrace that night would be enough to frighten her away from her dearest friend? He now knew that she was made of sterner stuff.

But if I had known he would arrive, would I still have come?

Banishing the thought, for she much preferred the notion that she would have accepted Nell's invitation regardless, she nodded firmly.

Of course I would.

Even better, whatever he might have wished to say to her about it had been suppressed, simply because his own guests were with him. How frustrating it must have been for him not to give her the sharp side of his tongue! She giggled, finally giving way to the mirth that had been bubbling up inside her all evening. The more she had sensed his frustration, the more comical it had seemed.

Oh, but you deserved it, for you should not tell any lady whom she may choose for her friends.

He had glowered every time she had opened her mouth to speak, and every time she had received attention or compliments from his friends. During the meal Mr Harting had been an entertaining companion, and sensing the Earl's irritation had simply encouraged Cecily to flirt and sparkle in a way that was most unlike her.

Afterwards, in the drawing room, Mr Carmichael had been equally attentive, while the Earl had become more and more morose as the time had gone on. By the time they had agreed to retire, his face had become as immovable as granite. He was clearly very, very angry with her. The thought, instead of being frightening, was strangely elevating. Perhaps seeing him simply as Tom's brother, rather than a monstrous ogre, had its advantages. And perhaps he could not, after all, banish her from Nell's life.

Her fear had gone, and with it her anger. Now she saw only obstinate brothers, as bullheaded as each other, and battles that hopefully did not run deep. Tom's optimism, as well as his kind words about his brother, had given her hope that all would, somehow, be well. And instinctively she knew that the Earl was not indifferent to her. There had been a certain look in his eye when Mr Harting had been flirting with her… The thought made her want to dance, to skip, to fly.

Being in the Earl's company was challenging, fascinating and exhilarating, at once. Pausing for a moment, she recalled one of the dark looks he had sent her earlier, and her expression broke into a grin. Still smiling, she crossed the room and rang the bell for the maid.

Jack stood in the Long Gallery, frowning. Carmichael and Harting had said their goodnights and entered their chambers, and he himself was paused near the portrait of his parents,

Lady Cecily had entered the Blue Chamber, and even now might be disrobing as she prepared for bed. Averting his thoughts swiftly, Jack instead made his way to the large Gainsborough featuring the Seventh Earl and his Countess. Mama was as beautiful as he remembered, but even at the time of this portrait, painted to celebrate their marriage, there was a sadness about her eyes. Deliberately, Jack looked at his father. The master painter had caught his essence—pride, arrogance, a hint of cruelty.

I am not the same as him. Not the same.

Not the same.

Unclenching his fist, he picked up a branch of candles from the nearby side table and made his way up the narrow staircase to the attics.

In the nursery, his valet was waiting, disapproval writ in the stiff lines of his figure. The man was clearly displeased that he was being forced to work in an attic nursery.

As if I am content to be sleeping here, Jack thought wryly.

As the man worked, Jack's focus returned, as it had on dozens of occasions this evening, to the conversation he'd had with Lady Cecily on Lady Jersey's terrace. Now that he knew her true identity, it was clear to see that she had been bewildered by his unwarranted verbal attack on her, yet had managed the situation with a coolness that had to be admired.

Each time he'd looked at her tonight, he'd been subjected to a whirl of conflicting emotions. Although his mind knew she was *not* Tom's wife, and had *not* trapped Tom into marriage, his gut was rather slower to catch up with this new knowledge. Meanwhile, his eye and his body generally were just as taken with her as before. The whole thing was entirely unacceptable!

The valet offered him one last, small glass of brandy, and he savoured it slowly. The man left quietly, discreetly, being careful not to disrupt his master's pensive mood. As soon as he had gone, Jack ran a hand through his hair, finally letting go of the social mask he'd been forced to wear all day.

Lady Cecily Thornhill. Quickly, he reviewed what he knew about her. She was Ash's ward, probably because her mother, Lady Fanny, was too flighty and unreliable for such responsibility. Lady Fanny was accepted everywhere, and generally well-liked, yet no-one could claim her to be anything other than bird-witted. How had he never noticed her daughter before?

He shrugged. Because, generally, he did not notice young ladies at all—except to admire a neat figure, plump bosom or pretty face in an almost abstract way. As he was not yet seeking a wife, society virgins were generally of little interest to him. It had never occurred to him to learn their names or even notice them fully. He would in future have to attend to such things.

He squirmed slightly, remembering Lady Cecily pointing out that they had met before. She had known exactly who he was. He should have verified her identity, he acknowledged ruefully, before beginning his tirade against her. He had been rude towards her, and knowing it gave him considerable discomfort.

And now she was a guest in one of his houses—the smallest of his houses, in fact, and he foresaw he would be forced to bear her company for the next few weeks. Was she, even now, regretting his arrival? He did not normally care overmuch what others thought of him. But he had behaved badly towards her, and it seemed important that he make things right.

Setting down his glass, he made for his bed. Being in his old nursery was playing havoc with his control over old memories. Here, he and Tom had slept, and eaten, and played. Here, Tilly had cared for them. Here, he had cried silently, night after night, after Mama had died and Tilly had gone away.

He sighed and blew out the candles. He did not expect much sleep tonight.

The housemaid who had been assigned to look after her had returned to assist Cecily in preparing for bed. A plump, middle-aged woman, she was warm and helpful without being pert, and as unlike a coolly efficient London housemaid as it was possible to be. Her name, she had informed Cecily, yesterday, was Molly.

Cecily sat before the mirror, now clothed in her nightgown. The maid began removing the pins from her hair, then brushed it out before dampening her side curls and wrapping them in rags, ready for the morrow. Cecily let the woman do her work, her eyes glazing over as her attention focused inwards. Her thoughts, as before, were entirely on one man.

Why am I not frightened of Lord Hawkenden any more?

She checked inwardly. There was nervousness, yes, but also excitement. The fear that she had carried before today was simply no longer present. Had she ever been truly afraid of him? Perhaps, for a moment when she had thought him to be mad, on the terrace.

Her change of heart had been partly due to Tom's reaction to the tale, she realised. If he could see the humour in it, perhaps the Earl was not so dreadful, after all. And Tom, presumably, knew the Earl better than anyone. They did look very alike, and Cecily could not help but wonder if they were alike in character. Tom had demonstrated a warmth and humour earlier that had impressed Cecily, despite her hitherto more negative impression of his brother.

At that very moment the maid dropped the hairbrush, which clattered off the fireplace with a resounding rattle. 'Oh, dear, miss,' she said loudly, suddenly all bustle and chat. 'Look what I've done, and you just getting all sleepy and ready for your bed. Now, you're all done, so let me pull back the covers for you. I put a warming pan in earlier, just like Miss Tillot used to always do for the boys, for who does not like a warming pan on a cool night such as this? Not that it is as cold as it can be in winter, naturally. But even in spring the nights can be cold. Why, I've seen snow at Easter, you know!'

She ushered Cecily towards the bed, all noise and fuss, and Cecily found herself between the sheets, the warming pan at her feet and a wax candle on her bedstand. Molly shuffled out with a cheery goodnight, and Cecily finally drew breath.

In the silence that followed, Cecily stretched out in the comfortable bed and allowed the events of the day to flit through her mind. Abruptly, the picture in her mind shifted to herself and Lord Hawkenden. Briefly, she tried to imagine him lying alongside her. The thought created a strange mix of emotions and made her insides churn in an alarming manner, so instead she pictured him as she had seen him earlier, lost in morose irritability. She stifled a giggle. Somehow, the exhilaration was still with her.

Blowing out the last candle, she turned on her side to sleep.

guests at such gatherings, and she could hide behind her mother's vivaciousness and the sheer numbers of people.

This time they were a party of six. Nell and Tom. Mr Harting and Mr Carmichael. The Earl and Cecily. The six of them would come to know each other well over the coming weeks, so she needed to be ready to adjust to new challenges.

How would he behave towards her today? And why, for goodness' sake, did it bother her so much? Already she could see that Mr Beresford—that *Tom*—was more than a match for his older brother in some ways, certainly from the dealings she had had with them so far. Tom seemed determined to protect his marriage from criticism, which Cecily had to admire. He would also, Cecily knew, assert Nell's right to maintain her friendship with Cecily, whom he now considered a sister.

As she nibbled her way through eggs and buttered toast, and sipped tea that was satisfyingly hot, the tightness in Cecily's shoulders began to loosen a little. Cool morning light was glowing through the multi-paned window, illuminating the rich wood panelling and the landscapes that adorned the walls. Outside, birdsong and breezes provided a soothing harmony.

The door opened, and the Earl strode in. He was the picture of health, good looks and vigour, and on sight of him, Cecily's stomach began its now familiar fluttering.

He bowed. 'Good day, Lady Cecily.'

'Good day, my lord.'

Thank goodness for the presence of the footmen! As the Earl helped himself to eggs, beef and sausages, and was served tea, he and Cecily made idle conversation—about the pleasant weather, the prettiness of the house, and their plans to walk out today. There was no sign of his suffer-

Chapter Twelve

Cecily entered the breakfast room with some trepidation, relieved to find only the footmen present. It was, she supposed, hardly surprising, since the gentlemen had probably all been a trifle bosky last night—she had noted the numerous bottles of wine they had collectively consumed at dinner—while no doubt Nell and her husband would rise late, as was apparently their usual habit.

Cecily herself had slept surprisingly well, but had awoken without that brazen confidence that had carried her through the evening. Nervousness had gripped her—perhaps because it was dawning on her that she would be constantly in the Earl's company for many, many days, and the advantage she had gained from catching him unawares yesterday was now gone. If he remained opposed to her friendship with Nell, then he might continue to show his disapproval throughout her stay.

She had expected a relaxed, quiet visit with Nell and her husband, enjoying the freedom of being away from Mama's scrutiny, but overnight the visit had become a house party. The smallest, the most intimate house party she had ever experienced. Normally there were at least a score of ing any ill-effects from last evening's rich food and fine wines. Indeed, he looked…he looked frustratingly good.

'Where are we to walk to, my lord?' She kept her tone light. Strange how they could seem so polite on the surface. The footman could have no clue of the history between them.

'We shall not be able to climb Thursley Hill today, I fear.' His tone was flat. 'I have already been out and the hilltop is beset by fog.'

'That is a shame,' she returned, despite having no idea of the location or significance of Thursley Hill. 'Your brother mentioned a woodland area?'

'Crow Wood, yes,' he returned. His gaze became unfocused. 'Tom and I would play there as children.' He shook his head slightly, as if trying to rid himself of the memory. 'It is an agreeable spot, and if the day remains dry we may wander there for quite some time.'

She raised an eyebrow. 'Forgive me, but I cannot see you tolerating such purposeless idleness.' *Lord!* She regretted the words as soon as they had left her mouth. She should not be commenting on his character!

His dark eyes widened briefly, then, as if despite himself, the ghost of a smile hovered at the edges of his lips. 'Why should you say so, Lady Cecily?'

There was no getting away from it. An answer was required. 'I— You seem so…so *vital*, somehow, that purposeless wandering just does not…' Her voice tailed away. He was eyeing her directly, and the swirling in her stomach had increased to a point where she momentarily felt quite breathless. Quite why this man above all others should have such a potent effect on her, she had no idea.

'Nothing I do lacks purpose.' His eyes pinned hers. 'Even when I err, I do so with resolve.'

Now it was her turn to react with startlement. Was he

acknowledging his error that night on Lady Jersey's terrace? She sent him a questioning look, and he responded with the slightest of nods. Clearly aware that his expressions were out of sight of the footmen, he grimaced, then shrugged ruefully.

'I note, Lady Cecily, that you and my brother's wife are close friends.'

'We are.' Her throat was so tight she could barely force the words out.

What will he have to say about the matter?

'Such friendships are of great significance among ladies, are they not?'

'Indeed. Even after marriage, it would be important to maintain previous ties, do you not think?' She swallowed, hoping he had changed his mind about her.

'Ideally, yes, but marriage may change things.' His gaze became unfocused, as though he was no longer thinking of her and Nell. 'Other ties may become strained, even when intentions are good.'

Was he speaking of himself and Tom? 'If everyone involved thinks it important to maintain those ties,' she offered softly, 'then I believe they can be maintained. Strengthened, even.'

His expression changed, became shuttered. 'Not always. Sometimes cracks are so severe they cannot be repaired.'

'And yet it is important to try, and to keep trying.' She eyed him levelly, unsure of the ripples around them, yet believing instinctively that their conversation had significance. 'There is my friendship with Nell, for example. Some might think that when a woman marries, she must leave her friends and focus only on her husband's family. That Nell should put behind her the entirety of her life as Miss Godwin and become only Mrs Beresford.'

He raised an eyebrow. 'Sounds like foolishness to me. Why should a married person give up who they were, simply because they are now married? Surely a woman—or a man—maintains a responsibility to those who depended upon them before the marriage?'

Astonishment made her jaw drop. 'I agree entirely, my lord.'

'Good.' He applied himself to his breakfast, as though the matter were settled.

'Then…you do not mind my continuing friendship with your sister-in-law?'

'No, why should I? It is none of my concern.' He eyed her closely, and her heart skipped a beat. 'Lady Cecily, at times I speak bluntly, and without thinking. It is a fault of mine—though one that I thought myself to have mastered. I—'

'Hush now, my lord.' She did not need to hear the apology he was clearly about to make. Whatever had caused him to speak so angrily to her that night, she was well past ready to let go of the matter, particularly since she now knew that he did not, in fact, disapprove of her as Nell's friend. 'I, too behave in ways I should not.' She dimpled at him, and he blinked. 'Particularly when provoked.'

He was outrageous that night, and I was rude.

Remembering that she had accused him of vulgarity, she flinched inwardly.

He smiled at her, and her heart sang. She had to admire such plain speech, and to match it with her own. It was unusual, and frankly refreshing, to enjoy such a conversation.

He is the best of brothers… Tom's words came back to her.

Reflecting on her own part in their first encounter, she frowned. 'Unlike you, when I…er… Afterwards I doubt myself, berate myself for acting unthinkingly.' Her tone was low.

Why did I admit such a thing?

'Some advice, Lady Cecily, if you will permit?'

She nodded, a little disconcerted by how rapidly their discourse had progressed from hilltop fog to this. Her heart fluttered again as his eyes met hers directly.

'Never doubt yourself. If you fail, embrace it fully. Learn from it, of course, make amends when needed, but primarily understand your true purpose and how your errors may, on the long road, still take you there.'

This was too much for the breakfast table.

My true purpose? Do I even have a purpose?

Her brow creased as she considered his words, as old uncertainties rose again within her.

What am I to do? Marry for security, for children, for company?

'For gentlemen,' she offered slowly, 'it is easier to discern a purpose. We ladies are told that becoming a mother should be the pinnacle of our life's achievement.'

He tilted his head to the side, considering this. 'I had not given the matter much thought. Are women not then content to bear and raise children?'

'Well, of course we are—many of us, anyway. But that cannot be our *only* design. Many women have other talents and skills—in running a household, or painting, or music. Others follow academic pursuits. But we are constantly told it is not seemly to involve ourselves in matters more commonly pursued by men. Matters of business, for example.'

His eyebrows were both raised. 'You have an interest in matters of business?'

'I do. Does that surprise you, my lord?'

'Surprise me? I am astounded. Though perhaps, given

what I know about you, I should not be surprised at all.'
His eyes narrowed. 'Lord Kingswood is your guardian,
I understand?'

'He is, and a better guardian I could not have hoped
for.'

He nodded thoughtfully. 'There are few men I would
trust for guidance, but he is one of them.'

She beamed at this praise for her darling Ash. 'His
wife, Lady Kingswood, is also a highly competent busi-
nessperson.'

'I had not known this.' His brow furrowed. 'How did
she learn to be so?'

Cecily snorted. 'In the same way that you have, I imagine.'

He shook his head. 'It cannot be so. Most business
dealings among the *ton* take place away from the eyes of
ladies. Agreements are made in clubs and in personal li-
braries. Conversations often take place at Tattersall's, at
the racing, and in the fencing clubs. Even—forgive me—
at boxing fights.'

'Oh, I understand *that*. But those dealings are often sup-
ported by many hours of laborious study, are they not? Details of financing, of legal matters, of timing and cash and
revenues?' She was quite enjoying his surprised expression. 'In addition,' she continued gleefully, 'do business
dealings not also take place at…' she gestured vaguely
'…country houses?'

He grinned, shaking his head with what looked like be-
musement. Her heart skipped to see how the smile trans-
formed his face. He was quite astonishingly good-looking.
She blinked.

'You have me there, Lady Cecily. So Lady Kingswood
assists her husband in making business decisions?'

'From what I have observed, they decide equally, although it is he who then holds the conversations. But they will always have worked out beforehand the various possibilities, and how they will respond to each.'

'My brother and I do the same.' He frowned. 'That is, normally we do.'

There was a silence, where the unspoken knowledge of the present rift between the brothers lay heavy in the air. His eyes dropped to his plate, and he busied himself cutting a slice of beef with what seemed to Cecily to be unusual care. A pang went through her, as she remembered his earlier comment about ties being strained.

It pains him that they are at odds over this.

'Well, I for one am looking forward to walking in Crow Wood today,' she affirmed brightly.

He gave a twisted smile, acknowledging her clumsy attempt to paint over any awkwardness. 'Lady Cecily,' he declared, 'I must admit for your ears only...' he leaned towards her conspiratorially '...that I do have some proposals planned for Mr Harting while he is here.'

This was better. Normality was restored. 'Ha! And so when we are wandering through the woods today, perhaps we shall not, in fact, be "purposeless"—not from your perspective, at least.'

His eyes were smiling. It was doing bewildering things to her insides. 'You have me there, Lady Cecily.'

Is Lord Hawkenden flirting with me?

She must have imagined it, for in the next instant his expression had settled back into its usual handsome remoteness. He sipped from his china cup and she tried not to watch. 'And Mr Carmichael? Is he here simply to make up the numbers?' She was genuinely interested, finding the entire conversation enthralling. Much more than she should, perhaps.

'Actually, Carmichael has indicated he has a proposal for me to consider. A new investment.'

Her eyes lit up with excitement. 'Oh, I love it when Lord and Lady Kingswood are considering a new investment, and they share the details with me! We spend hours poring over the numbers, and trying to consider the possibilities from all angles.'

'Indeed?' He looked as if he might say more, but at that moment the door opened again, admitting Mr Harting. He was clearly in good spirits, and his smile broadened when his eyes lit on Lady Cecily.

'Good day, Hawk. Lady Cecily.' He bowed.

The Earl, who had risen to greet his guest, took his seat again. 'Was your chamber adequate, Harting?'

'It was, and the staff excellent. I must admit to being impressed by Hazledene, Hawk. I wonder you do not spend more time here. Thank you,' he added as an aside to the footman who was serving him.

A shadow crossed the Earl's face, so fleetingly that Cecily wondered if she had imagined it. Why did he not spend more time at Hazledene? Oh, how irritating it was not to have had more time to continue their conversation.

'It is a tidy house, in a pretty setting, but too small for a full house party.'

'There I must disagree with you, my lord. Four gentlemen and two ladies is plenty for an intimate gathering. I declare I am delighted with the company!' He was looking at Cecily when he spoke, and she felt herself blush. She never knew how to behave when gentlemen openly admired her. Last night's bravado had vanished, and she was left with her normal cool reserve. 'I see we have a dry day,' Mr Harting continued, 'so we can persist with our plans for a pleasant walk in pleasant company.'

The Earl was leaning back in his chair. 'Pleasant as

you like, Harting,' he murmured, yet it seemed to Cecily that his expression had a cynical twist.

Mr Harting seemed not to notice, tucking into bacon, eggs and beef with alacrity. 'Has Carmichael surfaced yet? I declare he cannot be keeping Town hours when we are in this bucolic idyll.'

'I have not seen him yet, but he can lie as late as he wishes. We shall not stand on ceremony here.'

They stilled at the sound of conversation in the hallway, then the door opened, admitting not only Carmichael but Tom and Nell.

'Good morning, good morning, all!' declared Mr Carmichael, his round face glowing with delight. 'What a pleasure it is to be in such company, and in such a setting!'

They all exchanged greetings, the Earl and Harting retaking their seats and the others joining them at table.

'Carmichael,' declared the Earl with a hint of sourness,' I had forgot how jovial you are in the mornings.'

Carmichael, still grinning, hit him in the arm with a friendly punch, seemingly taking this as a compliment. The Earl, unflinching, went back to his food. Tom, serving his wife with eggs, toast and honey, at her murmured request, remarked, 'My brother is never jovial in the early morning, Carmichael.'

Carmichael nodded sadly. 'We cannot all be blessed with a cheerful disposition. Er, tea, please,' he added, to the footman at his elbow. 'And more of the ham.' He had already loaded his plate with a selection of everything within reach, including the last slice of ham. 'So, what are we to do today?'

Here we go again.

Social conversation was so empty, Cecily noted. The same greetings and pleasantries, endless conversations about the planned walk in Crow Wood, and whether the weather would be kind. Looking within, she had to admit to ongoing frustration that a promising conversation with Lord Hawkenden had been interrupted. He was altogether much more *interesting* than she had anticipated. This was surprising, but also strangely exciting. And now that she knew he no longer disapproved of her, why, anything might occur!

Jack's mood was uncertain. At some point during the long night his brain had seemingly finally accepted that Lady Cecily was not Mrs Tom Beresford, and that his error in confusing the two ladies was at the heart of his frustration with her. From now on he would treat her as though she were any other lady. It should not be difficult.

On seeing her this morning he had been almost surprised to note he felt no conflicting feelings at all. Instead, there was a simple sense of pleasure on entering the breakfast room and finding her there. She was undoubtedly a beautiful lady, and her quick mind intrigued him. He was now free to admire such beauty, uncomplicated by his concerns about Tom's hasty marriage, which must be considered separately.

Today Lady Cecily was wearing a gown of sunshine yellow—the *modistes* probably dubbed it jonquil or buttergold or some such nonsense—but he had to own it suited her. The daylight filtering through the mullioned windows sent a golden glow over her fair curls and delicate skin. She looked fragile, and slight, and he idly tried to imagine how small her chin might feel in his hand, how large his hand would be if it rested on her fine shoulder. Such thoughts would lead nowhere, he knew, for he did not dally with Almack's maidens.

His comments acknowledging he had erred that night had not been considered beforehand. In the secret work-

ings of his own soul, he now understood that if she had
behaved rather rudely in walking away from him, she had
had good reason, for his behaviour towards her had been
nothing short of egregious. As he recalled his blunt comments towards a young lady he did not even know, he had
the grace to feel rather ashamed of himself.

Ten minutes later, he had been surprised again—this
time by the content of their conversation. A lady interested in business? The knowledge that Lord Kingswood
involved both his wife and his ward in matters of commerce? The notion was entirely novel, yet now, as he let
the conversation among the others wash over him, he discovered that he found it credible. In his business dealings he had frequently encountered quick-minded women
among the traders and managers in commerce. Why, then,
should he be surprised that similar intelligence existed
among women of his own class?

Because they are not raised to it, he realised.

From an early age, young ladies, from what he understood, were trained in manners, and deportment, and the
arts, but not in business or commerce. The closest they
perhaps came to it was the skills involved in running a
household.

This led him to another notion. He had, naturally, secured excellent housekeepers for his larger properties, yet
one of the reasons he was looking forward to having a wife
was so that she could take from him the burden of managing Springfield Hall, with its army of indoor servants,
and constant harassment regarding supplies, staff manage-
ment, and chimney-cleaning. He already knew he would
bring the same dispassionate coolness to his selection of a
wife that he normally applied to matters of business. When
he eventually chose a wife, the lady he selected would
naturally need to meet his many requirements.

He glanced up to eye Lady Cecily speculatively. Beautiful, quick-witted, accomplished, herself daughter to an earl…might she be a candidate worth considering? Instantly, a strange kick hit him in the gut, powerful and disturbing.

Fear? Desire? Both?

He could not accurately discern it. But the fact that he had had such a strong reaction told him one thing. She could *not* be included in his list of potential alliances.

When he married, it would be a selection based entirely on rationality. Whatever his gut was saying, it was speaking much, much too loudly, and he was not having it.

Chapter Thirteen

Crow Wood was a gentle stroll from the house, on the far side of Hazledene village. 'Village' was perhaps too grand a name for the place, Cecily mused as they ambled through. In reality it was more of a hamlet. It consisted of a single street, with a medieval church, a row of pretty stone cottages, a few shops, and a handful of larger houses. There was a single crossroads in the centre, with the back roads to other hamlets crossing the main Portsmouth road. A narrow lane dotted with small cottages snaked upwards towards the famed Thursley Hill, the one they could not visit today. Cecily glanced towards it. Sure enough, the top was swathed in solid cloud, completely obscuring the summit. It was just one of a range of green hills in the surrounding countryside, most rich with the woodland typical of the western Weald.

The Earl, flanked by his two friends, was leading the way, with Cecily, Nell and Tom following. Cecily could not help but run her eye over the three figures of the gentlemen in front of her. Mr Harting, slim and tall—almost willowy, Mr Carmichael, shorter and rather portly, and in the centre the Earl himself. As tall as Harting, as solid as Carmichael, but of the three his figure was the most pleasing—broad, muscular, strong…

If I were to ever choose a man, she thought idly, *I should like one with a well-built figure such as this.*

She flushed at her own daring, understanding that her mama's sometimes shocking comments had made her more knowing about certain things than she should be. Glancing sideways at her friend, she was concerned in case Nell had noticed Cecily's hungry appraisal of the Earl's broad shoulders, encased in his well-fitted burgundy-coloured coat. Nell, thankfully, was not looking in her direction, her attention seemingly focused on her husband. Naturally.

At the very end of the village, where the track bent left, a stile on the right took them directly towards the woods. Tom handed both Nell and Cecily over the stile, then climbed across himself.

'I have not been in these woods since Jack and I were boys.' Tom's tone was reflective as they traversed the last few yards towards the line of trees. 'It used to be one of our favourite haunts when we came to Hazledene every summer. Thursley Hill and Crow Wood were places of adventure, of imagined dangers and elaborate games.'

So the Earl's given name is Jack. A strong, direct name. Cecily tried it silently in her mouth. *Jack.* It suited him.

The three gentlemen were stopped near the trees, having delayed while they caught up. 'We decided to wait for you before we crossed the line.' The Earl's tone suggested something of great significance.

'The line, my lord?' Cecily was intrigued. She peeked up at the Earl from under the poke of her bonnet, and had the satisfaction of seeing his eyes soften briefly in admiration before assuming their more usual expression. Her heart fluttered briefly in response.

My word!

Tom reached for his wife's hand. 'Here,' he pronounced, laughter crinkling his eyes, 'we leave the everyday world behind, and enter a realm of magic.' His voice took on a tone of dire warning, comical in its exaggeration. 'These woods contain witches, and dragons, and evil creatures that would seek to do us harm.' Nell's eyes widened theatrically as she joined in the joke.

'But fear not!' There was a humorous glint in the Earl's eye as he joined in the play-acting. 'For the scions of House Beresford can protect you from all harm.' He was gazing directly at Cecily as he spoke and, despite knowing it was all a game, she could not help feeling a slight thrill at his words and expression.

'The Hawkenden knights,' added Tom, 'have special powers that help us defeat any evil that comes against us or our loved ones.' His eyes met his brother's briefly, then they both glanced away.

Cecily felt a tightening in her throat as their childish game gave her a fleeting impression of how close the brothers had been, long ago. Friends, playmates, allies.

That is the first time today I have seen them look at one another directly.

The current estrangement between them remained strong, and Cecily was finding herself increasingly bothered by it.

The path ahead was narrow, admitting only two abreast. 'Lady Cecily?' The Earl offered his right arm, and Cecily took it, enjoying the sensation of her gloved hand sliding under his elbow and curling around his forearm. Tom and Nell fell in behind them, with the two gentlemen taking up the rear.

Three steps in, Cecily began to understand why the Beresford boys had believed they were entering another world. The pine trees and fern-filled undergrowth was tightly packed, meaning that daylight was dimmer here, and the everyday sounds of breezes and birdsong were silenced. Ten steps in, and they might have been in a cave, so dense was the forest around them. The ferns and ivy gradually disappeared, until Cecily found herself ankle-deep in brown pine needles. She lifted her skirt a little as she walked, enjoying the crunch and give beneath her kid half-boots. Lifting her head, she looked all around, enjoying the eeriness and the clean, refreshing scent of the pine trees.

Her eyes met his. 'Do you feel it?' he murmured.

'I do.' Her voice trembled a little. 'It is wonderfully frightening!'

His left hand moved across to cover hers. 'I am impressed that you can sense both—the frightening other-worldliness and the thrilling adventure of it. Such fancies are perhaps best left in childhood, and yet...' His voice tailed away. She could feel his warmth through her glove. It was making her hand tingle with pleasure.

'Places like this are perhaps how superstitions are created,' she replied softly. 'I *know* that it only seems different because the light and sounds from outside cannot easily get through. Yet the more primitive part of me *feels* as though there may indeed be dragons and witches behind every tree! I love how the light slants through here and there, lighting up small places as though they have great significance' She gestured with her free hand. 'It is...perfect.'

He grinned. 'Exactly.' Their eyes met again, and something flared between them. Something fervent, and wonderful, and *dangerous*. Something that took her breath and made her pulse race and left a hot warmth in the pit of her stomach.

My goodness!

Swallowing hard, she made haste to fill the silence. 'Who brought you here? As boys, I mean?' In her mind's eye she could see two sturdy boys, wooden swords at the ready, venturing through the half-light. 'Your father, perhaps?'

His expression hardened. 'Our father had no interest in games. Or in his sons, for that matter.' His face looked closed, his eyes narrowed. He had gone, somehow, having disappeared behind his usual wall of cold haughtiness.

She grimaced. 'I apologise. I should not be prying.'

He shrugged. 'No need. Our father was what he was. I have long since accepted it.'

Have you, though?

She kept the thought to herself but had not missed his clenched jaw and the tightness in his speech as he had spoken of his father.

A hundred questions were flying around her brain like starlings, yet to pursue the topic of his father would be too much. 'So who did bring you here?'

'Actually, it was our nurse, Tilly.' Now there was a different tone in his voice. Some deep emotion, too complex for Cecily to name at that moment.

'Well, good for her! She clearly understood the minds of small boys.'

His gaze became unfocused as he considered this. 'I suppose so. We—Tom and I adored her. She looked after us both, having been promoted from housemaid to help Mama when I was a baby. We spent more time with her than we did with either of our parents.'

'So was your mama also…busy?' Conscious that she was much, much too fascinated by him, she tried her best to maintain a reasonably neutral tone. But her attention was completely focused on understanding him. Had both parents been cold towards him and Tom? It would explain much, she believed. Had she not read somewhere 'Give me the boy until he is seven and I shall show you the man'?

'Somewhat,' he replied after a moment. 'She was affectionate and generous, but she left us with Tilly most of the time. She had a… I think my father was a difficult person to live with.'

'I see.' But she did not, not really.

He was pondering again. 'I had not understood this before,' he said slowly, 'but it now occurs to me that perhaps Mama was trying to protect us.' He was frowning, and his left hand had dropped back to his side.

'Yet a small boy, not seeing that, might feel unwanted,' she offered softly.

He looked momentarily stricken, before a mask of polite unconcern came over his features. 'The path widens out just around this bend.' He indicated the way in front, where, sure enough, a moment later, the forest opened into a clearing. Crows cawed, the breeze ruffled Cecily's curls, and the moment for sharing secrets evaporated like mist on a mountain.

'What an adventure!' Nell's eyes were shining as she and Tom caught up with them. 'I was just saying to Tom how lucky he was to have had such a wonderful place so close to the house!'

Cecily managed a smile. What had happened in the dimly lit woods had been unlike anything she had ever experienced. Not just the heated look that had passed between them, but the exchange that had followed. Never had she had such an intimate conversation with anyone, least of all a gentleman. Her mind was reeling with images of forlorn, sad boys and angry, arrogant men. Her body, meanwhile, was still reeling with his effect on her.

Making a conscious effort, she tried to breathe normally and focus on what was going on around her.

Nell lowered her voice as Mr Harting and Mr Carmichael emerged blinking into the clearing, and the Earl and his brother both turned to speak to them—partly, Cecily guessed, to avoid having to speak to each other. 'I am so sorry you were left with the Earl for so long, Cecily. I shall ensure that you have better company on the return journey.'

'I…' Cecily was unsure what to say. 'There is no need. He was agreeable company.'

'Really? He did not take the opportunity to insult you again?'

'No, not at all.'

'I suppose he can hardly do so in mixed company.' Nell sniffed. 'I do wish my darling Tom and his judgemental brother would be friends again.'

'I remember a time when Tom was not as agreeable as he is now,' Cecily pointed out dryly, stung into defending the Earl. 'At Christmastime, you and he had a terrible falling out, as I recall.'

Nell had the grace to blush a little. 'True, but Tom is essentially *good*, and generous, and honourable.'

Cecily shrugged. 'Appearances may deceive us. Perhaps his brother has also been misunderstood.'

Nell snorted. 'Why, you yourself have been on the receiving end of his arrogant disdain. He has barely spoken to me, and he and Tom are circling each other like bucks before a fight!'

'True.' Cecily frowned, as a sudden insight came to her. 'I believe he is behaving in a remarkably similar way to Tom, last Christmas. Before you and he came to an understanding.'

Nell opened her mouth as if to argue, then closed it again.

Cecily pressed on. 'He spoke to me earlier, about our disagreement at Lady Jersey's.' She frowned. 'Actually, he did not speak of it directly, for there were servants present. But he is sorry for his part in it, I am certain.'

Nell raised a cynical eyebrow. 'Did he say so? Did he apologise to you?'

'Not exactly, but—'

'Well, when he does so, I shall be prepared to consider forgiving him. But while he treats you, and Tom, and me with disdain, he cannot expect amity from me!'

This was entirely reasonable, and yet Cecily's thoughts about the Earl were confused. In the arrogant man she now saw the boy he had been, and it was changing her view of him. Today was proving to offer unexpected insights. Her head was still muddled, as all her notions of the Earl were contradictory. Yet she now knew she was willing to see the goodness in him.

She glanced across at him. He was engaging in some light-hearted raillery with his friends, his expression relaxed and open. Gone—for now, at least—was the cold, empty Earl. Gone, too, the hurt and confused boy who had briefly surfaced in the eyes of the man. She ought to have known, she supposed, that people were always more—and less—than what they seemed, and that one could never safely judge another.

Tom approached the ladies then, seemingly unable to stay away from Nell for very long. Seeing how her friend's face lit up when her husband was near created confusing, conflicting feelings in Cecily. While she was open to marrying one day, she could not be confident that she would enjoy the felicity of a love match. Love matches were rare, and there was no reason why she should be lucky enough to achieve one. Like many other ladies, she would likely marry a sensible suitor and hope for the best.

On the way back, Mr Harting accompanied the Earl, with Cecily and Mr Carmichael directly behind them, and Tom and Nell taking up the rear. Cecily suspected the newly-wedded couple to be kissing in the woods behind her, and was conscious of a pang of envy. She herself had not had a kiss for a long time—since last summer, in fact, when a handsome young man had been making up to her during their visit to his family home. She had permitted him one kiss and had forgotten the lad soon afterwards. What must it be like to kiss the same man a hundred times? A thousand? Her eyes flew to the Earl, directly in front of her. His dark hair was curling over his collar, and she imagined her own hands raking through it, disordering it and enjoying the imagined sensation of feeling its softness through her fingers. Her heart skipped a little, and—

'How do you, Lady Cecily?' Mr Carmichael was looking at her solicitously.

To cover her confusion, she gave a bright smile. 'I am not at all frightened, Mr Carmichael, I assure you!' On hearing this information, he looked rather disappointed.

'Well,' he declared, patting her hand where it rested in the crook of his arm, 'never fear! Should there be dragons, I shall protect you!'

Stifling a genuine smile at the notion, she dipped her head so her bonnet would hide her expression. In the mystical half-light, he could not see her properly anyway. Straining to hear, she caught snatches of the conversation between Mr Harting and the Earl. It involved labourers, and cottages, then later a field. Not particularly interesting on the surface, yet Cecily was intrigued by whatever business arrangements were being tentatively addressed by the two men during the walk. Partly because she was always interested in such matters, and partly because the Earl was involved.

Emerging into full daylight was as sudden a surprise here as it had been in the clearing. 'Oh, how bright it is!' she declared.

'The contrast is even more powerful on a sunny summer's day,' offered the Earl. She glanced at him. Was that an air of satisfaction? Perhaps the conversation with Mr Harting had gone well. Or maybe he was simply pleased that his guests had appreciated Crow Wood.

Tom and Nell emerged from the twilight forest, he nuzzling her cheek and whispering something that was making her blush. Cecily, glancing quickly at the Earl, was unsurprised to catch him lifting his eyes briefly to the heavens. She was helpless to completely stifle the low chuckle that bubbled up within her, but she turned it into a cough and hoped no-one would notice.

After a moment's general conversation they all walked onwards towards the stile. This time it was the Earl who handed Cecily over it, and she felt what was now becoming a familiar thrill when she was near him.

I declare I must be developing a tendre *for him! How inconvenient!* Inconvenient, and rather frightening in its intensity.

Once or twice before she had been aware of similar flutterings, when a particular young man had flirted with her. The feelings had been temporary, passing within days once her customary cynicism had reasserted itself. The same would undoubtedly occur in this case.

As they meandered companionably up the village street, she decided to simply accept the inevitability of it. She applied some sensible thinking to the situation. The Earl was handsome, well-built, and spoke to her as if she were a rational being. He also, she suspected, admired her looks. She was to be here for a few weeks only. Like her mama, why should she not enjoy a gentle flirtation to help pass the time? Unlike Mama, however, she would naturally *not* be inviting him to her bed.

Mama had recently begun to pass on such wisdom as she thought appropriate to Nell's stepmother, Mrs Godwin. Some of it had already come Cecily's way. 'One can be too subtle, my dear,' she had declared recently. "You must always let a man know when you are interested in him, for they are often too stupid to notice. Engage playfully. Compliment him. Listen carefully when he speaks, even when it is tedious."

A quiver of repugnance rattled through Cecily. She could not do such things. Not in a hundred lifetimes. No, she would proceed with a light flirtation to while away her visit, but she could only be herself as she did so.

Chapter Fourteen

Just as they came close to the Vicarage, the front door opened, revealing a smiling, balding vicar and a lady who must be his wife. They stood, quietly waiting, then bowed and curtsied as the party neared the gate. Cecily waited, knowing it was up to the Earl to acknowledge them—or not, if he so chose.

I do hope he is civil to them.

She need not have been concerned. He stopped and tipped his hat, and the pair hurried to the gate. They exchanged introductions, the vicar naming himself and his lady as Mr and Mrs Martin. The vicar looked a kindly sort, if distracted, for he flustered himself with half-sentences and delight. His wife, a middle-aged lady with an intelligent gaze, said little, and held herself back from them all.

They were invited inside for tea, an offer that the Earl accepted urbanely. The sitting room they were ushered into was comfortable, cosy and spotlessly clean. While awaiting refreshments, the vicar, to his wife's noticeable chagrin, then announced that they had seen the party pass on the way out and had sent to the baker's for some sweetmeats. These were duly produced, along with some welcome, warming tea, and pronounced by all to be of the highest quality.

They spoke generally of the area, of Crow Wood, Thursley Hill and Hazledene, and the vicar commented how welcome it was to have the family at home once again. 'For it is a shame that such a delightful house must be half-empty, the furniture hidden under covers and the shutters closed, for three-quarters of the year.' Tom and the Earl exchanged a quick look, Cecily noticed, then immediately looked away from each other. It reminded her of Mr Carmichael's comment, and the shadow she had seen crossing the Earl's face.

Why do they not stay here more often?

Hazledene was beautiful, and comfortable, and within easy reach of London. Most families, if they owned something like this, would make it their main residence for comfort, keeping their larger properties for entertaining.

'It is hard on the servants too, of course,' the vicar continued, sipping his tea from a delicate china cup. He laughed lightly. 'Not that you will be interested in the needs of the servants, my lord.'

Mr Carmichael responded immediately with a comment about how his servants loved him being away, for they had much less work to do when he was gone. This being such an obvious point, no-one had anything further to say for a moment.

The reverend, in response to Nell's polite question, gave details of the times of the Sunday service, beaming, and said he looked forward to seeing them all there on Sunday. The Earl agreed, and set down his cup, signalling that the visit was at an end. Five minutes later they were once again on the path back to Hazledene.

'A civil fellow,' commented Mr Carmichael, 'though perhaps something of a radical.'

'How so, Mr Carmichael?' enquired Cecily, although she suspected she knew.

He shrugged. 'He and his wife are quick to defend the servants, even though servants should be grateful for their positions.'

Cecily and Nell exchanged a glance. Both having experienced being taken for granted, they had an affinity for the needs of others that was unusual in their class. It was one of the threads that had bound them together as friends. Nell had been terribly ill-used by her stepmother, and Cecily was delighted that her marriage to Tom had ensured an escape from drudgery for her friend.

Mr Carmichael was still watching them. 'Naturally,' Cecily replied smoothly. 'Yet it is always good to remember their needs as well as our own.'

At this the gentlemen protested, and a lively debate ensured. Nell and Cecily would not concede defeat, even when it was suggested they were too tender-hearted.

'This is why women have no head for business,' declared Mr Carmichael, opening up an entirely new battlefront. 'They would be bankrupt within a month, for their hearts are too big and their brains too small to make difficult decisions.'

Cecily could feel her anger rising. 'Why should you say so? Surely the heart has a place in making good decisions?'

He laughed at this, calling on the Earl for support. 'What say you, Hawk? You are well-known for your hardheadedness in business.'

The Earl remained impassive. 'Of course. Rationality and the ability to master one's base emotions are the signs of a true man.'

'Then I am glad,' declared Nell hotly, 'that I am not a man. Money cannot be the only motivation.' She eyed her husband. 'Which is why I refused to sell you my home at Christmas.'

Tom grinned, seemingly enjoying the ladies' rebellious-ness. 'And you were right to do so, my love.'

Cecily could not help it. Her eyes went immediately to the Earl, expecting exasperation at his brother's romantical declaration. Instead, his visage had settled into a mask-like rigidity. 'You were not always so irrational, brother,' he offered, his neutral tone belying the tightness in his jaw.

'Indeed,' Tom replied coolly, his eyes flashing. 'But I find myself becoming wiser with age. You have always exhorted me to be open to learning.'

The Earl raised an eyebrow. 'To *learn*, yes. But foolish-ness masquerading as learning is not wisdom.'

Tom's brow was furrowed, and there was a tight silence.

'Of course, there can be exceptions,' Mr Harting inter-jected, acting as peacemaker. 'But in general I believe it is best to maintain a certain objectivity when it comes to matters of business. Lady Cecily, be careful, for the path is particularly uneven just here.' He continued with a pleas-antry about the weather, and then kept up a trail of benign enquiries and comments until they reached Hazledene. The party separated in the hallway, divesting themselves of boots and hats, and agreed to meet again for nuncheon in a half-hour.

Cecily was first to climb the staircase and was sur-prised to find Molly the housemaid in her chamber, reor-ganising all Cecily's gowns in the wardrobe.

'Oh!' she said, bobbing a quick curtsey. 'I apologise, Lady Cecily. I can finish this later but, you see, I have been busy all morning, making the nursery more comfortable, so this is the first chance I've had to see to your gowns.'

'The *nursery*?' Cecily could not, for a moment, under-stand this. 'Whatever for?'

Molly grimaced. 'I should not have mentioned it, my lady. Forgive me.'

'Why the nursery, Molly? I insist you answer me.'

'Lord Hawkenden is sleeping there. Normally he takes this, the Blue Chamber, but...'

Cecily's jaw dropped, then she swiftly calculated. Three main bedrooms, plus the suite that Nell and Tom were occupying. Of course!

'You understand, my lady, that there is nowhere else.'

'But the *nursery*? Was there really no other...?' Realising how inappropriate it was to debate the matter with a housemaid, instead she bit her lip and left.

According to the footman, the Earl was currently in a ground-floor room known as the library. She scratched at the door then opened it on hearing the command to enter. The Earl was there, and with him Mr Carmichael. The Earl was leaning back in his armchair, one hand draped casually across the arm, the other engaged in swirling a glass of amber liquid.

Mr Carmichael, in contrast, was leaning forward in his chair, his air one of frustration at the interruption.

'Oh, I apologise, my lord, Mr Carmichael. I can come back later—'

Both gentlemen stood, the Earl's face breaking briefly into what looked like a genuine smile. Despite herself, she returned it.

'Lady Cecily! How may I serve you?'

Cecily already knew she could not speak of it in front of Mr Carmichael. It was bad enough that the Earl was being forced to sleep in the nursery—the *nursery*, for heaven's sake—in his own home. It would be intolerable to shame him in front of his friend by revealing this fact in company.

'Oh, it is nothing,' she replied, making a vague gesture with her hands. 'Just a—a domestic matter.'

Was that a glint of humour in his eye? 'Domestic matters are not "nothing", Lady Cecily. On the contrary, it is of the utmost importance to me that all my guests are comfortable.'

'Oh, but I do not wish to give the impression— That is to say, I am very comfortable with the house, and with—with everything.'

'And yet you are moved to come and find me about a domestic matter?'

He was toying with her, enjoying her discomfort. However, he was doing so in a light-hearted way, and she appreciated his relishing the opportunity to fence with her like this. Her heart danced at the connection between them. It was as though they had their own language—one that others were not even aware existed. She hugged the feeling to herself.

Plus, her mind added, *here is further evidence of his lively mind, and the good side of his nature.*

He was awaiting her reply. A streak of devilment possessed her.

She raised an exaggerated eyebrow. 'I could not possibly interrupt your no doubt important conversation.' She nodded towards Mr Carmichael, who still looked cross.

'Thank you, Lady Cecily,' that gentleman replied shortly, looking at her from under his beetling brows. 'As it happens, we *were* discussing an important matter of business.'

'Then I shall leave you,' she declared firmly, nodding at them both. 'For the emotionality of having a woman present might cloud your discussions!'

On this defiant note she made her escape, pausing outside the library door. She did not feel comfortable returning to her bedchamber, where Molly still toiled, so instead she made her way upstairs to the yellow parlour to await nuncheon. Relieved to find the room empty, she closed the door carefully and seated herself on a comfortable settee covered in straw-coloured satin.

Enjoying the blessed silence, broken only by the ticking of the clock on the mantel and the sound of birdsong outside, she allowed her mind to drift to their trip to Crow Wood. The undoubted estrangement between the brothers. Tom's clear adoration of his bride. Her own reaction to being in the Earl's company. Her hand on his arm. His hand coming across to cover hers. The way he had looked at her...

She caught her breath. She could not recall, during her previous brief infatuations, ever feeling anything this strong.

Perhaps I am remembering it falsely.

But, no, never could she recall anything like this. Her fascination with the Earl of Hawkenden, Jack Beresford, was not simply down to admiration of his fine figure and handsome face. She was also intrigued by his mind, his character, his essence. She wished to understand who he truly was. Why she was so intrigued by him, she did not fully understand.

What she knew so far was puzzling to say the least. Despite his intelligence, wit and humour, she was also aware of something darker. The emptiness in him was clearly apparent to her here. There was a deep unhappiness within him, a sadness she had been unable to define until she had seen him here. In their previous passing encounters, she had never lingered long enough to see anything other than how he behaved. His arrogant disdain was, she thought, something of a suit of armour. He used it, it seemed, to maintain a distance from others, and to disguise some sort of pain within.

What she had learned of him today had given her pause. Both boys had clearly been hurt by their father's coldness, although it sounded as though they had had a nurse who loved them, which must have helped. *Tilly*, the Earl had called her. Miss Tillot.

Frowning, Cecily wondered where she had heard the name before, then it came to her. Molly the housemaid had said that Miss Tillot had always put warming pans in the boys' beds. Cecily's heart turned over at this evidence of love and warmth for little Jack and little Tom. With a nod of acknowledgement to that long-ago nurse, she turned her attention to the other gentlemen.

She forced her mind in another direction. Mr Harting continued to gently pursue her. Calm, gentlemanlike and intelligent, yet he offered no threat to her peace of mind.

This is a good thing, she told herself.

Even as she said it in her mind, she knew it to be a lie. Why?

Because of the other one.

Swiftly averting her thoughts from pursuing *that* particular notion, she allowed her mind to again wrestle with the conundrum that was Jack Beresford. He seemed genuinely concerned for his brother, and Cecily had to admit that it was not unreasonable, given the speed with which Tom had met and married Nell. The Earl clearly remained sceptical about Tom's sincerity, but since Cecily presumed him to be the person in the world who knew Tom best, she hoped he would eventually come to understand the true affection shared by the young married couple. Yes, Tom's marriage was at the root of the brothers' current estrangement, despite both, she suspected, being deeply unhappy about the rift between them.

The gong sounded for nuncheon. How quickly the time had passed! Putting her worries aside, Cecily stood, smoothed her pale-yellow day gown and descended briskly to the dining room.

Chapter Fifteen

Tom and Nell were ten minutes late for nuncheon, and arrived glowing with suppressed emotion of some sort. No-one commented on their tardiness, and they all made trifling conversation as Tom served Nell with food. His bride did not seem particularly hungry, contenting herself with a long cup of tea, some freshly baked bread with yellow butter, and doting looks from her husband.

While the others were talking, Cecily intercepted a look between Nell and Tom that she could only describe as heated.

My goodness!

It reminded her of how she had felt when the Earl had looked at her so intensely earlier.

Daringly, she glanced at the Earl. How handsome he was! And how her heart fluttered at the sight of him. There was a beautiful strangeness about it, and she resolved to enjoy the thrill of it all and attempt not to allow her mind to become clouded by unnecessary thoughts. Peace of mind, she decided, was overrated.

The gentlemen were planning a short ride in the afternoon, since the walk to Crow Wood had been completed so early in the day. They planned similar short rides for the next few days, teasing each other about how unused to riding they had become over the winter. Monday was the day fixed for a long hack, covering a full ten miles in a circular route. Cecily allowed the discussions to wash over her, having no interest in the detail of the routes they would follow on their various jaunts.

It seemed Tom would go with them, so she was looking forward to spending some extended time with her dear Nell. The men were animated, provoking each other as friends often did. They had, it seemed, almost forgotten the women quietly observing them. Or were they, even in their raillery, playing to them as an unacknowledged audience?

Nell, of course, mostly was fixated on her Tom, but Cecily noticed her also glancing at the Earl a couple of times from under her lashes, as if trying to understand him. Nell no longer seemed frightened of him, for which Cecily was grateful. If they were ever to become a true family, they needed to find a way to forgive each other.

The gentlemen, fired up at the notion of riding out, set down their cutlery, agreeing to leave in the next half-hour. The ladies waved them away, confirming that they were done with eating, and the party rose.

Nell accompanied her husband upstairs, and Cecily followed them. The Earl, catching up with her on the wide wooden staircase, spoke in a low tone. 'What was it you wished to discuss with me earlier, Lady Cecily?'

She glanced at him. 'Oh, my lord, I have just discovered that you are being accommodated in the nursery. I wish to say that I would be content to sleep in the Countess's chamber, if Nell would agree. She can share her husband's…'

Her voice tailed off, for he was already shaking his head.

'Unacceptable.' His tone was clipped. 'You will have a

chamber of your own, rather than be forced to sleep in an adjoining chamber. As host, I insist on it. There is nothing more to be said.'

'But—must you really take to the nursery? I cannot be comfortable at the notion that I—that *we*—are banishing you to the attic.'

He grinned. 'I shall take it as a reminder that I am *less* than I sometimes believe myself to be. Returning to the nursery will be a useful lesson in humility, which I would imagine should please you, Lady Cecily. After all, if I had not been so hard-headed, insisting on bringing my guests to Hazledene this week, there would not have been a problem.'

Taking this in the light-hearted way he clearly intended, she smiled. 'A good dose of humility should be a regular tonic for any of us burdened with titles and expectations. You are an earl. I am the daughter of one. What others do not always appreciate is the burden of expectations such blood requires.'

He grimaced ruefully. 'True. Although it has perhaps been easier for me, I admit, since my father did not do justice to his position or his title. But your father, from what I hear, was a good man.'

She beamed, filing away his comments about his father into a secret library in her mind, marked with his name. 'Papa was a very good man, and well respected. He died when I was twelve. And Ash—the Fifth Earl—is equally well seen.'

They were at the top of the stairs, at the entrance to the gallery. 'But tell me,' he continued, stepping to one side as Mr Carmichael and Mr Harting passed them, 'why should it be a burden to be the daughter of an earl, Lady Cecily?'

She considered this, tilting her head to one side. 'They expect me to behave with propriety and decorum at all times, to marry well, and to be *no-one*. I must hold no opinions, come to no-one's notice, and simply be a cipher to my father's title. I am to be grateful to be titled 'Lady' and to never disappoint in terms of my appearance, my behaviour, and my choices. I am, after all, a reflection of my mother, and of my deceased father, and of my guardian. I am never just—me.' She shrugged, recognising that she had answered the question in rather more detail than might reasonably be expected. 'Apart from that, there is no burden at all!' Her eyes danced with mischief, confident that he would understand her.

He threw his head back, laughing aloud. It was a beautiful sound. 'Lady Cecily,' he declared, 'you are a diamond! And I think we both know that you are very definitely "someone". Remember, I barely know your mother, and have the highest regard for Ash. But to me you are definitely yourself, Lady Cecily.'

There was a taut silence. After a moment he blinked, as if coming to his senses, and adopted a faux stern expression. 'Your behaviour, however, at times does leave a lot to be desired!'

Knowing he did not mean it, she twinkled back at him, glorying in the freedom of being fully herself. Returning to London and the rules of the season would be hard, following this heady liberty.

He leaned closer, his gaze glinting with humour. It made her heart race even faster, and her stomach now began to tumble wonderfully. 'So on that matter I must agree with society's judgements!'

'Sadly true,' she sighed, maintaining a degree of normality despite her racing pulse. 'I shall endeavour to do better in future.' She sobered, looking him directly in the eye.

I accused him of vulgarity.

'And while we are on the matter, I must properly apologise for my—'

'Shh! Stop!' He pressed a finger gently to her lips, making her heart race even faster and her mouth instantly desperate for his kiss. 'You have no need to apologise for anything, so I do not wish to hear it, Lady Cecily.' His hand fell away, leaving her lips bereft. 'Whatever you may have done, responsibility for it rests with me, for I was the one who—'

'Shh!' Now it was her turn to silence him. Greatly daring, she lifted her finger and touched it to his warm lips.

Instantly, and seemingly without forethought, he pursed his lips and kissed her finger. She snatched it away, blushing, yet knew that both her finger and her own lips were both tingling from his touch, and that every nerve in her body was suddenly alive and begging for more.

There was a breathless silence, during which they looked at each other, both seemingly frozen. She was acutely aware that they were in the gallery, where fellow guests and servants might appear at any instant. If not for that…

He was first to recover. 'Actually, perhaps I should accept an apology after all, Lady Cecily. Now that it comes to it, I confess I am a little daunted by my return to the nursery. Who knows what horrors await in the attics? My first night there was uneventful, but I am yet to be convinced there are not spiders, or mice, or worse!'

How was it possible to feel such disappointment and yet such relief at one and the same time? The pull between them just now had been exquisitely, wonderfully terrible, and Cecily was both glad and devastated that the moment had passed.

'I confess,' she said, 'to a certain curiosity, my lord. I

think I shall venture upstairs to view the attics while you gentlemen are all preparing to ride out—with your permission, of course? Tom showed us around the main floors, but we did not venture below stairs or to the attics.' She raised a quizzical eyebrow. Somehow, Hazledene held answers to questions she was puzzling over.

He bowed. 'Better than that, I shall accompany you, if you will permit?'

To be alone with him?

She had no hesitation, for it was the one thing in the world she wanted at this moment. The advantages of a house party and no chaperone… 'Of course! But I do not wish to make you late.'

He shrugged. 'I can change in approximately a third of the time it takes Carmichael, so I have no concerns on that score.' He indicated the way, and they walked silently together down the hallway towards the Blue Chamber end.

My chamber, normally his. She hugged the thought to herself.

A small, discreet door opposite the chamber led to a steep staircase too narrow for them to walk abreast. He followed, three stairs behind, and her senses were alive to his presence, behind and just below her.

I am to be alone with him!

At the top was a narrow corridor running the length of the house, with narrow doors on both sides and two dull roof windows letting in dim light. An old carpet, threadbare in places, dulled the sound of their footsteps. Unlike the rest of the house, which was ornately decorated, here there were no brocade hangings, rich colours or gilt-framed paintings. The walls were simple, unadorned whitewash.

'The nursery is here, next on the left,' he murmured.

'The rest are servants' quarters. Until yesterday I had not been up in the attics for many years.'

'Just like Crow Wood.' They had stopped outside the door.

'Yes. This is a time for past things to return, I think.' He opened the door, and they stepped inside.

The room was bright, the shutters having been opened to admit the spring sunshine. There was a faint smell of polish in the air, and it was clear that the chamber had just been cleaned. Cecily saw three beds—two small ones against the wall on their left, as well as an adult bed near the window on the right.

That is where he slept last night. Where he will sleep tonight. I should not be here, alone with him, and yet...

The Earl paused, looking around as if seeing the nursery again for the first time. 'This room...' His gaze flicked from the window to the dresser to the two small beds.

'Which one was yours when you were a boy?' Cecily asked softly.

'That one.' His voice croaked slightly. He walked across to the bed nearest the door. 'Tilly would tell us stories and kiss us goodnight.' He looked stricken, as if almost overwhelmed by the memories that must be flooding through him.

'What happened to your nurse?'

His face hardened. 'She left. A better job, with a higher salary.'

Cecily frowned. 'Really? That surprises me.'

'Why?' His face twisted. 'At the end of everything, money is the only certainty. There is no place for softness.'

She desperately wanted to challenge him, but her throat was too tight to speak. Tight with his grief. His, and Tom's.

He opened a drawer in the dresser and, bending, reached in towards the back. 'It is still here!'

She looked curiously at the small figure in his hand. Whittled from wood, the paint chipped in places, it looked like a knight. 'Tilly got the gardener to make this for me—a present for my sixth birthday. I used to carry it everywhere, even putting it under my pillow at night.' His voice lowered, he murmured, almost to himself, 'Soon after I came home from school to find her gone, I put it away in this drawer. I have not looked for it since.' Straightening, he sneered briefly, before handing the figure to Cecily. 'I think it is finally time to throw it away.' His voice was thick, his eyes narrowed, and his shoulders tight with—with something. Anger? Pain? Both?

'Are you sure?' Cecily eyed him calmly. 'This was important to you. I do not believe that you truly—'

'It was important to a boy, a long time ago.' His tone was curt. 'This man has no need of such things.'

Cecily knew better than to argue in such a moment. 'Very well. It is gone.' Opening her reticule, she dropped the figure into it. 'Now, may I suggest that I move to the Countess's chamber, for this is clearly not a suitable sleeping chamber for you.'

'Nonsense!' His tone was brisk. 'I have already informed you of my decision. The matter is not open for discussion.'

His tone brooked no argument. Striding back towards the door, he held it open for her. Stifling a sigh, she passed him, leading the way back down to the main upper level. Where had he gone, the man who had gently kissed her finger and looked at her with such warmth? As they emerged back into carpeted elegance, she stole a glance at him. His expression was blank, his eyes cold. He was every inch the Empty Earl.

Chapter Sixteen

Cecily was glad of her warm pelisse, for the village church was rather chilly. Before the service, the vicar had led their entire party up the aisle to cushioned pews at the front, and Cecily had been conscious of the whispered attention of the congregation. The pews faced the altar, so she could not satisfy her curiosity until the service was over. By the time they made their way outside, many of the villagers were already dispersing, although there were curious stares from those still leaving.

Naturally, the local gentry had remained, standing chatting in pairs and clusters in the porch, along the path and even on the edges of the graveyard. Cecily spied at least five different groups of richly dressed people, although the level of elegance varied. Despite trying her best not to be harsh, and with the half-heard words of the vicar's sermon still ringing in her ears, she nevertheless had to stifle her horror at the puce day gown on one lady, the over-elaborate feather headdress on another, and the almost slovenly appearance of a couple of the gentlemen. Others, though, looked perfectly respectable, including one family with a smiling young matron in an elegant scarlet redingote with fashionable braiding.

The Earl had chosen to stand directly beside Cecily. This made up a little for the fact they had been seated apart inside—he flanked by his two friends, Cecily between Mr Carmichael and Nell. Throughout the service, she had allowed herself to daydream of him, and had devised all sorts of scenes that ended with a warm kiss. Now he was standing dangerously close, and she had to remind herself that she had no right and no expectation of receiving kisses from him. Nevertheless, her entire side tingled with a delicious awareness of his nearness.

Mrs Martin, the vicar's wife, had naturally come to speak to them, and was soon joined by her husband. This encouraged the neighbours to hover more closely, awaiting introductions, and the vicar duly obliged. Cecily soon lost track of the names and relationships but managed to smile and curtsey and join in the conversation with what she hoped was graciousness. The general tone was that the county families were delighted to see the Earl in residence, along with his dear brother, sister-in-law and guests. The Beresfords had clearly met many of the locals before, although Cecily had no sense of any true friendships between any of them.

The lady with the feathers remarked upon the presence of the ladies with particular gladness, as it would enable her to call on them on the morrow, if His Lordship would allow? His Lordship smiled, and allowed, but Cecily could tell that he was not particularly comfortable with the notion. How did she know this? She shrugged inwardly. She just did.

Her assumptions were confirmed on their walk back to the house, when the Earl declared that one of the blessings of Hazledene being a hunting-box was that their parties had not before included ladies, which therefore meant they had hitherto been protected from visits, invitations and general intercourse with the local gentry. The Squire—the grey-whiskered gentleman wearing the red waistcoat—would apparently normally have made a social call, involving a half-hour's discourse smoothed with brandy, but apart from that the Beresford brothers had been, the Earl said, left in relative peace.

Tom, naturally, could not let this pass. 'My wife and her dear friend are perfectly welcome at Hazledene, brother, and if it is such an inconvenience to you, I wonder that you should have chosen to join us!'

Oh, dear!

Up until now the hostilities between the brothers had been conducted beneath a veneer of *politesse*. Tom, his dander up at what he perceived to be an insult against his Nell, had clearly been unable to resist a direct attack.

The Earl was quick to reply. 'Of course I meant no slight to the ladies, Tom. I wonder that you should even suggest such a thing.' His tone was flat, but Cecily spied a telltale flush along his cheekbones.

Tom snorted, but said only, 'I am happy to hear it!'

There could be no doubt that all was still not well between the Beresford brothers, and the knowledge of it niggled at Cecily like a splinter in her hand or a speck in her eye. She wished everyone to be contented. Tom and Nell. Jack. It mattered to her, much more than anything had for a long, long time.

Although, on the surface, the brothers joined in shared conversations, they rarely spoke directly to one another, and while the Earl frequently conversed with Cecily, he exchanged only occasional pleasantries with Nell.

His stubbornness is adding to the schism between him and Tom.

Cecily bit her lip. She so wished to meddle, to bang the brothers' heads together and give them both a sound trimming! Strange how the most capable of men could revert to childhood patterns, given the right circumstances.

The Earl, clearly making an effort, turned the conversation towards the ride the gentlemen had planned for the afternoon, and politely asked Nell what her intentions were while they were gone. She coloured, clearly uncomfortable with his unexpected attention, and murmured something about writing to her stepmama. Cecily, encouraged by this development, was still concerned. Nell had never been so timid before. Clearly, the Earl's disapproval was affecting her deeply.

'Yes, I am acquainted with Mrs Godwin,' he returned amiably. 'You are from Kent, are you not?'

'I am,' she returned, with a little more confidence. 'Wyatt House, where I was raised, is near the village of Chiddingstone.'

'A pretty area,' he commented. 'I once visited Tunbridge Wells, where my friend the Duke of Leyswood has a house.'

'Oh, Langton House is a delight!'

'You have been there?'

'Yes, many times, when I was younger.'

'My wife's mother's family, the Wyatts, are a notable and long-established family in Kent.' Tom's tone had a slight edge to it; he was clearly trying to educate his older brother about Nell's suitability to join the Beresford family. His message was clear: despite any vulgarity on Nell's stepmother's part, Nell herself was a Wyatt.

The Earl nodded. 'Your father is still alive?'

Nell shook her head. 'He died two years ago.' Her voice was tight with grief.

'Ah.' He frowned slightly. 'Actually, I recall now someone had told me of your father's death. I am sorry.' He looked and sounded sincere.

'Thank you.'

The conversation turned then, and Cecily let out a breath she had not known she had been holding. Some progress at last!

'Cecily, there is a carriage coming up the drive!' Nell stepped back from the window, anxious not to be seen by whoever was arriving at Hazledene. It was Monday afternoon, and the ladies were in the parlour. The gentlemen had been gone for hours, as today was their first long hack, and Nell and Cecily had been enjoying a relaxed day of conversation, reading and, currently, embroidery.

'Oh, thank goodness! I can put this away now.' Cecily eyed her handiwork ruefully. The handkerchief looked reasonable, with a cluster of primroses and forget-me-nots emerging in yellow, orange, blue and green silk in one corner. The reverse side, however, was the usual tangled mess. She could never figure out how to achieve reasonable neatness on the back. She stole a glance through the window. 'And here are the gentlemen, also returned!'

'Really?' Nell joined her at the edge of the window. 'It seems Tom and his brother both know these visitors, whoever they are.' Both Beresfords had brought their horses alongside the carriage, tipping their hats to the people inside. Mr Harting and Mr Carmichael were holding back, seemingly conversing with each other as their horses followed slowly up the drive.

'Well, I do hope they can change out of their hunting clothing quickly, for otherwise we shall be forced to entertain their guests alone!' They laughed nervously at their own shocking inhospitality, then quickly took their seats.

Jack called for his valet, aiming to change from his riding gear as quickly as possible. As host, he could not leave the ladies alone with the visitors for too long—particularly as he had only spoken with them briefly as their carriage had come up the drive.

The sense of urgency within him was strong, and it occurred to him that he would not normally have been so hurried. Was it that the locals did not normally visit, and he wanted to create a good impression? He had no doubt that the ladies were socially accomplished—indeed he had no worries on that score—yet this particular family, particularly the matron, had been known to sorely test his patience during his brief encounters with her in the village.

Being honest, he acknowledged that there was more to it. The truth was that he had been looking forward to returning to Hazledene, having been gone from the house for a number of hours. A sense of *home* had spurred him on. Such a notion was alien to him, yet today it had definitely been in his heart as he and Tom and the others had approached the house. It was an unfamiliar urge, something he had not felt since death and abandonment and boarding school had made him cynical, and he was astonished to find traces of it within him still. Summers in Hazledene had been his childhood idyll. No Papa. Just him, and Mama, and Tom, and Tilly.

And now Papa's ghost was a distant memory, and the old hurts seemed far away—for today at least. The character of the house was reshaping itself in his heart. Dinners, walks and afternoon tea with his friends, and his brother, and the ladies. It was becoming a place of joy, of comfort. Of safety even. Card games, and repartee, and a sense of deepening ties. He shuddered. Such ties were dangerous. His head knew it, yet his gut could not be denied. An image of Lady Cecily came to him, her pretty face lighting up in the way it sometimes did when he smiled with her. She was behind this change, he knew. She had brought light to his Hazledene.

'You rang, sir?' It was the valet.

'Yes. Help me change, please.'

'Very well. If you will permit…'

Jack was only half-listening. As he cooperated with the valet, his inner ear still retained his own words.

Help me change. Please.

It meant nothing, of course. He had been referring to his clothing. Why, then, did the words reverberate with such depth in his soul?

The ladies were the picture of elegant serenity when the footman opened the parlour door, announcing the guests. 'Squire Standish, Mrs Standish and Miss Standish!'

Together, Nell and Cecily rose to greet their guests, who were already sweeping in with effusive cheeriness. 'Good day, good day, Lady Cecily, Mrs Beresford!' It was Feathers Lady, although today she had contented herself with a purple satin turban. Since her dress was in multiple shades of purple and lilac, with contrasting roses in bright orange embroidered across it, the effect was just as frightful as her huge headdress had been the day before. Here, clearly, was a lady who liked to be noticed. The Squire, his whiskered face beaming in good-natured joy, bowed, and said all that was proper, and they re-introduced their daughter, a shy-looking damsel of about seventeen, who was wearing a hideous chartreuse green gown.

They all sat, and Nell, as hostess, rang the bell for tea. Cecily assisted her friend by taking a full part in the conversation, which focused mainly on the delights of the area, the ladies' impression of the western Weald and their plans for their stay. Tea arrived, Nell served, and they all bit into sweetmeats, smiling politely over their teacups.

'Tell me,' Cecily offered, 'do you yourselves live near the village?'

'We do, we do!' declared the Squire, his ruddy face animated. 'Not three miles from here, in a neat little house—'

'Oh, please, husband,' his lady interjected. 'You are too modest! Rywell House is a substantial dwelling, and—apart from Hazledene, of course—quite the most notable house in the district!'

'Indeed?' returned Nell, politely. 'Is it an old house like this one?'

'Oh, Lord, no!' Mrs Standish waved this away as if the very notion was abhorrent. 'Our house is only fifty years old, and with all modern conveniences. I really do not know how you put up with these old-fashioned windows and chimneys, Mrs Beresford!'

'I think they are beautiful,' Cecily declared firmly, 'although I understand the challenges of an old house. Over the past few years my guardian has made a number of improvements to my own family home, Ledbury House, including the chimneys.' Quite why she felt the urge to defend Hazledene, and its owners, from what felt like an attack, she was not exactly sure.

'I understand,' Nell added, 'that my husband and his brother have completed substantial renovations at Hazledene over a number of years.'

Mrs Standish sniffed. 'Well, an old house will always be an encumbrance, even if it is dressed up to look like new.' She laughed at her own wit, while Cecily resisted the temptation to look Nell's way. While itching to defend Hazledene, she decided to hold her tongue, having met people like Mrs Standish before. Such individuals, in Cecily's experience, had no insight into themselves, or the impact of their words, and they believed merit to lie in the simple act of having an opinion. Whether such opinions were well-informed or ill-informed was irrelevant, for they were convinced of their own wisdom, and of everyone else's folly.

Another notion struck her as she quelled her inner outrage. Somehow, she realised, she was aligning herself not just with Nell but with the Beresfords, too.

Hmm... While she understood why she had so quickly developed a sisterly loyalty for Tom, she knew that, somehow, Jack was all mixed up in her inner alliances, too. And her feelings for Jack, new and fresh as they were, seemed anything but sisterly.

'Of course—' Mrs Standish was still talking. '—I have not had the opportunity to see inside Hazledene before, although my husband and the Earl are, naturally, great friends.' Her husband looked rather taken aback by this intelligence, which was clearly fresh news to him. 'All of the ladies in the district have admired the Earl and his brother for many years but have never had the opportunity to cultivate their acquaintance before.' She sighed. 'Hunting-boxes are all very well, but it is such a pity when gentlemen keep to themselves, do you not agree, Lady Cecily?' Her smile and expectant air invited a response that Cecily felt unable to give.

'Yet here we are,' she offered brightly, after a pause, 'and so you are finally able to visit!'

Mrs Standish leaned forward, placing a large hand on Nell's small one. 'A pity one of them is now wed, although I am sure you will disagree with me. Still, at least it is the younger brother!'

Nell's eyes flashed fire at this. Concerned that she might forget herself, Cecily intervened smoothly, addressing the Squire. 'The gentlemen, as you have seen, have recently arrived from a long ride around the countryside. Do you also enjoy the sport?'

'I do,' he confirmed, his kind face creased with a smile, 'although my portliness means I cannot take the fences the way I once did.' He laughed. 'My horses now are stouter and slower—much like myself!'

Cecily blinked at his directness, while Nell made a noise that sounded extremely like a stifled giggle. Thankfully, at that moment the door opened to admit the Earl.

'Stand up straight, Lucinda!' Mrs Standish hissed at her daughter as they rose. The girl looked terrified.

If the Earl had heard the comment, he gave no sign of it. Following an exchange of greetings, they all took their seats again, the Earl choosing a spot beside Cecily on the straw-coloured settee. The fact that her heart was beating harder might be due to her annoyance at Mrs Standish's coarseness. Or it might not.

The indelicacy continued, albeit it now had a different tone. Mrs Standish, ignoring Nell and Cecily completely, focused her attention entirely on the Earl. She flattered, she simpered, and she dragged her poor daughter into the conversation at every possible opportunity. 'My Lucinda loves to ride—do you not, Lucinda?' 'Quite the prettiest girl in the district, so they say!' and 'My darling Lucinda is a wonderful dancer! Do you dance, my lord?'

'Not if I can help it.' His tone was flat. As the conversation had continued, he had gone from polite urbanity to withdrawn cynicism, although on the surface all seemed well.

Frankly, Cecily was embarrassed by Mrs Standish's performance. Embarrassed for her sex. While she had seen many matchmaking mamas during her London seasons, she had never before observed at close hand such tactics tried out on a discerning gentleman, and one that she had somewhat come to know. To a stranger's eyes, the Earl may have seemed polite, even engaged at times. Cecily, who was beginning to read the tiny signs of his true feelings, was able to see the true impact of Mrs Standish's shameless vulgarity.

Still, when the Squire's wife invited the entire party to her home for an evening soirée, the Earl could only agree. Since Mrs Standish had already established that they were to remain in the district for at least another three weeks, he could hardly refuse. He thanked her for the invitation and did not even flinch when she replied that she would be the envy of all the neighbours.

'For, my lord,' she declared with glee, 'I have managed to do what no-one has ever done and persuaded you to a social evening in the district. Mind…' she wagged a teasing finger at him '…it will be a simple country affair, my lord. Just the local families coming together for a bite to eat and maybe a country dance or two.'

'It sounds delightful.'

'It will be.' She rose, with the air of a person who had just accomplished a difficult feat. 'Come, Lucinda, we must not take up any more of His Lordship's time.'

They all rose, her husband draining his teacup in one long gulp before setting it down on the side table. Clearly, their sudden departure was a surprise to him. He pumped the Earl's hand with smiling enthusiasm. 'A pleasure to see you again, my lord.'

Goodbyes were exchanged, and the Standish family finally moved out to the hallway. Cecily, Nell and the Earl accompanied them to the front door, where they waved them off. As they turned back inside, Tom appeared, descending the staircase. 'Have they gone?' he asked, with an exaggerated tone. He was grinning, his face alight with mischief.

The Earl shook his head. 'Tom, Tom. You wound me!

You abandoned us—two defenceless ladies and your own brother—to the mercies of the entire Standish family.'

'I have no doubt you were well able to manage them. Besides, I was changing my clothes. I could not come to the parlour while smelling of horse!'

'I too was out riding, in case you had forgotten.'

'Ah, but you have the knack of changing clothes in a flash. Must be that valet of yours.' He turned to his wife. 'How awful was she?'

'Mrs Standish? Well, she did express disappointment that one of you was now married...'

Both brothers grinned at this, exchanging rueful glances. It warmed Cecily's heart to see it. Might there be a thawing in the coldness between them?

'But she then declared her relief that at least it was the younger brother!'

They could not help it, all laughing at the absurdity of it. At that moment Cecily was conscious of feeling in charity with all three of them. Invisible threads, as subtle as any embroidery, were needling through them and between them, creating a picture of greens and yellows, deeper oranges and blues. The finished pattern was unclear, and under the surface the threads tangled terribly, but something—she was unsure what it was—*something* was possible.

'Sadly, without your presence as my aide-de-camp, I was unable to evade the trap of her invitation,' the Earl continued.

Tom groaned. 'Let me guess. Dinner at Rywell House?'

'Worse. A soirée.'

Tom put a hand to his head. '*Years* of successful evasion, of avoiding her outside church, of telling her we were already committed on whatever date she suggested. Yet now you have succumbed, and all of us must pay.'

The Earl grinned. 'It is all your fault, brother, for you are the one who got married!' He winked at Nell to take the sting out of his words, making her blink in surprise.

'Have our guests gone?' Mr Harting now joined them.

'They have, sadly,' the Earl replied, perjuring himself without hesitation. 'Still, they have invited us to a soirée at their house on Thursday.'

'Splendid, splendid,' declared Mr Harting, seemingly unaware of the suppressed humour of the party. 'I shall look forward to it.'

Chapter Seventeen

'Surprisingly, I am truly looking forward to tonight's soi-rée,' Cecily confided to Nell. Both young ladies were in Cecily's chamber, and the maids were almost done dressing their hair for the evening. Cecily loved the feeling of anticipation she sometimes enjoyed with Nell when they were preparing for an evening event together. Even with all the tiresomeness of unwanted attentions from bosky gentlemen, of crushes, of overheated rooms and a lack of air, there was something wonderful about wearing a pretty gown, having one's hair dressed, and going out.

Tonight Cecily had donned a gown of gold transparent gauze over a gold-and-yellow satin slip, while Nell had chosen a pale green silk, trimmed with a full fall of lace. Both dresses were long in the waist and cut low around the bust, in line with the current fashion. With glossy curls, matching fillets, satin slippers and white kid gloves, both ladies were now almost ready.

'Me, too,' Nell agreed as their eyes met in the dressing-table mirror. The maids finished their task and departed, taking the curling irons with them, and the young ladies smoothed their dresses and picked up their fans, ready to descend.

Cecily grinned, sensing that Nell's excitement matched her own. 'Although I am enjoying our quiet sojourn in the country, I confess an occasional soirée is always welcome.'

'I care not whether we have soirées, or walks, or whether we simply stay in beautiful Hazledene all the while. What I care about is having you and Tom with me. At times I still cannot believe my good fortune!' She frowned. 'There are still worries, of course. But I do not feel unsupported.'

They both knew there was no time to speak of important matters just now, which was something of a relief, since Cecily wondered if Nell had noticed the flirtation she had begun with the Earl, and if she had, what Nell made of it.

In a turn of events she had not anticipated, Cecily's own time and attention had been happily taken up simply by being at Hazledene. She was fast building firm friendships with the entire party, and for the first time in her life could plausibly claim to have friends who were men. She had come to know them all fairly well already, and was developing something like affection for all of them.

Needless to say, her burgeoning friendship with the Earl was complicated by that thrilling attraction she felt towards him. They frequently walked out together, and Cecily had come to rely on the thrill of being in his company, of learning more about him, and of the tingle of excitement that she always felt in his company. They discussed all manner of topics—none of them personal—but she had come to understand him a little more, while also gradually sharing more of her own thoughts and opinions with him.

She lived for those occasions when he would give her a look that made her senses tingle. He had not done so at any point today, she realised. The thought left her feeling a little bereft, so she immediately dismissed it, focusing instead on the delights of the evening ahead. Would he dance with her?

As she and Nell walked along the gallery, making for the wide stairway, she mused aloud, 'Earlier, I was thinking about tonight's party, and I realised I am strongly reminded of the time Prinny came to one of my Mama's soirées.'

Nell's eyes widened. 'The Prince Regent himself? What happened?'

'As you may imagine, Mama was exceedingly excited, but also terribly nervous. She planned everything down to the last detail.' Cecily chuckled. 'At least, she *talked* of every last detail. At great length. I, naturally, did the work.'

Nell lifted her eyes to heaven in sympathy. They both knew Cecily's mama well. 'But why should you be reminded of that tonight? We have had no preparations to worry about, beyond our own toilettes.'

'Ah, it was not *us* I was considering, but Mrs Standish.'

Nell lifted a gloved hand to her mouth to stifle a giggle. 'It is true! As far as Mrs Standish is concerned, securing the Earl for her soirée is a significant achievement. Who knows how much preparation she has insisted upon?'

'I actually have some sympathy for her. It must be hard, having an Earl always just out of reach, and with a daughter to fire off!'

Nell snorted. 'If she thinks he has any interest in her daughter, she is mistaken.'

'Indeed. And yet, when gentlemen marry, they often choose meek debutantes like Miss Standish. There is no accounting for it!' Just for a second, Cecily imagined him married to the shy Miss Standish.

Why, he would terrify the poor girl!

The notion of his marrying Miss Standish—marrying *anyone*— disturbed her, so she shrugged it off. They turned the corner and paused at the top of the lower staircase, hearing voices below.

'And here they are!' Mr Carmichael had clearly been watching out for them. 'Ladies!' He gave a deep bow as the other gentlemen turned to greet them.

All four were dressed in the required evening dress—evening breeches, snowy-white shirts and cravats. The only difference was the colour of their jackets. The Earl's was a moss-green, and clung perfectly to his frame, while the other gentlemen were in russet, black and dark blue. Cecily barely noticed them, for her eyes had met the Earl's, and the way he was looking at her brought a blush to her cheeks. The brief flirtation was still in place, then, on his part as well as hers. Something suspiciously like relief raced through her.

'Beautiful!'

'You look simply divine!'

Mr Harting and Mr Carmichael were fulsome in their praise. The ladies accepted the compliments graciously, while Tom kissed his wife's hand, whispering something in her ear.

The Earl stood by mutely. He had murmured a polite greeting but had held back on any praise for the ladies' appearance. As ever, this evidence of his discomfiture was a little amusing. For a man normally so assured, so serene in his knowledge of his own place, he clearly struggled at times when in the company of Cecily and Nell. For different reasons, perhaps. Besides, his eyes had already let Cecily know he admired her appearance tonight.

'We shall use both carriages this evening, rather than all trying to fit uncomfortably into the coach.' The Earl had found his voice, it seemed, but his tone was flat, his face expressionless.

'An excellent notion, Hawk. Lady Cecily, might I accompany you in the first carriage?' Mr Harting, moving swiftly, claimed Cecily's hand. Mr Carmichael, not to be outdone, declared that he, too, would travel in the first coach. Since Tom and Nell would undoubtedly travel together, that left His Lordship with two poor choices; accompany the lovebirds as an unwanted third, or squeeze into the first carriage with Cecily and his two friends.

Seeing his brow furrow, Cecily caught her breath.

Oh, dear!

Reading his expressions was one of her favourite pursuits, although working out the source of his current discomfiture was not difficult. She reflected on this as they donned their cloaks and made for the carriages. How had she come to know him so well?

She shrugged. She just had. She now could read his moods, could sometimes almost read *thoughts* as they flitted fleetingly across his handsome face. At other times he appeared shuttered, closed off from everyone. At those moments she suspected he was slamming his inner doors on thoughts or feelings he did not wish to entertain. His solution, she guessed, was to choose to feel nothing.

Automatically, she replied to Mr Harting's comment, and a few minutes later they set off, Mr Harting joining Cecily on the forward-facing seats. Mr Carmichael had secured the seat facing her, while the Earl had joined them at quite the last minute, squeezing in beside the rotund Carmichael. Seeing his thunderous expression, Cecily swiftly turned her gaze outside before her amusement became obvious.

He remained silent during the entire journey, which took no more than twenty-five minutes. The horses pro-

ceeded sedately and carefully along the dark road, flambeaux helping them find their way. The homeward journey
would be a little easier, for the half-moon would rise later.

Cecily was well-entertained, for her two admirers tried
to outdo each other in comment, and wit, and queries after
her comfort. The fact that she was unaffected by the two
gentlemen's efforts to secure her attention was, she believed, obvious to anyone with an eye to see it. The more
they exclaimed, however, the less the Earl seemed to like
it. Cecily almost felt sorry for him, but she was enjoying
his frustration too much to do so. If it had been socially
permissible for him to raise his eyes to heaven, he would
have done so, she had little doubt. Eventually, he gave up
any pretence of following their conversation, and gazed
outward into the darkness.

Instantly, she felt rather forsaken, as though the sun
had gone behind a cloud.

*I must not take this flirtation with too much serious-
ness.*

To do so could be dangerous to her inner tranquil-
lity, which, at this instant, seemed to have abandoned her.
Firmly, she told herself not to be foolish. An entertaining
evening lay ahead. There was no need to think overmuch
on one person's opinion of her.

Jack was sorely regretting inviting Carmichael and
Harting to Hazledene. Yes, he had swiftly secured Harting's agreement to sell him the field he wanted, but he
could surely have contrived a way of doing so in London.
And while it was true that Carmichael had a business
proposition for him to consider, Jack kept, for reasons unknown, deferring the necessary conversation about it. His
mind was strangely disinterested in matters of business.
He currently wished he had agreed to meet Carmichael

in his club or his library in the townhouse, or a blasted gaming den, for all he cared. Having the man continually dancing attendance on Lady Cecily was beginning to grate on his nerves.

Cannot he see that she has no real interest in him?

Lady Cecily, intelligence glinting in her amber eyes, was co-operating with Carmichael's games, although her fancy was clearly not engaged. She tolerated the man, being polite and even friendly towards him, but he might as well be a chimney sweep, Jack knew, for all the chance he had with the lady.

Harting was a different matter. Lady Cecily seemed to genuinely like and respect him. And, indeed, why should she not? Harting was known to be a good fellow. Jack frowned. Something about the situation was profoundly unsettling.

He glanced at Cecily again. She had had her hair done in one of those elaborate evening styles that women favoured. It suited her, as did the elegant golden gown, he grudgingly admitted, though the thought of her beauty being even more apparent than usual gave him no joy. His peace was already destroyed, and he had now almost resigned himself to a bleak existence where he was condemned to eternally dwell upon Lady Cecily's beauty, and Lady Cecily's charm, and Lady Cecily's kindness.

He lived for their walks, their conversations, and for the looks that occasionally passed between them. Lived for them, and yet at the same time resented them. He, who prided himself on rationality, on detachment, was in danger of losing his sanity. There was safety in separateness, peril in passion. At least with Cecily, who had somehow sneaked past his usual defences to cause him untold torment.

His heart lurched as he recalled them standing together

in the nursery last week, and how she had seemed to pry open heavy iron doors inside him that he had thought shut many, many years ago. *Danger*, his mind had shrieked. And so he had run. Away from Lady Cecily, away from the memories, away from that infernal carved knight. In those brief moments, years of careful control had been shredded. He had spent the hours and days since carefully rebuilding the armour of logic, of reason, of detachedness. He could not risk leaving himself vulnerable to abandonment ever again.

And yet, somehow, his obsession with Lady Cecily was now as much a part of him as breathing. Each time he tried to rebuild the walls that kept him safe, she eased her way through them, as fine as mist, as subtle as breath.

Deliberately, he pulled his gaze away from her, although it made little difference, for he could see her yet in his mind's eye. With something akin to desperation, he turned his attention elsewhere, but his damnable mind replaced one frustration with another, for it settled upon Tom and his bride, who were probably even now enjoying some form of marital relations in the other carriage.

His new sister-in-law seemed reasonable enough, he supposed, and there was nothing to criticise in her demeanour and her manners. Indeed, if he were forced to admit it, he would allow that she was pretty-behaved, attractive, and *not* bird-witted, as he had first supposed. Indeed, he was finding himself developing something of a liking for her. The fact that Lady Cecily was so fond of her meant something too, for Lady Cecily had wit and discernment.

Nell also had, it was clear, a genuine *tendre* for Tom. Quite why it troubled him so much to see her devoted attentions towards his brother, he did not know. Yet each time he noticed evidence of her caring for his brother, some stab of pain went through his gut. Perhaps it was simply that it underlined his own estrangement from Tom. Or that their togetherness emphasised his ultimate solitude.

'I think we have arrived!' Carmichael, stating what was obvious to them all. As the carriage slowed and the candlelit windows of Rywell House came into view, Jack wrenched his thoughts away from Tom, and Nell, and Lady Cecily, and braced himself for the horrors of Mrs Standish's soirée.

Two hours later, and he was searching in his mind for a more accurate epithet. 'Horror', as it turned out, was too strong a word, for Mrs Standish had, surprisingly, put together a reasonable evening of entertainment. The food was a little over-elaborate, as was Mrs Standish's feather headdress, but the wine was excellent, the house unexceptional, and the company not unreasonable. He and his two friends had enjoyed a few rounds of Hazard with some of the local gentlemen, and the Standish servants had been on hand to unobtrusively refill their glasses at every turn.

Standish himself had been gruffly welcoming, adjuring them to consider their own comfort above all. 'After supper,' he had confided, 'Mrs Standish plans some dancing, but you must not feel compelled to participate, no, indeed!'

Jack appreciated the sentiment, but understood that it would be the worst of social solecisms to fail to dance with Miss Standish. Which meant he would also be forced to dance with the ladies of his own party, as not to do so would be seen as a snub. Sighing inwardly, he finished his light supper, then abandoned his place at the card table with some regret, making his way to the large salon that had been cleared for dancing.

'My lord!' His hostess had been hovering near the en-

trance to the salon, and glided forward to greet him in a
bustle of orange satin, nodding feathers and effusiveness.
'I do hope you are entertained by our simple soirée. As I
said, nothing formal, just a few local families coming together to honour your presence in our midst!'

Since there were at least fifty guests at the soirée, all
sparkling in fine gowns, evening coats and glistening jew-
ellery, Jack found himself momentarily at a loss to respond
to Mrs Standish's description. He need not have worried,
for she had enough empty utterances to fill both sides of
the conversation.

'I see you enjoy your cards, my lord. While I myself am
partial to a little whist on occasion, I have not the patience
for prolonged attention.' He was unsure what to say to this.
Should he agree? Disagree? Sympathise? Thankfully, she
had already moved on. 'Let me get you some wine.' She
signalled to a footman, who approached with a tray of
wine glasses. Jack took one, noting absently that the glass
was well cut and that the ruby-red liquid within was reflecting the glow of the hundreds of candles in the salon.

'If you wish to dance then your timing is superb, my
lord, for the dancing is about to begin.' She indicated the
musicians on a raised platform at the far side of the room,
seemingly awaiting a signal, for they were all regarding
her fixedly. At her nod, they struck up a strain that sent a
murmur of excitement around the room.

Jack knew his duty. 'Might I secure the hand of Miss
Standish for the first dance?' he offered politely.

Mrs Standish seemed to grow two inches at this. 'Well,
of course you might. Lucinda!' Lucinda, her eyes round
as saucers, hurried towards them.

Avoiding gazing at Miss Standish's gown, which was
in an unbecoming shade of yellow, and which made her
look even more sallow than usual, Jack focused instead on

doing what he could to put the girl at ease. She murmured a polite acceptance of his request for the first dance and allowed him to lead her to the dancing area in the centre of the room. Throughout the figures, he kept up a string of easy platitudes, which she responded to without animation, seemingly focused on remembering the steps of the dance.

How is it that both Miss Standish and Lady Cecily are in yellow-gold gowns, and yet the one looks sallow and the other glowing?

He had been about Town long enough to know that Lady Cecily's taste was much more refined than that of poor Miss Standish's mother, and yet there was more to it. Had the gowns been reversed he was certain he would still prefer Lady Cecily. But, then, at this point he should probably prefer Lady Cecily even if she were attired in rags.

Harting had beaten Carmichael in the race to secure Lady Cecily's hand for the first dance, and Jack's portly friend was currently glowering at them both from near the fireplace. Tom was, naturally, and in contravention of current convention, dancing with his own wife.

For the second dance, they performed as might be expected. Jack took his sister-in-law to the dance floor, and was pleased to discover she danced well, looked well, and held up her end of the conversation with, it seemed, no difficulty. This could not fail to impress him, as they both knew he continued to disapprove of Tom's hasty wedding and had been anything but welcoming to Nell.

Yet she behaved with grace and propriety throughout, and he could not help feeling a glimmer of unexpected pride in her. Almost as if she somehow was becoming part of the Beresford family. He sighed. Yes, the wedding had been hasty, but the marriage was permanent. While he still struggled to understand Tom's speed, he was gradually accepting that Nell was now a permanent fixture.

My sister-in-law.

A female in the family.

Will she leave him someday? If so, how am I to support him?

There was no logical reason that he knew of to assume that Nell would go, or that Tom would suffer the agonies of bereavement or separation, and yet the irrational being in Jack's gut was terrified for his brother's sake. The legacy of Mama's death and Tilly's betrayal was like a scar that would never fully heal.

The emotions this generated were both unwelcome and deeply unsettling, so he distracted himself by allowing his gaze to fall briefly on Lady Cecily, currently navigating the dance floor with a beaming Carmichael.

My, she puts all these other ladies in the shade! Like a golden moon in a sky of pale stars.

Such a thought was hitherto unknown to him. Never had he indulged in poetic nonsense about women. His gut was suddenly tight with vexation as he endured a wave of inner mortification at his own thoughts.

He returned his focus to the present. Despite his determination to resist the unlooked-for fixation with Lady Cecily, he now had a new challenge. The next dance should be hers.

I shall dance with her, and be unmoved, he told himself, knowing he was lying.

Approaching her was not difficult, for Nell asked to be taken to Lady Cecily as their dance ended. Tom met them there, and immediately secured his wife's hand again for the next dance. 'For we have been apart for too long, my love,' he added, making Jack's face twist cynically.

Unable to help himself, Jack met Lady Cecily's gaze.

Her eyes danced with humour and he knew without asking that she was experiencing a similar response to Tom and Nell's sentimentality. She agreed with alacrity to his invitation to dance, and led the way to the centre, giving him a brief yet delightful view of her back, her white shoulders and the nape of her neck.

I should like to kiss her there.

He pictured himself bending to touch his lips to her delicate skin, imagining the feel of it—

'My lord?' She had turned and was eyeing him curiously.

Abruptly, he slammed his usual expressionless mask into place, hoping that he had not revealed anything of his thoughts to her. 'Lady Cecily.' He bowed, for the musicians were striking up the tune.

The next few minutes went by in a haze. He completed the familiar steps unthinkingly, his attention completely caught by the woman in front of him. Her beauty enthralled him, her character captivated him, and some part of him decided, just for these moments, to abandon his inner resistance to her. He could always recover his control after the music stopped. As the whirling melody surrounded them, he allowed his fingers to drift upwards, until he achieved the merest contact with her smooth skin. Dimly, part of his mind was aware that he was allowing himself to feel things that could turn him into just the sort of fool that Tom had become, but at this moment he simply did not care.

She did not speak, which was something of a relief, for Jack doubted he would have been able to create anything like a sensible conversation. Instead, they moved together and locked gazes when they could, and he gave himself over to the joy of being near her, of being the focus of her attention.

The room was now very warm, which might account for the flush on her cheeks. It did not, however, explain the heat in her gaze as her eyes met his.

She feels it too!

Suddenly it became imperative that he find a way to be alone with her. As the music came to an end, and they bowed and curtsied to each other once again, he cleared his throat and asked if she was feeling uncomfortable at the heat in the room. She confirmed it, and he led her towards the terrace. The servants, on Mrs Standish's instruction, were serving iced punch, and a number of people were drifting out through the three sets of double doors, glasses in hand, seeking relief from the warmth of the ballroom.

Jack and Lady Cecily stood together at the very edge of the terrace, where candlelight gave way to the darkness of the gardens. He did not dare suggest a walk in the wilderness, much as he wished to. They avoided speaking, simply enjoying the cool spring air and ignoring the conversations of the others. Their shared gaze was turned to the heavens, and as his eyes became accustomed to the darkness, the stars began to show themselves alongside the newly risen half-moon. Ursa Major. The Pole Star. Cassiopeia.

Jack's heart was thundering in his chest, and the haze of Lady Cecily's witchcraft still surrounded him. The music, somehow, was still playing in his head. He remained acutely aware of her, and all his senses seemed sharpened. He tracked each party of guests as they turned and went inside, until, finally, they were alone. At any moment, more guests might drift outside.

Now is the time.

Chapter Eighteen

'Cecily.' His voice cracked.

Tension apparent in the line of her shoulders, she turned to him. No further words were needed, for they were, it seemed, as one in their desire. He could not say whether he had reached for her or whether she had stepped towards him. He only knew that she was in his arms and now, finally, they would kiss.

The conflagration within him threatened to overwhelm them both, so, using every ounce of his self-restraint, he forced himself to meet her lips gently at first. Her starlit face was upturned to his, and as his eyes drifted closed the imprint of it stayed with him. At this moment, he believed it would stay with him forever.

His arms snaked more tightly around her, pulling her close, even as his lips met hers. Their first touch was feather-light, almost questioning, but before long all notions of restraint were lost as they devoured each other, hunger matching hunger. He could feel the length of her body pressed against his, sense the outline of her shape through her thin gown. His hands stroked her back, from the nape of her delicious neck down the track of her spine. Daringly, he flicked his fingers over her bottom briefly and she reacted as if stung, pressing herself towards him. With a groan, he slid his hands back there, this time pressing, grabbing, kneading. A gasp escaped her as her hips pressed against his, and her arms tightened across his back. Their tongues were dancing now, adding to the sensual delight as they both gave themselves up to each other.

Leaving her mouth briefly, he trailed kisses across her cheek and along the line of her jaw. Cat-like, she raised her chin to allow him access to her neck, and his heart thundered at this continued evidence of her enthusiasm.

'My lord,' she murmured, 'what is it that you are doing to me?'

'Jack,' he muttered. 'I am Jack.' He needed to hear his true name on her lips. His inner name. His childhood name.

She duly obliged. 'Jack.' She pulled back to look at him, bringing both hands up to his face. 'Jack.' This time, it was she who swooped on his mouth. He waited, enjoying the delicious anticipation, and when their lips met he felt as though he were a drowning man breathing air again.

The kiss ended, the only sound that of their ragged breathing. 'Good God, Cecily!' Never had he felt anything like this, and he had had his fair share of escapades.

Dimly, he sensed one of the ballroom doors opening, the noise from inside abruptly increasing. As one, they moved apart, turning their backs on the ballroom, seemingly fixated on the sky.

'That bright one is the Pole Star, is it not?' The tremble in Lady Cecily's voice would, he hoped, not be apparent to whomever was joining them on the terrace.

'It is. And can you see Cassiopeia?' His own voice sounded alien even to himself. How could he pretend that all was well after such a thunderous embrace?

'Ah, there you are, my lord!'

Jack turned, sensing Lady Cecily moving with him. It was Mrs Standish. Behind her, another three or four people emerged onto the terrace, exclaiming about the relieving coolness. They moved to the right, away from where he and Lady Cecily stood. There was already a couple there—presumably the first to emerge following his brief tryst with Lady Cecily.

'They are to play another set shortly, and I would not want you to miss out.'

'Thank you. I certainly would not.'

'I do hope you were not too warm.' She tittered. 'I believe I am the victim of my own success, for everyone of note is here tonight, so it is a sad crush!'

Through the far door another couple of people emerged.

Why, it was as busy as Rotten Row during the midday parade! They were lucky to have secured a moment alone just then.

'Indeed, and an excellent evening's entertainment it is,' he offered smoothly.

'Lady Cecily, might I offer you some iced punch?'

'Er…yes, of course. That would be delightful.' The slight tremor in Lady Cecily's voice was barely noticeable now, but it thrilled him nevertheless.

'I should enjoy some, too. Although punch is not typically my beverage of choice, the notion of ice will reconcile me to it.'

What on earth am I babbling about?

Mrs Standish beamed. 'Our icehouses are renowned in the district, my lord. Should you ever suffer a want of ice, I should be most happy to oblige!'

As they walked back to the house, Mrs Standish looked around the terrace, her gaze inspecting the various parties outside together in the cool darkness. It was clear she had no idea that he and Lady Cecily had been alone. A wave of relief went through him as he considered the alternative. To have risked compromising Lady Cecily was unforgivable.

He had stolen kisses on many occasions over the years, but only rarely with society maidens. Everyone knew that such kisses were only permissible if they remained secret. It would have been mortifying to both Lady Cecily and to himself if they had been discovered in a passionate embrace at a soirée. He groaned inwardly, remembering his hands on Lady Cecily's exquisite bottom. There would be no arguing that it had been a chaste salute on *that* evidence.

I must stay away from her.

He voiced the thought inwardly, needing it to counter the instinct to remain glued to her side for the remainder of the evening. He had no wish to compromise her, no confidence in his ability to resist doing so, and a need to escape from the whirlwind of emotions that was even now swirling through him.

Instead of seeking her out, he danced twice more with ladies suggested by Mrs Standish then, his duty done, he forced himself to return to the card room, away from even a glimpse of Lady Cecily. The run of luck he had experienced earlier seemed to have left him—possibly due to the fact he found himself strangely unable to concentrate.

Wine.

Wine was the answer. He signalled to a nearby footman and watched with anticipation as his glass filled with ruby-red oblivion.

Chapter Nineteen

'Lord! Gentlemen can be so frustrating!'

Cecily looked up from her breakfast to raise a quizzical eyebrow at her friend. 'How so?'

'Tom was so drunk last night that I had to help the valet to get him out of his coat. He was trying to dance me around the bedchamber at the time!' Nell giggled, belying her stated frustration. 'Why do gentlemen enjoy so much drinking to excess?'

'I know not!' Cecily reflected on her own journey home in the darkened carriage. She and Nell had travelled together, along with Tom and Mr Carmichael, while the Earl and Mr Harting had waited for the smaller carriage. All of the gentlemen, from what Cecily could see, had been entirely drunk.

Castaway, disguised, foxed.

She ran the epithets through her mind. Even the Earl.

Quite why this was so disappointing to her, she was unclear. Perhaps she had hoped for more attention from him. Perhaps she had wanted to see whether the fire between them was still there. Perhaps she simply wanted to see how he would behave towards her following that momentous kiss on Mrs Standish's terrace.

Was he already drunk when he kissed me?

As it was, no-one had been able to get a word out of him as they waited for the carriages, and Cecily had already been mounting the stairs when the second carriage had reached Hazledene.

She frowned, taking another sip of delicious chocolate. Had their embrace been as momentous to him as it had been to her? Perhaps he was used to such things. She was decidedly not. Indeed, she had never experienced anything like the passion that had flared within her when he had kissed her.

Jack. Jack kissed me.

The notion sent her heart fluttering, and a warm glow grew in her belly. Remembering his 'Good God!' and the way he had said her name sent her heart from fluttering to pounding. Her hands trembled. Carefully she set down her cup.

'He is yet in bed, you know, sleeping as if he had not a care in the world!'

'Excuse me?' Shaking her head to try and dispel the image of a handsome, sleeping Jack, Cecily eyed her friend. 'But it is afternoon! I had assumed the gentlemen were breakfasting in their chambers. I did not realise they might yet be asleep!'

Nell grinned. 'My Tom is a champion sleeper—particularly after too much wine. Nevertheless, I expect the gentlemen will appear soon—and they will miss breakfast entirely!'

She proved to be right. Less than an hour later, they were all seated in the red parlour with the fire lit, for the day was cold. The gentlemen were all clearly nursing sore heads and feeling rather under the weather.

'Lord!' Carmichael sipped at his tisane, making a face

at the noxious taste. 'Nights out are all very well, but the after-effects of intoxication are most unpleasant.'

'And yet,' Harting added, 'we never learn.'

'I tell you sincerely, Harting, I shall choose never to learn for the rest of my days.' Carmichael looked in earnest. 'Even now, with blacksmiths pounding in my head.'

'While I,' Tom declared, 'am determined to learn. I am no longer one-and-twenty, and wine seems to take its toll now in new and painful ways.' He looked decidedly uncomfortable. 'I was drunk as a wheelbarrow last night!'

Nell had whispered to Cecily that Tom had been violently ill a short time ago, when he had finally awakened. 'It serves him right!' her friend had added, a glint of humour in her eye.

She glanced at the Earl. He looked unruffled, and as handsome as ever. However, he was even more taciturn than usual, and had, she noted, accepted a cup of the chamomile, mint and honey tisane brought by a housemaid on Nell's instruction.

Well, I hope he is suffering!

Stung by his now clear avoidance of her, Cecily could not help feeling that all of the gentlemen deserved their headaches. Including Lord 'Silence' Hawkenden.

She sipped her own tea, enjoying the fresh flavour, and munched on a freshly baked sweetmeat. The Hazledene staff, once again, had proved their worth, for the food and drink remained uniformly excellent.

After the tea tray was removed, they all stretched, and shifted. Tom moved to take his usual place by Nell's side and they began conversing, heads close together. The Earl glanced their way then averted his gaze.

Mr Harting, with a shy smile, came to sit with Cecily. 'How do you, Lady Cecily?'

She gave him a bright smile. 'Very well, Mr Harting. And you?'

'Ah, I, too, am suffering from the legacy of overindulgence.'

She tutted. 'Now, now, Mr Harting, you have only yourself to blame.' Out of the corner of her eye she saw Mr Carmichael moving to sit with the Earl, near the fireplace.

I'll wager Mr Carmichael gets no conversation from him!

Mr Harting smiled ruefully. 'True, true, and yet at the time it seemed an entirely reasonable thing to do.' He sent her a sideways glance. 'I must say again that you looked delightful last night—as you always do.' He hastily added the last, as if concerned that she might misunderstand him. Looking decidedly anxious, he scanned her face. 'You are always beautiful,' he stated simply.

Sensing his sincerity, she felt herself flush. 'Thank you.' She dropped her gaze, unsure of what to say. Mr Harting was an amiable and pleasant gentleman, and she did not wish to hurt him or disappoint him.

'Did you enjoy the dancing?' His tone was more prosaic, and she lifted her eyes to reply.

'I did! I love to dance.' She could tell he was preparing to compliment her dancing skill, so she pressed on. 'Do gentlemen, generally, dislike dancing? I sometimes have the impression they only take part because they are compelled to do so by determined hostesses.'

In the background, she could hear Mr Carmichael talking about 'a unique opportunity' that Hawk must surely be interested in.

The business proposition!

Despite herself, she could not help but be curious. Here she was, condemned to parry compliments and discuss nothingness, while the Earl and Carmichael had the felicity of discussing something stimulating, and interesting, and complex. The specifics were, of course, none of her concern, yet it galled her that gentlemen had opportunities that ladies did not.

Mr Carmichael was mentioning the library—perhaps referring to the conversation she herself had interrupted more than a week ago. Carmichael must not have yet had the opportunity he craved to speak fully with the Earl about his business proposition.

Now, would the Earl engage? Surely this was the one topic that might encourage him to converse? Or perhaps not. The morning after a night's drinking might not be the most suitable time to approach a man about matters of business. She shrugged. That had been Mr Carmichael's judgement, and he, presumably, understood his friend better than she.

'I shall let you in on a secret, Lady Cecily.' Mr Harting leaned forward to speak quietly in her ear, then sat back, his eyes smiling. A sudden pang went through her at the realisation that such an agreeable man could do nothing to her insides. No fluttering, no heat.

Such a shame!

'A secret? Do tell!'

'In truth, many of us enjoy dancing just as much as ladies do. When we protest, it is all bluster, I'm afraid.' His eyes danced. 'Although I should make it clear that I do not speak for *all* gentlemen.'

'Indeed? This is useful to know, Mr Harting. Now, tell me…' She touched his hand playfully. 'How are we ladies meant to work out when a gentleman's protestations are real, and when they are feigned?'

He laughed at that and leaned forward again. 'That, I shall never divulge!'

They continued, easy, friendly conversation flowing

like a babbling stream. No tension, no hidden depths. Cecily still occasionally caught snatches of that other conversation. The Earl had engaged, and was sitting upright, quizzing Mr Carmichael. He was replying with numbers, and dates. She strained to listen to Mr Carmichael, intrigued to learn more, but, frustratingly, she could not hear enough to catch the thread of their conversation. Unthinkingly she sighed, her frustration needing an outlet at that moment.

'Lady Cecily? Are you unwell?' Mr Harting was all concern.

'Not at all.' She flushed, fearing that others would notice their exchange. Forcing a smile, she added, 'I am quite well, Mr Harting, thank you. Just a passing thought.'

'Are you certain? I should hate for you to feel any distress.'

Moved by his genuine concern, she patted his hand. 'I am sure.' Inwardly, she was still intrigued to discover the details of Mr Carmichael's proposal, and frustrated that she might never do so.

Why should gentlemen have all the opportunities to use their brains, with us women expected to speak of nothing and keep to our embroidery?

Somehow, hearing the Earl discussing these matters, yet excluding her, felt more than unfair. Oh, it was irrational to blame him, she knew, for apart from that one conversation at breakfast where she had shared with him her fascination with matters of commerce, how was he to know that she would be interested to join him and Mr Carmichael? Still, she could not help but feel cross, and frustrated, and—almost *slighted* by him.

Jack was experiencing quite the most difficult day of his adult life. His head was pounding, his stomach threatening to dispel its contents, and his heart was in turmoil. Last night—

Last night—or at least, that part when he had decided to douse his head in wine—was a haze of memory. He clearly recalled his decision to get drunk, and the enthusiasm with which he had encouraged the footmen to keep filling his glass. However, he had no notion how he had made it to the carriage at the end of the soirée, or to his chamber, or to his bed. He could only hope he had behaved appropriately.

Stifling a groan at his own foolishness, he sipped at the tisane. It was surprisingly pleasant and seemed to be settling his angry stomach a little. He glanced at his sister-in-law, who had instructed the staff to prepare the tisane.

Perhaps, after all, it is unhelpful to always surround oneself with gentlemen.

He shook away the thought. He and Tom had never needed ladies before—beyond the obvious, short-term desires—but, still, Tom should not have made such a hasty change, particularly without Jack's approval. Recognising his own thoughts as churlish, he reminded himself that he was quite warming to Nell. So why was he so determined to be cross with Tom?

He considered the matter. Although he was learning to appreciate Nell's good qualities, Jack's simmering resentment at Tom's unlooked-for marriage remained. It had the whiff of betrayal about it. Betrayal. Abandonment in a different way, yet still abandonment.

Things will never again be what they were...

The thought made his guts twist, enhancing the wine-induced nausea, so he quickly diverted his mind to other matters. Like the lady who was, as ever, dominating his attention.

As Carmichael prattled on, Jack barely heard him. His

awareness, quite against his own wishes, was entirely devoted to the scene on his right, where Harting was successfully engaging Lady Cecily in light-hearted conversation. Lady Cecily was a picture of beauty, he allowed, grudgingly. Her amber day dress emphasised her beautiful eyes. He could not recall ever noticing such things in a lady before. His gaze dropped to her captivating mouth, and he looked away quickly.

Ignoring his visceral reaction to their whisperings, he reflected, sadly, that he himself was incapable of light-heartedness today. He had slept badly, waking every hour or two to drink cool, clear water and moan at his aching head. Nothing, however, could flush out the copious amounts of red wine he had imbibed. Or the memories of that embrace. That, naturally, remained astoundingly clear in his memory.

His head pounded, amplifying his sense of misery.

How could I have allowed myself to lose control so spectacularly? To abandon the habits of years?

He was not sure if he was referring to his drinking or his embracing Lady Cecily. Either way, there was nothing he could do about it. He would simply have to endure the effects of his foolishness until they decreased.

Wine. And punch.

There had been iced punch as well as wine, had there not? He and Lady Cecily had drunk some after returning from the terrace. He should have persisted with only wine.

Diverting his mind away from Mrs Standish's terrace, and the events that had taken place there, instead he forced himself to ask Carmichael some questions about his proposal. It was, after all, the reason why he had invited Carmichael to Hazledene. He had known that the man had wanted to talk to him for days, but there had never, until now, been a suitable opportunity. They had had two or

three half-conversations—including one in his library—
but Carmichael had not yet come to the nub of his proposal.

I am not certain that today is suitable either.

But he should give his friend the courtesy of listening.
And, besides, he was always interested in new business
ventures. Hunger for wealth had been his inspiration ever
since Papa's death, after all.

He reached inside himself for the familiar vigour—one
that had enabled him to hold business 'meetings' in unusual situations over the years. Memories flitted through
his mind—on a yacht, while feeling decidedly unwell,
in a tavern in York, half-drunk, even at a boxing match.
Yet today his body and heart and mind seemed unable to
focus on Carmichael. He gleaned enough to understand
that Carmichael was seeking a significant investment for
a shipping business ripe for taking over, and promising
significant returns.

'Very well.' He cut the man short. 'Let us speak of this
further tomorrow. Might I ask you to do something for
me, though?'

'Of course!' Carmichael's face was red with pleasure.

'Can you write some of this down for me? Numbers
and sizes of ships, their condition, the goods they trans-
port, and by which routes. Anything you know. I also wish
to understand precisely how much this would cost me—
would cost Tom and me—and what our returns would be.'

Carmichael looked a little crestfallen. 'I do not have all
of that information in my head, Hawk. But I shall write
down as much as I am able.'

'Thank you.' His tone denoted finality, and thankfully
Carmichael took the hint.

Nell, rising, excused herself and left the room. She

looked serene, but Jack noticed how Lady Cecily's gaze followed her friend, a slight frown of puzzlement on her brow.

Have the lovers quarrelled?

He glanced at Tom, who seemed his usual self. Well, that version of himself suffering from the delights of too much wine.

Despite his resolution to avoid the feelings that sprang up in him each time he looked at Lady Cecily, he could not resist looking back at her. Their eyes met, and hers slid away immediately.

Something about her response caused his instincts to come to full alertness. Where he had become accustomed to holding her gaze for an instant longer than was strictly acceptable, just now she had deliberately avoided him.

Damnation!

He might have known that their kisses last night would change things. While the physical memories for him held mainly delight—although the delight was unfortunately accompanied by some deeper, unsettling emotions—he had not stopped to think about how a sheltered maiden might view their encounter in the cold light of day. Yes, at the time she had been a willing—even an *enthusiastic*—participant. Yet it went against every rule that society made for unmarried maidens to do what Lady Cecily had done last night.

It had been no chaste embrace. It had been raw, and sensual, and filled with naked passion. For just a moment he indulged himself by allowing the memories to wash over him fully. Her face upturned for his kisses. Her tongue dancing with his. The feel of her delectable body pressed against him. Her passion, matching him breath for breath.

Lord, she is glorious!

Swallowing hard, he gazed into the fire, using every ounce of inner strength to regain mastery of himself. Once calmer, he diverted his attention to considering further how Lady Cecily might be remembering their encounter. He smiled ruefully to himself. He suspected she might never have felt intense desire before. Maybe it had frightened her.

He shifted in his seat, sensing something like terror at the edges of his own consciousness.

Have I ever experienced desire so intense before?

He was experienced in bedding women, and knew the delights of the flesh. But Lady Cecily inspired him with more than her beauty, more than her exquisite body. And that was, frankly, terrifying.

No. He could not allow his thoughts to veer in that direction. Instead he needed to divine how best to remedy the situation. Might Lady Cecily think he planned to ruin her? Society knew he was not seeking a wife. That may lead her to assume he was, instead, seeking a lover. He needed her to understand he was no rake and had not the habit of seducing and discarding virgins of any class. He glanced at her again. She continued to converse with Harting, but there was a different quality to her smile now. To him it looked brittle, as if she were masking some inner discomfort.

His heart sank. Never would he wish to cause her distress! His pulse skipped as he took in her beautiful profile, the elegance of her pose, the grace of her white arms, hands resting neatly in her lap. He also noted the continued slight frown on her brow, the fixedness of her smile.

Cecily!

Could no-one else sense her distress? He glanced around. Tom's eyes were closed as he took the opportunity to doze in his armchair. Carmichael, seemingly intent on wasting no time, had made his way to the writing desk by the window and was even now sharpening a pen.

Only Harting was focused on Lady Cecily, his gaze rapt as he looked at her.

And why should he not be? Jack's insides twisted. *After last night, she might believe that Harting's civility is preferable to my savageness.*

How could he comfort her when he might well be the source of her distress?

This was a complication he had not anticipated. At the time, he had been thinking only of his need to be alone with her, to kiss her, to press her close. It had seemed then as if tomorrow might not come.

Unfortunately for all of them tomorrow had indeed come, and it wore a vengeful visage.

Chapter Twenty

When Nell had still not returned after a half-hour, Cecily decided to go and look for her. Her own conversation
with Mr Harting had eventually lapsed into silence, aided
by her gradual polite disengagement. Tom was sleeping,
Mr Carmichael was writing, and the Earl had not lifted
his gaze from the fire for an age. It was unusual for Nell
to be away from her husband's side for so long.

Murmuring a polite farewell, Cecily made for the door,
wondering if the Earl had even looked up. Straightening
her shoulders, she refused to glance back. At this moment,
she could not bear to meet his gaze. Between uncertainty
over the aftermath of their kiss, and feeling irrationally
excluded from matters of business, looking at him brought
too many complications.

An obliging footman informed her that he believed Mrs
Beresford to be in her chamber. Hurrying upstairs, Cecily
scratched on Nell's door. 'Nell, it is I.'

'Come in, Cecily.'

On hearing the muffled response, Cecily wasted no
time. Closing the door behind her, she made her way towards her friend, who was lying on her side on top of the

bed facing the door. Her knees were drawn up and she was wearing a familiar pained expression.

'Ah, Nell, what is it?' She asked the question, although she had already guessed the answer.

'Just my monthly flow, but I think it will be a bad one this time.' She reached out a hand and Cecily took it, sympathy rushing through her.

Not wishing to call a housemaid straight away, Cecily helped her friend unlace and undress. Once Nell was in her nightgown, without the restrictions of corset and gown, she sighed with relief. Cecily tucked the blankets in around her, but Nell immediately loosened them, needing to thrash about a little.

Cecily's brow creased at her friend's discomfort. 'I shall ask for a tisane, with your permission?'

'Please, do.' Nell gave a short laugh as Cecily walked across to the fireplace to ring the bell. 'The gentlemen need tisanes for their drinking, and we for our womanly concerns!'

'Indeed, but at least they had a choice in the matter!'

Luckily, it was Molly, the amiable older housemaid, who answered the call-bell. She immediately bustled into action, securing a well-mixed tisane and a hot brick for Nell. 'Now, you just hold that brick close to where it hurts, my love,' she said kindly. 'I shall light the fire, and all will be well.'

Molly left them to it, with a strong recommendation to Nell not to be worrying that she was not yet in the family way. 'There is plenty of time for that, ma'am, and it often happens that the first baby may take a year or two to appear!'

Nell did indeed seem to take reassurance from this, and thanked Molly for her kindness.

When the maid was gone, Cecily shook off her slippers

and climbed onto the bed beside her friend. They chatted for a while—mainly recalling each moment of last night's soirée, which they had both enjoyed. Cecily was tempted to tell Nell about the kiss from the Earl but held back. She did not know whether Nell would react with delight or horror and, frankly, she did not wish to know.

Her own feelings flailed wildly between the two. Delight that she had experienced such a wonderful, amazing, peace-shattering embrace. Delight that he, Jack, had kissed her. Delight that he had, seemingly, been moved by it, too.

Then there was the horror. Horror at her own display—hardly the actions of a demure young lady, daughter to an earl. Horror at the notion that they might have been seen at any moment. Horror that she had become so lost in her *tendre* for him that she had forgotten his arrogance, his aloofness, the cold-hearted emptiness that she had long seen in him. He had treated Nell terribly badly—although, to be fair, he was now making an effort to deepen his acquaintance with his brother's wife, though it was largely limited to trivialities.

She squirmed. Here at Hazledene she believed she was beginning to understand him a little. And dimly she was aware that there were reasons behind some of his actions. Reasons for his steely armour. She could not forget their conversation in Crow Wood, or the wooden knight, which still nestled safely in her reticule.

'Tell me, Nell…' the words were out of her mouth before she could stop them '…has Tom ever spoken to you of matters of business? What is his view of involving you in his decisions?'

Nell looked up at her. 'No—I—We have never spoken of it. But I have no doubt that Tom will share his worries with me, and his triumphs.'

Cecily nodded. 'I am glad to hear it. But would you not wish to be involved in the detail? Numbers, projections, all the facets of a decision that must be considered?'

'Possibly.' Nell's tone was vague. 'I have not much thought of it. But, yes, why not?' She eyed Cecily curiously. 'Why do you ask?'

'Oh, for no particular reason.' She stood, feeling a surge of restlessness. 'Now, I shall go and seek an interesting book, so I might read to you.'

The chiming of the ormolu clock on the mantel awoke Jack with a start. Between the heat of the fire and the effects of last night, he had succumbed to the comfort of an afternoon nap—something he could not recall indulging in for many years. But, then, he had not been quite so drunk for many years. Almost guiltily, he glanced around the room, stretching in his armchair as he did so. All three gentlemen were sound asleep—Tom in his armchair and Harting on the settee, while Carmichael was stretched out on the window seat, snoring gently. Of the ladies there was no sign.

Lord! Did they return and see us all collapsed?

Jack felt his face flush a little at the notion. They were all four bachelors, unused to the presence of ladies. Their habits reflected it.

No, Tom is married now, he recalled.

The notion still surprised him, even now. The usual stab of pain went through him as he remembered, although it was perhaps a little less sharp than usual.

Still, it was impolite of the ladies to have stayed away for so long. Had they returned, an intervention as subtle as a polite cough would likely have brought the gentlemen back to consciousness—perhaps with an additional prod required for Carmichael, who seemed deeply asleep. Jack frowned as he speculated on the reasons for the ladies' prolonged absence. Were they even now huddled together somewhere, criticising the gentlemen? It was a novel and disturbing thought.

Suddenly he felt the need to escape. Fresh air, perhaps, and a break from all of it. Rising silently, he made his way out of the salon and into the hallway. Lady Cecily was just descending the staircase. She hesitated slightly when she saw him, and an uncertain expression flickered across her face.

'Oh! There you are, Lord Hawkenden.' Her smile seemed forced, raising indignation within him instantly. What had she been saying about him? Had she told Nell about their embrace?

'Might I borrow a book from your library, my lord? I am in need of something to read. In fact,' she continued, the words tumbling out of her in a rush, 'I mean to read something to Nell.'

He raised an eyebrow, awkwardness, disappointment and frustration all rising within him. 'So your friend is brooding in her chamber? Have the lovers, then, finally quarrelled? I knew it would come to this eventually.' Hearing his own words, he tried to soften them with a smile, but he was, it seemed, too late.

She flushed, vexation in her expression and in the sudden stiffening of her shoulders. 'Indeed not! As far as I know, there is no quarrel between them. Nell is simply indisposed.'

Perhaps he could tease her into charity with him again. 'If you think me a fool, only born yesterday, then you may think again, Lady Cecily! I have heard it said that ladies are frequently "indisposed" when they mean to punish gentlemen for some imagined slight. There is no sickness in this house—no fever, or anything like it. The only mem-

bers of the household who are truly indisposed today are
the gentlemen—and that is because we overindulged in
wine last night. So tell me honestly, what have we done to
offend you?' His tone was light-hearted, but there was a
genuine plea in his words, which he hoped she would hear.

*Have I offended you, Cecily? Please, tell me, that I may
make all well between us again.*

He eyed her closely, observing her reaction, and his
heart sank. She was gripping the handrail, knuckles
showing white, and there were two spots of colour on
her cheeks.

Lord, I have truly angered her!

'Lady Cecily—' he began, determined to speak to her
in a more straightforward fashion. 'I—'

'If you must know, my lord, Nell is unwell because of
her monthly courses. She is, even now, in bed in great
pain.' Cecily's eyes blazed with fury. 'The housemaid has
brought a tisane and poor Nell is pressing a hot brick to her
stomach in an attempt to endure the pain.' Her lip curled.
'Gentlemen have no idea what ladies suffer!' She glared
at him, then belatedly clapped a hand to her mouth. 'Oh,
Lord, I should not have—' Overcome by her own confusion, she turned around and fled back upstairs.

Jack, stunned, watched her go, his jaw hanging loose
and his mind awhirl. Shock was too small a word to describe the turmoil within him. Since childhood, the only
women he had encountered, apart from superficial social
interactions, had been servants and courtesans. Although
he vaguely knew a little of womanly matters, generally
women avoided speaking of such things to bachelors. So to
discover that women could suffer so during their monthly
time was shocking, if fascinating, new information.

Vague memories came to him, as he abruptly made
sense of certain episodes in the past. A host's sister dis-

appearing from a house party for two days as she was 'indisposed'. Housemaids unaccountably replaced for brief periods, disturbing the rhythm of his routine comforts. Courtesans 'indisposed' for some days each month—and losing money from it. Indisposed, indisposed, indisposed.

Well! Who would have thought it?

Intellectual curiosity surged within him. What was the reason for women to suffer so? How could their menfolk best care for them? How on earth did a hot brick assist them? Although chilly, the day was not freezing cold.

He sighed as his gut caught up with his brain. He had bungled his conversation with Cecily, his attempt at lightheartedness falling flat. Their first conversation alone together since that momentous embrace, and he had made a complete mull of it. His misjudgement entirely.

Never before had he missed his footing with a lady. He always knew exactly what to say, in any situation. Yet, with Cecily, he sometimes found himself unsure, hesitant and sorely lacking in judgement. And yet their conversations when they walked out together were among the easiest he had ever known. Just one of the many ways in which her effect on him was unique.

Another notion struck him.

Does Tom know?

He pictured his recumbent, wine-suffering brother, stretched out as he had last seen him in an armchair, and chuckled.

Most certainly not!

There was no way on this earth that Tom could be aware of his darling's suffering and yet not be by her side. Even if she had sent him away he would be fretting about her.

Briefly Jack allowed himself to imagine how he would feel if Cecily were in agony, pressing a hot brick to her

stomach in search of some relief. His gut twisted as he
realised he, like Tom, would wish only to ease her pain.
Briefly, he closed his eyes and swallowed hard. His growing feelings for Cecily, unlooked-for as they were, at least
gave him some insight into Tom's heart.

So it was with part sympathy, part responsibility that he
returned to the salon of sleepers. Touching Tom's shoulder, he placed a finger on his lips to hush his brother, who
had opened his eyes and was now frowning. Beckoning
for Tom to follow, Jack left the parlour for the second time
in ten minutes. Once they were in the hallway, the door
safely closed, Jack wasted no time in explaining himself.

'It appears your *beloved* is indisposed,' he offered
bluntly, unable to prevent adding an ironic tone to the
endearment. Old habits remained, despite his dawning
understanding. 'Women's trouble, I understand.'

'Lord, no! Is she very ill? Must we get the doctor?' The
colour was draining from Tom's face, and Jack could not
prevent a pang of sympathy. Tom clearly cared for his wife.

'I know not. Lady Cecily has been with her. Tisanes
and a hot brick have been secured. Tom—' for his brother
had already spun towards the staircase '—do let me know
if anything more can be done to ensure her comfort. I
know little of these matters, but…' He paused, his words
fading into silence.

Tom nodded, gratitude in his expression. 'Thank you,
Jack.'

'You are welcome,' he responded gruffly, his throat
tight. Spinning on his heel, he made for the back door,
calling for a footman to fetch his boots. He needed that
fresh air more than ever.

Lady Cecily made for her own chamber, entirely mortified. How could she have mentioned such matters to a gen-

tleman? An unmarried gentleman, at that? Having been raised partly by Marianne and Ash and knowing how sympathetic Ash was towards his wife any time she suffered, Cecily, as she often did, had come to judge all men by the standards of her guardian. She knew, of course, that such matters were generally unmentionable, and that bachelors in particular would likely be disgusted or alarmed by unwanted knowledge. She had witnessed shocked aversion on certain faces occasionally if a woman had needed to be brought home early from a picnic or a theatre trip, or if—horror of horrors—a woman needed to quickly don a borrowed cloak.

Jack does not even have a sister!

She put a hand to her head as she recalled again his shock and stillness after her mortifying outburst.

How could I?

Oh, Lord, as if matters were not confused enough already.

Stepping away from the door, for she had been leaning on it as if to ensure that reality could not intrude, she began pacing up and down the chamber, memories of her various encounters with him flooding through her mind. That look between them at Lady Jersey's. Their argument on the terrace there. His arrogance and disdain towards her and Nell.

Then the other side of him, seen at Hazledene. Their developing friendship. Their walks together. Their conversations. The nursery. His mother's death. The little carved knight. He had rejected it so firmly, and yet she had kept it, feeling that it was important to do so. Even now, it remained in her reticule.

Trying to be fair, she remembered their shared amusement at Tom and Nell's endless dalliance, the understanding—never voiced—that the marriage had occurred after a worryingly short period of time. While she could not support the disdain he showed at times towards the loving pair, she at least understood the concern behind it.

Then there was their own embrace last night, the storm of passion that had overwhelmed her as they had kissed. Overwhelmed them both, perhaps. And yet today there had been no sign that he saw her as pleasing in any way. He had been detached, distant, almost rude in his withdrawal. Mr Harting's kind attentions did little to assuage the hurt inside her, for it came from a need for Jack. Jack, and no other.

Finally, she allowed herself to relive the moment just now, when she had spoken to him of matters that must never be discussed. Sinking into an armchair, she pressed her hands against her hot cheeks, rocking backwards and forwards as if comfort could be achieved from it.

She would never be able to look him in the eyes again.

Chapter Twenty-One

Dinner was a strange affair. Jack took his usual seat at the head of the table, while Tom sat opposite. Harting and Carmichael declared their appetites to be fully restored—a fact reinforced by the way they attacked the food, enjoying each course and devouring copious amounts of meat, vegetables and side-dishes with gusto.

In contrast, Tom picked at his food, his attention seemingly elsewhere. Until today, this would have caused Jack severe irritation. Tom had not appeared downstairs again until the dinner gong, and Carmichael had greeted him with attempted raillery about him dallying with his wife in the afternoon. Tom had reported that his wife was indisposed. The moment was then saved by the arrival of Lady Cecily, who had not heard Carmichael's ribald words. Or at least Jack hoped she had not. She had seemed rather uncomfortable since she had arrived in the dining room, and had said little. He was desperate for an opportunity to make things right between them, but so far she was avoiding his eye.

She is clearly still angry with me.

She had not spoken directly to him since dinner began, he noted. Indeed, she had not even looked in his direction.

He knew this because meeting her gaze had, somehow, become important to him. To have her withdraw from him like this today was unexpectedly wounding. Every part of him was eager to mend what he had broken, to restore the amity that had become so essential to his peace of mind.

He caught his own thoughts and frowned into his wine glass.

I am becoming absurd! It will not do.

Why should it matter to him what one young lady thought of him? He had been impervious to the opinions of innumerable young ladies for most of his life. Yet, somehow, this was different. Lady Cecily was different. The way she made him feel was different.

How? Why? He could not understand it. He had encountered any number of young ladies over the years. Almack's was full of them. Matchmaking mamas would fling their daughters in the paths of gentlemen such as him without any trace of embarrassment or remorse. Until now, he had been entirely impervious to the ladies' charms and their mamas' machinations. Until now.

Lady Cecily behaved differently from other ladies. Where they flirted and fluttered, she could slay him with a level gaze. Where they simpered and preened, she appeared entirely unaware of her own beauty. It should have meant he was less interested in her. In fact, the opposite was the case.

As an earl, he knew he had a certain standing in society. As daughter to an earl, she matched it. He did not understand why this caused him discomfort. A possible explanation occurred to him.

Have I become arrogant?

He shrugged. And what if he was? Why should he be concerned with the opinions of others, when such matters had never bothered him before? A weariness came over him, swiftly followed by anger. He was suddenly tired of Lady Cecily Thornhill, tired of Tom's tiresome bride, tired of carrying all his burdens. It seemed that Tom did not need or appreciate him, or his concern, in the way he once had. Cecily, too, had withdrawn from him—an event that was hurting him much more than it should.

The thought of his estrangements—from Cecily, from his brother—brought a familiar sinking feeling to his stomach. He knew his thoughts were irrational, his hurts petty, yet he could not stay them. The unhappiness that drove him was deep, and huge, and rooted in events that had occurred many years ago, yet it was the uncertainties around Tom, and Cecily, and Nell that had shaken him to his core and were now awakening a sleeping giant of pain within him.

He sipped his brandy.

I should be impervious to every one of them.

Yet he was not.

Tomorrow, he decided, he would start afresh, considering only his own needs, and not those of others. It was the only way to master this.

Three hours later he climbed the stairs wearily, yet there was no refuge to be had in his old bedroom. Too many memories lurked in the shadowy corners of the nursery. The bed was uncomfortable as well—too narrow, the mattresses too thin. It had been many years since he had suffered the indignities of such poor accommodation. Internally, he added this to his list of grievances. Yet he knew that the problem was not the mattresses, or the nursery, or any of the trivialities with which he had been distracting himself.

None of this was his doing. If Tom had not been so foolish as to marry a provincial nobody with nothing to recommend her beyond a decent figure and a wide smile, he would not be in the position of having to endure such a change in the relationship between himself and his brother. He also would not have been forced into acquaintance with Lady Cecily, or experienced her rejection of him—a rejection that seemed to have hurt him in places too deep for comfort.

Has she truly rejected me?

Perhaps he could still make things right between them. Yet his gut was not listening. Tom was gone. Cecily was gone. Just like Mama. Just like Tilly. Once more, he was alone.

Tomorrow beckoned. Another day to endure. Tom and his indisposed bride irritating him. Lady Cecily cold and distant. Carmichael hounding him with notions of a business investment, while Harting made sheep's eyes at Lady Cecily. Part of him knew that such matters, in normal times, would not affect him in this way. But there was something about Hazledene, and Cecily, and that damned wooden knight… If only he could escape from all the people, and the places, and the memories. He generally avoided Hazledene as much as possible, and was now being punished for his own obstinacy in coming here when he should have known better.

At least there were plans for the gentlemen to ride out on the morrow. One more day trapped in the house would likely be too much for him. He felt as though his sanity, his very self, was hanging by a thread.

Jack's mood at breakfast was just as listless as at dinner the night before. Bleary-eyed from lack of sleep, he found he could barely manage the required pleasantries, while his fellow guests today seemed equally lethargic. Only Carmichael, his bluff demeanour impervious to hints, chattered freely, opining on everything from the mild weather to his anticipated enjoyment of the day's sport. Jack played his part in their discussion of the route they would follow, while trying not to look at Lady Cecily, who was currently engaged in sipping tea, her gaze unfocused. She had wished him a polite good morning, yet there had been nothing of intimacy in her glance towards him.

Very well, then.

Yesterday's alcohol-related ailments had worn off, yet still there was an air of discomfort among the group.

Jack himself was oppressed by a pervasive sense of futility. He was determined to fight the sense of exhaustion that was menacing him, and yet was conscious of a huge hulking monster of pain within, barely controlled. Matters he had ignored for years were awakening, threatening, planning to overcome him. He sensed it but was now too tired to fight any longer.

Nell had not joined them for breakfast, and Tom's furrowed brow was causing Jack great irritation. Yes, he had no doubt that Nell was suffering, and understood that Tom must feel concern for her, but their strong connection with each other emphasised his new distance from Tom. There was a vague recognition that he envied Tom. Envied him the felicity he had found with his Nell. It made Jack's solitude all the more apparent.

I am alone.

'Apologies, Carmichael. What did you say?' Carmichael had just asked him something. Jack had caught the tone but not the content. Shaking himself, he determined to behave properly, even with this ennui lying upon him. He could do no less.

'Oh, just that I have prepared the written information

you requested. Hoping you can have a look at it today.'
He tapped a paper he had placed on the table beside him.

'Capital! I shall read it on our return.' In truth, his mind
remained strangely uninterested in matters of business.

Inconceivable!

One more sin to lay at the feet of his heedless brother
and the lady causing such havoc to Jack's previously well-
ordered life. Lady Cecily Thornhill.

Once breakfast was done Carmichael and Harting rose
first, eager for the ride ahead. They departed, leaving
Tom, Jack, Lady Cecily and a strained silence. Lady Cecily had still not spoken to Jack, apart from the basic cour-
tesies, and she was now frowning in his direction again.
Or was she? He glanced her way again. Her expression
was as smooth as glass, and just as brittle. There was no
sense of their previous connection, none at all.

She has left me.

He picked up Carmichael's paper, idly playing with it,
and entirely aware that Lady Cecily was watching him
closely. He could not bear the knowledge that she thought
ill of him.

The footmen, gathering some dishes, left for the kitch-
ens. Tom wandered to the window, staring outside, his
shoulders hunched and a general air of misery surrounding him. With a single, exasperated glance in his brother's
direction, Jack refocused on the lady who continued to
disturb his peace with her very presence. He waited until
she returned his gaze.

'Your attention to matters of business continues, my
lord?' There was an edge to her tone, something he could
not quite identify. Where had she gone, the Cecily who
was his friend?

'Naturally,' he lied, shrugging, then glanced towards
his brother's back. 'Someone in this family must continue

to attend to matters of importance. We cannot all spend half the day in bed and expect decisions to be taken as if by magic.'

His brother stiffened.

A hit? Good. For I am done with niceties.

Perhaps Tom would listen to him now. Perhaps Tom would see him. Perhaps Tom would remember that he had a brother.

He picked up Carmichael's paper and pretended to read, knowing he should not be doing so at the breakfast table.

'Might I enquire,' Lady Cecily asked in a creamy tone, 'about Mr Carmichael's proposition? Only if you are willing to discuss such matters, of course. I would understand it if you would prefer to maintain privacy, and of course your business affairs are none of my concern.'

He frowned, unsure of her meaning. 'It is no secret, I suppose.' His eyes narrowed. Here, perhaps, was an opportunity to shake Tom out of his lovesick lethargy. 'A shipping line is in difficulty, Lady Cecily, and is up for sale. Carmichael is keen to invest but knows he has not the experience to make a success of it. Hence, he brought it to us. He says he will follow my lead.'

This had the desired effect. Tom turned, his face twisted with sudden anger. 'Shipping? But you know that I usually handle matters related to shipping. Why have you not discussed this with me?'

Lady Cecily, Jack noted, was looking from one brother to the other, her expression suddenly concerned. Jack barely had time to consider this for here, finally, was his opportunity to take Tom to task. The angry creature within him demanded it.

'My dear brother,' he drawled, 'you have shown no interest in matters of business since your unfortunate and hasty wedding.'

'That is not true!' Tom's face was flushed. 'I have signed every paper required of me! And it is only natural that I should wish to devote my time and attention to Nell for now. She is—and will remain—my wife! And I consider marrying Nell to be the most fortunate event of my life!'

Jack gave a bark of cynical laughter. 'Were you even aware that Carmichael had a proposal for me to consider?'

'For *us* to consider,' Tom replied pointedly. 'Yes, of course. He is not exactly subtle about such matters. But…' he shrugged '…you invited him here. You were handling this one. It was up to you to include me if needed. We both know that at times we have each taken on different schemes, for ease. But I did not know his proposal involved shipping.'

'No, for your mind has been elsewhere.' Jack injected as much venom into his tone as he could manage. The monster within was wide awake now and roaring with rage. 'Why, even this morning we were all forced to endure your woebegone face at breakfast. I declare it was enough to quite put me off my food!'

Vaguely, he knew he should have waited for Lady Cecily to leave before unleashing his frustration on Tom. Yet somewhere in the back of his mind was a sense that he might be able to trust her. That showing his true self, his true frustrations, might not necessarily be a bad thing. Was it even possible that she might understand him? She had before.

He knew that he was behaving outrageously. Knew it, and yet at that moment he seemed unable to control the anger within. Dimly, he was aware that he was not, in fact, angry with Tom, but with Mama, and Papa, and Tilly—with all the people who should have cared for the boy Jack, yet had not. A lifetime of refusal to look their failures squarely in the eye had led to this day. His mind awhirl and his gut filled with rage, he now avoided Cecily's eye.

'Are you accusing me of discourtesy towards our guests?' Tom's tone was tight, his hands fisted by his sides.

Deliberately, Jack leaned back in his chair, knowing such demeanour would anger his brother further. 'You barely spoke this morning. Why?'

'Because Nell is—is unwell, and I am concerned for her! You know this!' Tom seemed to have forgotten Lady Cecily's presence. And yet her presence might be the only thing currently preventing them from taking their grievances to fisticuffs. Oh, how Jack would welcome the release of a bare-knuckle fight! Had he been in London, he could have made his way to Jackson's Boxing Saloon, there to be soundly beaten by that master of the art. But he was in Hazledene, with no prospect of escape from the memories that surrounded him, thick and dense as any forest.

'Oh, yes, I certainly know it! But there is no need to make such a tragedy out of it, surely? Our guests expect better!'

'And I suppose your not attending to Carmichael is acceptable? You starting this argument in front of Lady Cecily—also a guest—is acceptable? Brother, you are becoming uncouth, and I have no further interest in this conversation! I shall see you shortly with our guests, and I expect you to have mastered yourself by then!' Turning on his heel, Tom stalked out, leaving Jack's rage with no target.

In the tense silence that followed, Jack met Lady Cecily's frowning gaze. 'Well?' he barked defiantly.

Uncouth? He calls me uncouth? How dare he?

She spread her hands wide. 'I can say only that I am relieved not to have had brothers, if this is how you go on.' Shaking her head slowly, she added, 'You are each as bad as the other, you know.'

He laughed shortly. 'Not so! It is not I who has abandoned his responsibilities and is lost in a malaise of *love*!' The final word was uttered with loathing.

'You think love a malaise?' Her tone was mild, but her eyes flashed fire.

'There is no love! There is only self-interest, and no-one acts from pure motives.' As he spoke he was hazily aware that she, too, was suffering his irrational anger. But she, like Tom, threatened his fragile self-control. He was better alone, without anyone to betray him.

'Not true! Love is real, and it makes people act *against* their own interests at times. I know, for I have seen it.'

This did not suit his current argument, so he made haste to take her down a side road. 'You are just as concerned about their sudden marriage as I!'

'I was, at first. But I accepted it. And seeing them together here, I now feel more confident of their true connection.' She tilted her head to one side. 'They seem truly devoted to one another.'

'Devoted? Such an idea is nonsensical.' His gut was entirely twisted now. 'Until he met Nell, Tom was like me. His priority was to restore our family pride and glory, to undo the harm to our name committed by our father.'

'What is your notion of glory, my lord?'

'In our case, it is our fortunes. To restore what my father destroyed.'

'So in your view, glory is simply wealth? Or might it also be goodness, generosity, doing good for others? Might *love* be part of glory?'

He snorted. 'People may *speak* of such things, but should be judged on their actions, not their words.' Old memories screamed again within him.

Loss, betrayal, absence, abandonment.

Lady Cecily was now openly glaring at him. So much for trusting her to be his second. So much for believing she might sympathise with his frustrations.

What she said next shocked him to the core. 'So, my lord if someone loved you—someone like your brother, for example. Would you reject that love?'

Her question mentioned Tom, yet something in her tone, in the steady gaze of her amber eyes seemed to cause his heart to stop momentarily. His mind had leapt to an unanticipated conclusion. Bypassing entirely the question of whether there was love between himself and his brother, he allowed himself to think of love in relation to Cecily herself.

What if she loved me? If Cecily loved me?

For a moment he felt lost, as hope flooded through him. The floor beneath his feet felt soft, and he heard a strange roaring in his ears.

Almost immediately, reality returned. *No.* It could not be. He had trusted in love before, as a foolish child, and had received only betrayal. He had trusted Tom, but Tom had found someone better to love.

Working hard, and using all the experience of his thirty years, he managed to smooth his expression, to hide the pain and the hope and the fear and the joy that her words had created inside him.

'Lady Cecily,' he managed, his tone deceptively silky, 'as enlightening as this conversation has been, I believe I must take my leave of you. We are to ride out shortly.' He stood, dimly realising that the predominant emotion piercing through him, throbbing in time with his heart beating, was fear.

He bowed, turned and left, pain from old, old wounds attacking him from within and without.

Chapter Twenty-Two

Cecily watched him go, feeling as though her heart might break in pieces. His argument with Tom she could vaguely understand. It was clear to her that the brothers cared deeply about one another—even though Jack would likely not ever admit such a thing. They were both in pain and were causing even more pain to each other. She sighed. Nominally their disagreement related to their business affairs, and Jack's clear frustration that Tom was currently more focused on his wife than their financial concerns. At a deeper level she suspected Jack was feeling a sense of betrayal. He and Tom had only had each other for many years, and Nell had come along and changed all of that.

It was clear to her that he and Tom shared a deep and abiding affection, yet just now Jack could not allow himself to admit to loving his brother. When she had asked the question, something of her own heart had been in it, too. Overcome with mortification at her own foolish boldness, she buried her head in her hands.

Lord!

Jack had known he was behaving irrationally, she could tell. She had been well on the way to defeating his flawed logic when he had retired from the fray. Yet underneath she had sensed some sort of gigantic struggle within him.

Her hand closed around the knight in her reticule, as it often did. It was key to her understanding of him. Was she reading too much into his words that day? And why was she so desperate to understand him? He had behaved badly just now, and yet she saw pain beneath his anger, hurt underneath the frustration.

Am I being too kind?

She had a tendency to see the best in those she cared about.

Catching her own thoughts, she gasped.

I care about him.

The realisation was unsurprising, even though it was the first time she had voiced it in such a way. And 'care' was too weak a word for what she was feeling at present.

Discomfort raced through her.

I care about both of them.

There! That was better. Nell's husband and his brother would naturally be more of her concern now that her darling friend had married into the Beresford family. Yes, it was perfectly reasonable to be developing an interest in their affairs.

Such tepid language did not match the tumultuous passion within her, yet she, like Jack, knew that she needed to hide from whatever reality was occurring—for now at least.

She sat on, gazing in an unfocused way through the mullioned windows, and reviewing all she knew of Jack, and of Tom. 'To restore what my father destroyed.' Her impression of their father was not a good one, although to be fair the childhood Jack described was not uncommon. Many fathers took little interest in their offspring when they were small and were seen mainly as figures of authority. Her own experience—a loving father followed by a loving guardian—was rare. Yet she saw the lack in Jack and Tom—a lack they may not even realise existed.

She mused on, her mind now considering the matter of womanly influences in the boys' early life. She shook her head, reviewing the matter of their mother's death, followed soon after by the departure of Tilly, Jack's beloved nurse. She had only the basic facts, and needed to know more. Fishing in her reticule again, she pulled out the little carved figure, which she still had no notion of throwing away. The edges were smooth, rounded by hundreds of hours of play and handling from a little boy, long ago. Pain stabbed through her for that little boy, now a complex, unhappy man. Did he even understand how unhappy he was, how meaningless his life without love?

Perhaps he is beginning to understand.

His current anger was out of character, she knew. Jack would never normally show emotion, she surmised. There was trust in it, and an implied compliment. Since Tom and Nell's marriage, she suspected the Earl's previous calm emptiness had left him, his cold serenity replaced by new or long-buried emotions that he was struggling to contain. He was not empty at all. He was filled with pain. She nodded to herself.

I shall continue to think the best of him.

Slipping the carved figure back into her reticule, she rose. At least the gentlemen were riding out this morning. Hopefully the exercise and the clean country air would calm some agitation and enable them to resolve the morning's argument, at least. In the meantime, she would check on Nell, and consider what she could do to help the situation.

* * *

Jack spurred his stallion on, thundering across the wide meadow. To his left and his right, the other gentlemen rode, all letting their horses have their heads and gallop as fast as they wished in the safe openness of the greensward. Hedgerows and trees flashed by in the edge of his vision as he focused entirely on the terrain ahead, navigating nimbly to avoid divots and holes.

Normally, such exercise helped purge Jack of any unseemly emotions, but today it was serving only to intensify the vexation in his heart and mind. Such had been his lot ever since Lady Cecily had come into his life—no, ever since he had been greeted with news of his brother's marriage. Frustration with Tom was only the start of it. His obsession with Lady Cecily grew stronger by the day, and this morning's incident had left him reeling. For the first time he had allowed a lady to see something of his true self, and it terrified him.

Anger, hurt, fear and confusion coagulated within him to form a solid, sullen mass of heaviness. It was too dull for pain, too inevitable to be surprising, too familiar for him to expect relief. He knew this feeling, for it had lived within him for a lifetime.

You are worthless, it said.

Despite all the years of financial success and high social standing.

You are useless, it whispered in his father's voice.

Others would never see him as being of value. Good people would know him to be inferior. Despite the title, the wealth, the status. He was unworthy of 'Earl'. What did 'Earl' even mean, anyway?

Despair had lain buried within him for years, hidden beneath years of cold armour, and Tom, Cecily and Hazledene itself had managed to unearth it. How he wished for a return to the cold calmness of his previous existence!

Cecily's words pounded through his brain in rhythm with the horse's thunderous gallop.

Is glory simply wealth? What of generosity and goodness?

At that moment he had defended his worldly view that wealth and fortune were paramount. He *knew* this to be correct. So why did her words haunt him so?

On he went, the sense of erring, of worthlessness strong within him. Always with him, normally so deeply hidden that he could pretend it was not there. Oh, he had occasionally had temporary relief from it. As a child, while pretending to be a knight. At school, on the occasions when he had done well in an examination or earned praise from a tutor. As an adult, feeling the attention of society, or the adulation of a woman inexplicably infatuated with him. Yet none of it had pierced deeply enough to heal the self-hatred dwelling deep within him.

His father's disdain, his mother's death, Tilly abandoning him... Long ago he had come to understand that he was unimportant, unworthy of consideration. *Very well!* He had made it his business to stand alone, to protect himself and his brother from disappointment. And now Tom himself had turned on him. Until it had happened he had never dreamed it possible.

It was strange, he mused, how normal everything seemed. Here they were, four gentlemen on a pleasant ride together through pretty countryside. Tom, as if to make up for any potential incivility on Jack's part, was all charm. His calm urbanity served only to heighten Jack's disconnection from any of it.

It was all rather prosaic, humdrum, commonplace. Yet inside Jack, emotions flared and stabbed, depriving him of any true pleasure in the ride, the company or the occasion. He sighed inwardly.

This is my life.

It was, after all, no more than he deserved.

Nell was feeling better, and the young ladies had come downstairs to sit together in the parlour. They planned to spend the day in ease, talking, reading and perhaps walking out, for the day was mild and clear.

Cecily, concerned by the worsening of relations between Jack and Tom, knew she could wait no longer for Nell to come to her. Once the servants were gone she lost no time in turning the conversation to intimate matters, and bluntly asked Nell about the situation between Tom and Jack. Nell was unaware of the details of the argument that morning, but Tom had been, she said, blazing with anger as he had been preparing to ride out.

'While I abhor the distance between them, Cecily, I do think that it is Jack who is behaving unreasonably here. At least Tom has me to confide in.'

While Jack has no-one.

Nell was still talking. 'I truly believe, Cecily, that Tom needs me just as much as I need him.' Nell's voice caught slightly. 'He and I are both orphans, you know. There is something in that, even though we are now both of age.'

'I can only imagine. I have been blessed to have Mama still with me, and to have such a kind guardian as I do.' Her eyes danced. 'Although I must admit my mother is not, perhaps, an ideal parent!'

'I could not possibly comment!' Nell's eyes twinkled with humour, then her smile faded. 'Tom's mother's death was hard on him. He was only a little boy, you know.'

'Yes, indeed. It would be hard for any child to lose a parent—as we both know.'

'But we were both a little older when we were first bereaved.' Nell frowned. 'I was almost fourteen when my mama passed away, and you were twelve or so when your papa died, were you not?'

'I was.' The old pain of loss had faded, although Cecily still wondered how different her life might have been if Papa had lived. She would not have had to keep such an eye on Mama, that was certain.

'Tom was troubled when I met him.' Nell's gaze was unfocused. 'It took him a long time to understand that he needed to be loved, but once that became apparent to him, everything changed.'

Abruptly, Cecily's thoughts swerved away from her mama, away from Tom, and towards the other troubled man—the one who had been taking up most of her attention. Nell's words hit her like a thunderclap. Unthinkingly, she declared, with feeling, 'He needs to be loved, but he does not understand this. Of course!'

'Oh, but he understands *now*. That is why I am so certain that his affection for me will not fade.'

'What? Oh, yes. That makes sense, Nell. How old was Tom when their mama died?'

'He was five. Still quite a baby, really.'

'Yes.' So Jack had been seven. Far too young to lose one's mama. 'But Tom and his brother had had each other.'

'Until recently, they were everything to each other, I believe. Jack, from what I have learned, has always wished to protect Tom from harm.' She sniffed. 'I suppose Jack's nose has been put out of joint by Tom's marriage to me, for Tom did not consult him first. As head of the family, Jack can be most particular.'

Cecily shook her head. 'There is more to it, I believe. Yes, Tom's marriage was undoubtedly a shock to the Earl, and it *is* unfortunate that you married so quickly in that regard.' She reached for her friend's hands. 'No, do not be angry with me! I am trying to be fair to all of you here.'

'Please, do not criticise me, Cecily! You, who are my greatest friend, and who know me better than anyone?'

'I do not criticise you, not at all! And, yes, I know you well. But, Nell, I did not know *Tom* when you married. Or at least, what little I did know of him gave me good reason to be concerned for your happiness.'

'You are referring, I suppose, to the Beresford brothers' reputation for cold-heartedness.' At Cecily's nod, she protested, 'But I did not know anything about his reputation when I agreed to marry him. I only knew that he loved me, as I love him.'

'And that is precisely why, as your friend, I had to be concerned. Do not mistake me—I support your marriage. I am merely trying to explain why someone might be concerned.'

Someone like Tom's brother.

'And so I must point out that I also remember...' she took a breath '...how Tom hurt you. At Christmas.'

Nell lifted her chin. 'Cecily, you clearly do not understand. I shall tell you, as best I can.' She thought for a moment, then lifted her head to meet Cecily's gaze again. 'It was worth it. Love is worth it. I was not fully alive until I loved Tom. He was not fully alive until he loved me.'

Cecily eyed her in puzzlement. Nell's words were creating deep currents within her, swelled by her existing enthralment to the Earl. She could feel the danger in it, but could not grasp Nell's assertion that putting one's heart into danger was in any way sensible.

A maid arrived, bringing tea, and Cecily held her tongue. For now.

Chapter Twenty-Three

The gentlemen had reached the far side of the long meadow and pulled up, allowing the horses to recover. Jack joined in the whoops and expressions of exhilaration, aware that he was simply not feeling what the others were feeling. A brief easing of his pain at the height of speed, that was all. He avoided looking directly at Tom, but was conscious that his brother had still been rather pale and decidedly stony-faced as they had set off.

It was well past noon, and they had been riding for almost two hours, their route taking them over hills, across rivers and through woods. Opportunities for a gallop had been rare, so they had made the most of this wide meadow. By agreement they turned back now, wishing to return to Hazledene in good time for dinner. Tom, naturally, had argued strongly in favour of heading for home. Jack had had to press his lips together to prevent a scathing comment emerging. He felt himself to be continually on the edge of losing his hard-earned sense of control. Arguing with Tom. Kissing Cecily...

No. He must not think of that. She was too dangerous to his peace of mind. Once she was gone he would be better able to rebuild the fortifications he needed around his heart. Thankfully that day would soon arrive. Before the month ended she would go, and he would regain his equilibrium. Dealing with Tom was enough. The last thing he needed at the same time was an inconvenient obsession with a lady who was even now judging him as harshly as his father ever had. It was all very well to regret her having witnessed his unseemly spat with Tom, but he had no way of undoing what he had done and said.

Carmichael was speaking, and Jack glanced towards him. He was all red-faced good humour, and for an instant Jack was conscious of something like envy. Carmichael had no self-consciousness, no airs, no deep-set wounds. He was comfortable simply being who he was. Vaguely, memories of Carmichael's extended family floated through Jack's mind. His parents, both bluff country types. His sisters, their husbands and numerous offspring. The relaxed chaos that had permeated their family home on the one occasion Jack had visited. Jack had, of course, held himself aloof from it all, yet now some part of him, he realised, yearned for the unspoken affection and acceptance that permeated the Carmichael home.

It is not for me.

Today he had finally let go of all such notions. There was too much peril in it. He now knew that his life would be one of business matters, of marrying and securing an heir with a like-minded maiden who also embraced solitude and a proper distance. Briefly, he thought of the child, growing up in such a household, and felt a little nauseous.

Yes, well, plenty of time to marry.

He would wait until he was sure he had found the right person to be a suitable countess.

And when the time came, he would hire a nurse who was warm and loving and he would pay her enough so that she would not leave.

* * *

After a couple of hours of lighter conversation, Cecily decided to be brave and dive into deeper waters again. 'Nell,' she offered tentatively, 'remember our conversation earlier about your marriage, and the Earl's reaction to it?'

'Yes. I have been thinking about it ever since.'

'You have? And have you reached any conclusions?'

'I know you care about me. And so, if you think it helpful to try to look upon events as if from the Earl's perspective, then I am open to doing so.'

Cecily embraced her. 'You are such an open-hearted person! I know it takes courage to do this, so I thank you.'

'Do not thank me yet,' Nell offered wryly, 'for I may yet conclude that Jack is the most heinous person and is not worth Tom's concern.'

They chuckled a little, yet Cecily knew she must tread carefully. If the breach between the brothers was to be healed, they would have to each understand the other. That meant Nell needed to influence her husband. This was only the first step of many.

'I have been considering your words from earlier—about how the death of his mama affected little Tom. How do you imagine it affected his brother?'

Nell frowned. 'He would have been seven, so also very young. I do not doubt he felt her loss every bit as keenly as my Tom.'

'They are very alike in many ways.'

'In looks, yes. But not in character!'

'Are you certain of that? I see two stubborn, strong-willed gentlemen, both with an equal reputation for cold-heartedness and an eye for wealth and wealth alone.'

'That is unfair! My Tom has changed!'

'Yes, you see a change, and I trust your judgement. But has the stubbornness changed?'

Nell smiled ruefully, acknowledging the hit. 'Not at all! He is quite the most immovable person, once a notion has taken root in his head. He— Oh! I begin to understand.' She rubbed her chin thoughtfully. 'Yes, very well, I concede that in some respects there are similarities.'

'Now consider this. If Jack had married hastily, to someone Tom did not know, and Jack was professing himself to have become vastly enamoured of the lady, how might Tom have reacted?'

'I believe Tom would have welcomed it, for he has spoken to me of his longing to see Jack happy.'

'What of the *old* Tom? The Tom who had never himself been in love?'

Nell opened her mouth, then closed it again. Cecily pressed her advantage. 'And what if the marriage was contracted within weeks of his first meeting the lady?'

Nell's hand fluttered to her brow. 'He would wonder if the lady's motives were pure. Or if Jack had become lost in a temporary *tendre*. Of course he would.'

'So the Earl's reaction to *your* marriage might not be wholly without rational basis?'

Nell's jaw dropped. 'No. Why, it might be an unsuitable marriage in a number of ways!'

'Precisely.' They looked at each other, and Cecily could almost *see* her friend's understanding become clearer.

'But… Jack has met me now. Surely he can see that I am not so unsuitable, and that I truly care for Tom?'

'Indeed. I do think he begins to appreciate you, Nell. Some of his persistence will be to do with sheer stubbornness, I suspect, and Tom battling with him just makes both of them obstinate in opposition to one another.'

Nell sighed. 'This I already know. They each make the distance between them greater each time they debate this.'

'There is more. Earlier, when you spoke of their mother

dying, I wondered if there was another reason for Jack's harshness.'

'What is it?'

'I have been trying to imagine their entire household at the time of their mother's death. We have been told that soon afterwards the boys' nurse also left. With regard to their father, I know little of him, but he does not strike me as a warm-hearted papa, such as yours and mine were.'

'No, indeed! I understand he was a remote figure, not a loving one. He treated the boys with some harshness, I believe, and had also made their mama unhappy.'

Cecily shook her head, feeling another pang of pity for the two motherless children. 'So who cared for the boys, then?'

'There was a nursemaid. Tilly. But she went away.'

'So who loved them then?'

Nell looked at her blankly, her eyes bright with unshed tears. 'No-one,' she whispered. 'No-one.'

Cecily swallowed. 'You mentioned before that Jack has always sought to guard Tom from harm.'

'Yes. They went to the same school, and Jack protected Tom from some of the older boys who thought it a great game to tease and hurt the little ones.'

'Jack would have been there for two years by himself before Tom joined him.' Cecily shuddered. 'I cannot imagine his time there to have been pleasant for, unlike Tom, he had no older brother to shelter him.'

Nell looked stricken. 'Poor little Jack!'

Cecily spread her fingers, breathing deeply. 'Nell, perhaps our imaginations are running away with us in this. Many schools are perfectly reasonable.'

Nell shook her head slowly. 'Not this one. It was called Herald's Hall, I believe, but Tom told me the boys who attended it dubbed it Hell's Hall. Cruelty was part of its nature.'

They paused, just looking at each other. Cecily was unsurprised to find herself trembling a little.

Poor Jack! Poor Tom!

'We have both known the grief of losing beloved parents. Only my mama remains. Yet we have never had to feel unloved.'

'Unloved.' Nell's voice shook. 'I did feel it after Papa's death, before I met Tom. It is—it is the most terrible feeling. I should not wish it on anyone.'

'Tom is lucky to have found you, and to have opened his heart to love again.'

'It frightened him.' Her voice was almost a whisper. 'That is why he broke with me.'

'Of course it did.'

Jack is afraid, too.

She closed her eyes as her own fear surged within her, fear of giving Jack control of her happiness. Opening her eyes again, she looked at her friend. 'Love means being open to hurt, and that is terrifying.'

Nell's eyes widened. 'Do you speak from experience, Cecily?'

Cecily paused, before replying carefully. 'Yes and no. I know enough of the world to have seen people battle with love and fear and have experienced enough weakness of position to have exposure to a similar type of fear.' Her feelings for Jack were too nebulous to be voiced, too raw and frightening to be scrutinised. She shook her head, turning the conversation away from herself, and back to those motherless boys.

'We see Jack as the Earl of Hawkenden. Powerful, wealthy, cold. But we have also gained an understanding of the boy that he was.' Could she help her friend create a bridge between the unloved boy and the Earl, as she herself had done? 'Jack may have only ever allowed himself to love one person since their mama and their nurse went away.'

Nell nodded. 'Tom.'

'Tom.' Cecily waited.

'And Tom...' Nell's voice tailed off as she worked it out.

'Tom loves someone else now.' Cecily said the words that Nell seemed incapable of uttering.

'Me.'

'Yes,' Cecily whispered. She cleared her throat. 'So Jack is completely alone. Or so it might seem to him.'

Chapter Twenty-Four

Making an effort, Jack joined in various light-hearted conversations as the horses picked their way up hill, down dale and through fields and woods. His heart remained heavy, and he looked forward to seeing Cecily again with a mix of wonder and dread. At times it had seemed as though she truly liked him, but this morning's conversation had turned everything backwards. Once again, he had gone back round the endless wheel of hope and loss, and now was back to hoping that she could forgive him for being such a hot-headed, hurtful, ill-disciplined fool.

He dared not think of her passionate response to his kisses, and was nervous about dwelling on the affinity that had seemed to have been developing between them these past weeks. He needed to remain cool-hearted, or else risk pain when she left him, as she inevitably would.

His heart clenched somehow, as a strange tension came over him. Just when had she become so important to him? She was no-one in particular, after all—just another young lady. He shook his head, knowing that this was unconvincing even to himself. It should not matter to him what her opinion of him was. Should not. But did.

How could he rebuild that friendship that had become

so essential to him? Surely there must be a way. She had shown an interest in matters of business generally, he recalled. Perhaps he could offer to involve her in reviewing the information provided by Carmichael? Yes, that might do it. His mind racing, he imagined them poring over documents, heads close together… From there, it did not take much for him to begin to indulge in more carnal thoughts—how he could contrive a private moment when he could create the opportunity for more kisses.

Again he shied away from his own thoughts, since the notion of kissing her disturbed much deeper feelings, and ones that he did not welcome in the least. Kissing Cecily was the one thing he desired most, yet it opened the door to the very fears that were causing him such anguish today.

With a sigh, he directed his attention back to the present. 'Harting,' he called, 'how have you found your mount today? I have taken him out frequently myself, and always enjoy him.'

His friend replied, and all thoughts of Lady Cecily's haunting gaze were banished—for a moment at least.

Cecily and Nell, both restless, had decided to take a turn about the gardens. Cecily was still feeling perturbed from the conversation earlier, and she guessed Nell was experiencing a similar disquiet. They strolled arm in arm around the perimeter of the house and along the few garden paths, enjoying the signs of a burgeoning spring.

In addition, though unspoken between them, was the calculation that the gentlemen should have been back already, as they would undoubtedly wish to wash and change before dinner. They could therefore reappear at any time.

Naturally, this engendered the usual feeling of a flock of butterflies flittering in Cecily's stomach, although today the excitement was accompanied by a strong feeling of dread. Impossible to deny for very long, Cecily acknowledged the dread related to the feeling that she and Jack were somehow estranged. The memories of their conversation at the breakfast table haunted her. Desperately she wished to be at one with Jack again, for his friendship was important to her.

Friendship? Something did not ring true about her mind's choice of word. She frowned as she walked, puzzling it out. Friendship was in a sense accurate, for during her time here she and the Earl had developed something of an affinity. But she had had friends before.

None had ever come accompanied by internal hosts of butterflies.

None had kissed her.

None had left her with such turmoil and obsession, fear and hope.

'Cecily,' Nell announced, bringing her back to the Hazledene gardens, 'I am decided. I intend to speak with Tom again about their childhood. It is not something he finds easy, so I shall have to persuade him. But I should like him to think about how Jack might be similarly affected. I also understand better now how our marriage might have been seen by a brother who cares for his sibling, and I intend to open Tom's eyes, as you have opened mine. Thank you.'

She embraced Cecily, and Cecily felt unexpected tears start in her eyes. 'I do hope that they can heal this rift, Nell. It is difficult for everyone to see how they continually bruise each other. And they are each on the receiving end of those blows. It seems clear to me that they are both unhappy.'

And I hope that I can reach Jack, change his notions of love.

'Until today, I thought only of Tom's unhappiness. But now I see that Jack is unhappy, too.'

'It is the same unhappiness. It lives in the breach between them.'

And there is another unhappiness, she added silently, knowing it instinctively. *One that lives within Jack alone.*

'Yes! What a clever way to describe it, Cecily. Oh, I am so glad to have you as my friend! All will be well, I know it!'

'I do hope so.'

Overhead, a single magpie called, before flapping its way to a nearby oak tree. At the same time a gust of chill March wind swirled around them. Cecily shivered, drawing her cloak more tightly about her. Wordlessly, they walked on.

The gentlemen now found themselves on the last stretch of their return journey. There, less than half a mile distant, was Hazledene.

Cecily.

What had she done all day? Had she spoken to Nell about the argument in the breakfast room? With Hazledene now in view, Jack sensed rather than saw Tom pick up the pace, and his irritation returned in full measure. 'Keen to reach Hazledene, brother?' Even he could hear the slight sneer in his tone, yet, once again, he felt helpless to prevent it. He could barely look at Tom without seeing his brother's younger self—the Tom who had needed him.

Tom bristled. 'Naturally. A good day's riding, but I am eager for home. Perhaps a bath before dinner.'

'And a reunion with your wife.'

Tom looked at him directly, and for the first time Jack saw a hint of bewilderment beneath his anger. 'Nell has

been indisposed, as you know, Jack. Of course I am eager
to know how she is faring.'

Tom's bewilderment was Jack's undoing.

*I am hurting him, hurting everyone around me. Every-
one I—I care about.*

Loathing rose within him, loathing for himself, how
he was behaving, who he *was*.

Seemingly, he could not find it within himself to be
glad that his brother had found happiness. That Tom was
truly loved by Nell.

In contrast, he had been so frightened by Cecily's hold
over him that he had managed to push her away.

Emotion finally boiled over within him. 'Then let us
not keep you, brother! Hya!' Spurring his horse, he began
cantering across the field. A moment later he heard Tom's
stallion move from trot to canter, then gallop. Neck and
neck they raced, carefully avoiding hazards but each unwilling to concede. Somehow it became vitally important
that Jack should reach Hazledene before his brother. The
other two gentlemen had dropped back, no doubt con-
demning the brothers as fools, and would reach the house
in their own time.

A low hedgerow loomed before him. There would be
a drainage ditch on either side, Jack guessed. Using all
his experience, he urged his mount to jump at exactly the
right moment. Landing perfectly on the other side, his ears
instinctively strained to confirm that Tom had also landed
safely. Reassurance came a moment later, and Jack knew
he was free to push his horse for the final part of their
impromptu race. He glanced back as he spurred the horse
on, finding gleeful delight in Tom's grim-faced frustration. He must maintain his advantage, slight though it was.

Through a stand of trees he went next, dipping to avoid

a low tree-limb that could have caused him serious injury had he not seen it in time.

'Branch!' he instinctively warned, throwing the word behind him. If he were to win, it would not be because Tom failed to navigate a hazard that he had not been warned about. The light increased as he reached the far edge of the copse, and there, on a low rise before him, Hazledene was once more in view.

'Hya!' he urged again, and his horse responded beautifully.

This must be what it feels like to fly.

Certainly it was the fastest gallop he had enjoyed since the reckless days of his youth. Tom, more cautious, was maintaining a reasonable gallop rather than a heedless one and was beginning to fall back.

The thrill of victory would be momentary. Jack knew it, yet he continued. Everything had been threatening to overwhelm him for days—Tom, Hazledene... Cecily. For this one moment he could be free of all of it.

In an instant, everything changed. He felt the horse stumble at high speed.

Rabbit hole.

As the thought was forming, he was already flying through the air, sky and grass rolling and rotating in his line of vision. An instant of pain, of force, of impact, then nothing.

Chapter Twenty-Five

Cecily and Nell both heard the sound they had been waiting for at the same time. Horses approaching. Quickly they
moved to peep over the hedge at the side of the garden,
just as a rider emerged from a stand of trees near the bottom of the field. A moment later a second rider emerged.
While they were too far away to see who exactly they
were, Cecily had no doubt it was the Beresford brothers
on their matching black stallions. Her heart lurched at
their speed. She could never understand gentlemen's pursuit of danger. They seemed to seek it out in everything
from fencing and boxing to carriage racing and riding at
breakneck speed.

As her heart began to pound with nervousness, she
tried to reassure herself that gentlemen did not ride with
the added complication of side-saddle, as ladies must.
She had been told many times how much easier and safer
it was for gentlemen, with their full saddle. It gave her
little comfort now as she watched both riders gallop flat
out up the slight incline.

Just as two further horsemen emerged from the copse,
her eye was drawn back to the lead horseman. Something… The horse was stumbling, the man thrown from

his seat like a child's rag doll. She saw a sickening impact as he landed awkwardly on the ground. The horse ran on, riderless. The man did not move.

Cecily and Nell were themselves already running, through the side gate and down the hill. Cecily's cloak billowed behind her while her bonnet threatened to loosen itself, so she put one hand to the back of her head to keep it in place as she ran.

'Tom!' Nell cried.

Jack! was Cecily's answering thought. Whichever brother he was, he still had not moved.

The second rider had now reached the injured man and jumped down from his horse. Quickly, he crouched down beside him. The dark riding jackets were similar. The shape was similar.

Who?

'Tom, Tom!' Nell called. They were nearly there.

He turned. It was Tom, ashen-faced.

'Oh, Tom! I thought you dead!' Nell flung herself at him, and his arms immediately enclosed her.

'Hush, my love. I am well, but Jack—'

Cecily had sunk to her knees beside the fallen man. 'Jack? Jack, can you hear me?' His chest was rising and falling as he breathed. 'He is alive!' Her eyes and hands were seeking and noting his injuries. A wound at the back of his head, bleeding profusely. His left shoulder, with a strange sickening lump. *Dislocated.* Chest, stomach, legs…nothing unusual visible, thankfully. She returned to the head wound. Gently reaching beneath him, she felt a fist-sized stone beneath that part of his head. Her heart sank. Her hand came away covered in blood and she wiped it on her dress without even thinking about it.

'Alive? Thank the Lord!' Tom's voice shook. 'I cannot— My brain has frozen, I'm afraid.' Tom sounded as dazed as Cecily felt. Nell was weeping softly, and still clinging to Tom.

Someone needed to take charge. All Marianne's no-nonsense training now came to her. 'We need to get him to the house.' Cecily's voice was low but sounded surprisingly steady. 'And someone needs to fetch a doctor.'

'Yes, of course! Thank you, Lady Cecily. I could not think what must be done. I can—I shall go to the house immediately and send a groom for the doctor. Will you stay with him?'

'I shall.' To her own ears, it sounded like a vow.

'Thank you. I shall bring back a pallet perhaps, or a board.'

'A board would be better.'

'Very well.' Disentangling himself from his wife, he made off up the hill. Nell watched him go, fumbling for a handkerchief at the same time.

'Nell, I shall need your assistance.' Cecily spoke firmly, hoping that Nell's sense would return to her now that Tom was both safe and gone.

'I am ready, Cecily. I am sorry for—'

'No need to be sorry.' Taking a clean handkerchief from her reticule, Cecily folded it and pressed it against the head wound. Glancing down the slope, she saw that Mr Harting and Mr Carmichael were almost with them. Both looked suitably concerned.

'Lord! That was quite a tumble! Is he dead?' Carmichael's words were blunt, but he looked entirely discomposed so Cecily had to forgive him.

'Not yet, but we need to get him indoors, where a doctor can see him.'

'Tom has gone to fetch a pallet,' Nell announced. 'He is sending a groom for the doctor.'

'Capital!'

'How can we assist you, Lady Cecily?' Mr Harting spoke calmly, dismounting.

'Can you bring Nell to the house?' Nell was *not* helping. Cecily could not think straight while her friend was still so visibly distressed. At Nell's protests, she spoke firmly to her. 'Someone needs to prepare his room, so I need you to speak with the servants, Nell. The Earl will, naturally, be put in the Blue Chamber, and I shall move to the nursery. I shall need to clean the wound.'

'Hot water, towels, bandages.' Nell, bracing her shoulders, was trying to control her emotions. Having a task to make her busy would assist her in doing so, Cecily hoped.

'Exactly. Thank you.'

Squaring her shoulders, Nell set off, Mr Harting accompanying her. One of the Beresford horses was nearby and Carmichael rode after it, lifting the reins so the horse would not accidentally trip itself. The other stallion—Jack's, Cecily reasoned—was running free at the very bottom of the hill. A groom would have to be sent to fetch it, once one could be spared. Carmichael began leading Tom's horse up towards the house.

Alone with Jack, Cecily allowed herself to look at his face and remember that it was him. His skin was corpse-grey, his handsome features rendered strange by the lack of healthy colour and the utter relaxation of his face.

He could be sleeping, Cecily told herself. *He is not dead.*

To reassure herself, she shuffled closer, still on her knees beside him, and maintaining the pressure from her left hand to keep her handkerchief in place beneath his head wound. Setting her right hand on his chest, she felt it rise and fall gently. After a moment she took his hand, taking a little comfort from its warmth.

Silence grew around them both. The breeze stilled, birds quietened, and the rest of the world seemed far away. There was only Jack and Cecily, Cecily and Jack.

Something strange then happened. Cecily felt as though she were spinning, or as though the world were spinning and she along with it. The feeling came from inside her chest, spiralling out so that it encompassed everything— the field, the horse, the trees, the sky. Everything in her life until now had brought Cecily to this man, and this moment.

'Jack!' she pleaded. 'Please, do not die.' The thought ripped her heart, it seemed, wide open, and freed the words that had been unspoken within her, the words she had been avoiding admitting to not ten minutes ago. 'Jack, I love you. Please, do not die.'

Jack groaned, pain lancing into through him and reaching, it seemed, every part of his body. His head was afire with agony, his left arm and shoulder sending him dagger-like pains. Someone was with him, he knew. There were vague memories of a voice, bidding him not to die.

Am I dead, then?

But, no, the pain was too great.

The horse stumbled.

He moved his hands a little, moaning as his left arm, shoulder and neck sent needles of torment through him.

At the same time, he realised someone was holding his right hand.

Who?

All his thoughts took only an instant, and he opened his eyes to discover where he was and who was with him. He opened them—to blackness.

Is it night? No, I am returning from the ride.

Desperately, he closed his eyes tightly and opened them again. Still blackness.

'I cannot see!' The howling cry erupted from him. 'I am blind!' Terror rushed through him. Never had he felt so helpless, so frightened. Instinctively, he gripped the hand that was holding his, and heard a gasp.

'Hush, my lord.' Cecily's voice was calm and soothing, but how could he be soothed when he could not see?

'Cecily? Why can I not see?'

'You have had a bump to the head, Jack. The effect is probably momentary only. Just be still, if you can. Your brother has gone for assistance.'

Tom!

'I am a damned fool! What was I thinking, galloping so fast?'

'My thoughts exactly, my lord.' Her tone was wry. 'Still, it seems you have managed not to kill yourself, so for that we should be grateful, I am sure.' There was a strange tone to her voice, and was her hand shaking? He concentrated on that for a moment and confirmed that, yes, she was trembling.

'I apologise for distressing you. I would not have wished to do so, not for the world.' He swallowed. 'This must have been quite a shock.'

'Indeed, my lord, but we shall see you well again, I am certain.'

Panic still lurked behind his eyes. He tried opening them again. Still darkness.

'My horse?'

'Is uninjured and running wild at the bottom of the field. They will send a groom to fetch him.'

'Good.' His voice was gruff. 'My foolishness has not harmed him, then.'

'I see your brother is returning, with two grooms and

Mr Harting.' Her voice sounded different, and he guessed she was looking up, away from him. 'They have brought a board to carry you on.'

Shame now added an extra layer of discomfort—on top of pain, fear, regret and anxiety. He groaned. 'All of this because of my hot-headed foolishness! My injuries are fully deserved.'

'Nonsense!' Her tone was brisk, and he could tell she was looking at him again. 'No-one deserves to be injured so!'

Oh, but I do. You have no idea how worthless I am. How headstrong, how selfish, how obstinate.

'Jack!' Tom sounded breathless.

Instantly, Jack opened his eyes, then squeezed them shut again against the terrifying darkness. 'Tom! I am sorry for the trouble I am bringing you this day. I am being well punished for my foolishness.'

'Nonsense!' Tom's tone was surprisingly similar to Lady Cecily's a moment before. 'Though it would have served you well had you broken your neck!'

'True.'

Have I broken my neck? Or my back?

His arms seemed functional—although there was definitely some injury to the left one, for it was agonisingly painful. Tentatively, Jack moved his legs a little. They responded, to his great relief. There was a silence, and Jack sensed there was some communication going on from which he was excluded. 'What is happening?'

'They are setting the board down beside you and will shortly slide you onto it.' Cecily's voice soothed him a little. She had maintained her grip on his hand, for which he was profoundly grateful.

The next few moments were agonising. Strong hands

reached under him and, on an agreed word, moved him from where he lay onto the smoothness of a wooden board.

An old door, he suspected.

He could not help but cry out, and when they began to walk with him, the pain jarred at every step they took. Abruptly, sounds and senses faded to black, and he knew no more.

Chapter Twenty-Six

'His unconsciousness has returned.' Tom's tone was terse.

'I am glad of it,' Cecily replied, in an attempt to soothe him. 'He would be better staying so until we can get him to his bed.'

She had managed to mouth to him news of Jack's affliction, and his jaw had loosened in shock. 'Is he truly blind?' he asked now.

'He could not see at all just now. That does not mean he is truly blind. His eyesight may return…' She paused. 'I hope.' Fear for him threatened to overcome her, but she pushed it away with determination. 'Has a doctor been sent for?'

'Yes. There is a surgeon who lives on the road to Edenbridge, so hopefully he can be with us within the hour, unless he is from home.' They paused, having reached the gate, and navigated their way carefully through the gap, their precious burden still oblivious. Cecily held her breath until they had him safely through the narrow space. He had not moved again.

A few moments later, after a precarious journey up the Hazledene staircase, they reached the Blue Chamber. Nell was there to greet them, and she was, to Cecily's great relief, much calmer. Between them, she and the housekeeper had stripped and remade Cecily's bed, ready for the Earl. A fire had been lit in the grate—a welcome sight for Cecily, who was shivering with cold after her prolonged time kneeling in damp grass. How much colder must Jack be?

Thankfully, his valet appeared almost immediately, and Tom and the ladies were ushered out while the valet and one of the footmen attempted to make the Earl more comfortable. Nell took the opportunity to hug her husband, who clung to her like a child, while Cecily sank onto a satin settee in the gallery and tried to make sense of it all.

He was badly hurt, she knew, although the fact that his oblivion had not lasted too long the first time was encouraging. His current unconsciousness was undoubtedly related to pain from the necessary journey from the field to the house.

The blindness, though, was a terrible development. How would a proud, independent soul like the Earl manage if such a change were to be permanent? She shuddered. It did not bear thinking about. In addition, the bang to the head could ultimately prove fatal, and they all knew it.

The other injuries were less urgent. A dislocated shoulder could be reset—hopefully by someone with the right skills. 'Is the surgeon skilled in bone-setting?' The words were out before she had considered them. It would have been better to wait, to give Tom and Nell some more time.

Tom disentangled himself from his Nell—at least enough to turn his head to speak to Cecily. 'Yes, he is well known in these parts as a gifted bone-setter, I am told.'

'Thank goodness.'

Silence descended again. This time, Cecily's thoughts went in a different direction. Closing her eyes, she gave herself over to the knowledge that she loved him. She loved Jack Beresford, Earl of Hawkenden.

It was not even a surprise to her, for her heart had known it for a long time. They had begun badly, of course, with her prejudice about him being cold and empty, and their clash on Lady Jersey's terrace. She shook her head gently. That might have been a hundred years ago, it was so far removed from the man she now knew. Oh, he was difficult, and complex, and broken, and he felt things very deeply. But he was also kind, and caring, and loyal, and when he looked at her in a certain way it deliciously disturbed every part of her.

Seeing him here, in Hazledene, had been the key to unlocking his mystery. Her hands moved to her reticule. Through its fabric her hand closed on the little carved knight. The boy Jack had been was at the heart of the man he now was.

Tom's present distress was also strangely reassuring. It confirmed that he loved Jack as much as Jack loved him. If only Jack could recover, Cecily was confident that, between herself and Nell, they could heal the distance between the brothers.

The chamber door opened and the footman emerged, bidding them enter. They did so, Cecily following Tom and Nell, anxiety rising within her as she prepared to face the reality of his injuries again. The valet stepped forward, explaining that while he had managed to remove His Lordship's boots and nether garments, he had not dared touch his jacket and shirt, for fear of exacerbating His Lordship's injuries. His report made, he stepped away from the bedside and took up his place near the window.

On the bed, the Earl moved his hand and turned his head slightly. 'Who is there?'

He is awake again!

Cecily's heart skipped as Tom listed their three names, his voice cracking a little.

'Tom.' Jack lifted his right hand. Crossing swiftly to him, Tom took it.

'I am so sorry, Jack. Such a fool I have been! I—'

'It is I who have been the fool. My damnable temper, Tomkin.'

Tom leaned down, pressing his cheek against his brother's. His shoulders shook. Reaching for each other, Nell and Cecily held hands and tried not to sob. Silent tears were rolling down Cecily's face, and she knew Nell to be similarly affected. Near the window, the valet stared steadily ahead, although Cecily's brief glance noted a muscle twitching in his tightly clenched jaw.

With a nod to Nell, Cecily indicated the armchair by the fireplace. They moved towards it together, Nell sitting facing the fire while Cecily stood, warming her hands in its welcome blaze. After a few moments she felt warm enough to untie and remove her cloak, which she set on the floor by the hearth.

'Oh, Cecily, your gown is quite ruined!' Nell's expression was aghast. Cecily looked down. Sure enough, there were grass stains, blood, mud and even a slight tear along the hem. Cecily could not remember acquiring any of them but, then, her attention had been elsewhere. In the background, the brothers were talking quietly together, and Cecily was glad she and Nell were too far away to hear what was being said. They continued to converse about unimportant matters in order to give the brothers the time and the privacy they undoubtedly needed. Nell informed Cecily that her possessions had been removed to the nursery, and that Molly was even now preparing that room for her use.

'You are so good, Cecily. Thank you for being so capable. I declare I did not know what I must do, down in the field.' She shuddered. 'I was overcome with fear that Tom…' Her voice tailed away.

'I understand.' She did. For the first time Cecily genuinely understood why her hitherto sensible friend became so distressed at times. Loving someone meant you were open to new fears, new hurts, new weaknesses.

I am helpless now in a way I have never been before.

And that helplessness was already exposed by the worry that Jack might yet die or be permanently blinded.

I love him!

It still seemed miraculous that she finally understood what it meant to be in love.

Jack. I love you.

Cecily's gown was quite dry and she was feeling much warmer when Tom finally called them over to Jack's bedside. Cecily's eyes ranged over his beloved face. Eyes closed, with surprisingly long lashes resting on his skin. Strong lines in his cheekbones. Aristocratic nose. Angled jaw. He was still pale, but not as grey-faced as he had been outside. Perhaps it was just the firelight, but she would take it as a hopeful sign. The bleeding from the head wound had slowed significantly and perhaps had even stopped, judging by the light stains on the towel that had been placed on his pillow.

'Nell?' He held out his good hand and Nell took it.

'Yes.'

Eyes still closed, he turned towards Nell's voice, wincing a little as he moved his head. 'I wish to apologise to you for being so unwelcoming, Nell. As I have told Tom, I do understand that you and he share a true affection for each other, and I am glad you have brought him happiness.'

'Thank you.' Nell bent and kissed his cheek. 'Thank you, brother.'

Cecily squeezed her eyes tightly shut for a moment, for fear her tears would again overflow.

'And where is Lady Cecily?'

'I am here.' Nell gave way, and Cecily took his outstretched hand. How warm he was, and how strong and smooth his hand!

'Thank you for staying with me, in the field. It helped.' He swallowed, and she pressed his hand gently. He returned the pressure and they just stayed like that for a moment. Then, as if the silence bothered him, he added, 'I am enormously embarrassed by my poor riding prowess, you understand.'

She heard the attempt at jocularity, understood both the gratitude and the genuine mortification behind it. 'As you should be, my lord. I had thought you a better horseman than this. To take a tumble in an open field, without a hedge or a ditch in sight…tsk, tsk!'

He laughed a little, moving his head, then grimaced.

'Now,' she said briskly, 'let me inspect the wound on your head again.' She touched his face. 'If you will permit, my lord?'

'For you, I shall permit anything,' he murmured, turning his head so she could see the large gash at the back of his head. Trying not to react to his words by giving them more meaning than he perhaps intended, she parted his dark, blood-matted hair, but it was difficult to see how extensive the wound was. Beckoning the valet across, she asked for a flagon of warm water and some clean towels, and a candle to see better by. The daylight was fast waning.

'Yes, my lady.' Within minutes she had all she needed, and set to work.

It took time, and more than once she heard sounds of protest, quickly stifled. She worked as gently as she could and needed four changes of water before she was satisfied. The wound was bleeding again slightly, but she was relieved to find it less extensive than she had feared. There had been a lot of grime in it, though, which she had tried her best to clean away. Tearing a thin towel into pieces, she folded one to create a pack to cover the wound. The surgeon could decide whether stitches were needed. Placing the pack gently over the wound, she touched Jack's face again to bid him turn his head back. He sighed, and thanked her, and something in his tone made her smile.

'It is clear to me that you have been cursing me under your breath all this time, my lord.'

'You have come to know me too well, Lady Cecily.' He opened his eyes briefly, gazing sightlessly at the ceiling above, then closed them again.

'Not *too* well, surely? *Well*, certainly. I agree.' He did not seem to be listening. He had opened his eyes again and was frowning. 'What is it?'

'I think I saw something. Yes, I can—there is something…light, I believe.'

Throwing a wide-eyed glance towards Nell and Tom, Cecily picked up the candlestick from the small table beside her. Rising, she leaned directly over him, candle in hand. Tom had already reached his other side, Nell following quickly.

'Can you see this? I am holding a candle over you.' Leaning further forward, she looked directly into his eyes. At first there was no recognition, nothing, then—then their eyes locked, and he looked directly at her!

'Cecily,' he breathed. 'I can see you.' He frowned. 'At least, I can see some of you.'

'What do you mean?' Her voice shook. It felt as though she were witnessing a miracle.

'It is the strangest thing. It is as though I am looking directly at the horizon but am permitted to see only the sky. The land below is denied me.'

Tom let out a whoop of delight. 'But the blindness is leaving you—and so quickly! This is good news, Jack!'

They all agreed and discussed more with Jack the strange gap in his eyesight. He could see the top half of everything, but not the bottom half. He had seen Cecily's face when she had leaned over him but had been unable to see her shoulders.

A sudden flurry of activity in the hallway outside heralded the arrival of the surgeon. He was a genial man in his middle years, who, following introductions, insisted upon washing his hands thoroughly before touching the Earl. 'For I have noticed, my lord, that it seems to lead to fewer infections in my patients. Now, let me see. Well, as you have no doubt realised, this shoulder is dislocated.' He turned to the valet. 'My good man, can you fetch the box of splints and slings from my carriage, please?' The valet, bowing, departed. 'Now, what else? A head wound?'

'He was blind for almost an hour,' Tom stated, his flat tone belying the worry Jack's blindness had caused them all.

'And can you see perfectly again?'

'No.' Jack explained, and the doctor spent some time holding his fingers in different places, before declaring himself fascinated by the Earl's unusual recovery.

'But his blindness will go away fully, will it not?' Tom asked anxiously.

'It is certainly likely, given that this recovery is already far advanced, and so soon after the accident. Now, my lord, let me inspect your head wound.' Jack turned his head, and Cecily, watching, winced for his sake. The movement would sting terribly.

'Ah, someone has done a capital job of cleaning you up, I see.'

'That would be Lady Cecily,' Tom reported, and Cecily blushed at the doctor's penetrating look.

'Indeed? Thank you, Lady Cecily, for you have saved me some work here. Hmm…still a small amount of debris, I see.' Taking a set of tiny pincers from his bag, he extracted a few small pieces of grass and soil, while the Earl gripped the bedclothes tightly with his right hand. Once content, the surgeon declared that no stitches would be required, and covered the wound again, securing the soft towelling in place with a bandage.

'Now for this shoulder, my lord.' The Earl groaned. 'Yes, I know, but it must be done. I shall need assistance.' Glancing around, his eyes flitted past the now sick-looking valet, who had returned with a box of splints of various lengths and an assortment of slings and broad bandages. His gaze settled on Tom. 'Can you aid me with this, sir?'

Tom nodded grimly. 'Of course.'

'Ladies, I could do with another assistant, if one of you has the stomach for it.'

Cecily and Nell eyed each other, both knowing who was better suited for the task. 'I can do it,' Cecily affirmed, though inside she was quaking. She had been avoiding looking at that misshapen lump in Jack's left shoulder, as its wrongness caused a terrible queasiness in her stomach.

Once the valet had left the room, along with Nell, the surgeon got to work. 'First we need to cut away the jacket and shirt,' he declared, taking a pair of tailor's scissors from his bag. Tom and Cecily, working together, removed the pieces of fabric as the surgeon cut, with as little disruption to Jack's left arm as they could manage.

As he worked, the surgeon pushed the bedclothes down as far as Jack's middle, and Cecily was now glorying in the sight of Jack's wonderful chest and flat stomach. There was a sprinkling of hairs over his breastbone and around his flat male nipples, and a thicker line of hair heading southwards from his navel. His skin looked tantalisingly smooth, the outline and swell of muscle emphasising the masculinity of his strong frame. Cecily's fingers itched to touch him. Now there was an entirely different feeling swirling in the pit of her stomach, and one that was deliciously exciting.

Admonishing herself for having such carnal thoughts while Jack lay there in pain, she pulled the blankets up as far as his ribs and lifted her eyes back to his face. That was safer—except that now her love for him washed all through her again, like a swelling wave moving inexorably to its destination.

'My lord, drink this.' The surgeon was offering Jack a flask.

'What is it?' Jack's tone was suspicious, and the doctor flashed him a smile. 'Brandy, with some medicine added.'

'Brandy, eh? Very well.' Lifting his head, he drank, and Cecily, now entirely lost in him, watched compulsively as his Adam's apple moved while he swallowed. He rested his head back on the pillow. 'Well, that must have been very strong brandy. I declare the room is spinning.' He grinned, half-foolishly.

'Brandy mixed with laudanum, my lord,' the doctor confirmed. 'It will help you get through the next few moments.'

Laudanum.
Jack had never, to his knowledge, had it before. It ex-

plained the bitterness in the doctor's concoction. Jack's mind, almost lost at times with the maddening pain and fear that had threatened to overwhelm him, had now, thankfully, been restored. His eyesight was returning. The relief of it was immense—and how fitting that Lady Cecily's beautiful face had been the first thing he had seen.

If her face was the last thing I ever saw, he thought now, *I should die content.*

His own foolishness had brought him to this, but in stripping away all the niceties, all the surface fears and everyday concerns, he lay raw, and exposed, and self-aware, for perhaps the first time in his life.

Tom, my brother.

How petty he had been to punish Tom for marrying. It was clear that he adored his Nell, and that she returned his affection.

And how did he know this?

Because he had found his own heart, and it belonged to Cecily.

Cecily, my love.

He was done fighting the monster within. Fear had lived in him for a lifetime and had been quietened by the only thing capable of doing so. *Love.*

How he longed to thank her, to tell her of what his heart sang! How fortunate he was that on his day of greatest need, she had been there to hold his hand with her soft one and reassure him with her gentle voice and her quick humour. How lucky he was that she had tended his wounds and remained calm and strong when she had every right to break down in a bout of weeping, as he suspected Nell had.

Even if he could never call her his own, he had at least had her company through the most distressing situation he had ever faced. Even the fact that the doctor had asked her to assist in the bone-setting signalled how capable she was.

She is so much more accomplished than any other woman I have ever met.

Accomplished, and good, and generous, and far-seeing. He closed his eyes as the effects of the laudanum increased. His thoughts were less logical now, more capricious, but the feeling of love, and of gratitude, suffused every part of him.

He had been vaguely aware of the surgeon's voice, issuing instructions, but now, suddenly, his arm and shoulder were being moved and wrenched with great force. He heard himself scream in agony, then blessed darkness settled over him once again.

Chapter Twenty-Seven

Cecily sank into the armchair by the fire, trembling from head to toe. What they had just done to the Earl had been necessary, she knew, but she felt sick at the movement of bones she had just seen and felt through her own hands resting on him, and at the pain they had caused him. Thankfully, the manoeuvre had been successful on the surgeon's first attempt, and Jack's shoulder was back where it ought to be. A stiff bandage had been strapped around Jack's shoulder, chest and upper back, and the surgeon had issued strict instructions for the Earl to rest his left arm and shoulder during the coming days.

Having pronounced himself content, the doctor was now packing up his bag. Hearing him give Tom further instructions for the Earl's care, Cecily stood again.

I should listen to this.

It was straightforward enough—changing the bandages on his head and ensuring there was no sign of pus or poison. Ensuring he kept to his bed and rested until the surgeon decreed otherwise. Checking that the shoulder strapping remained tight, yet not too tight. Using the sling provided any time he sat upright.

'There is one more thing.' The surgeon paused and was

looking at them both directly. 'It can be difficult to measure the correct dose of laudanum. The Earl is tall and broad, so I gave him quite a large amount in the brandy. He may show some delirium over the coming hours, so should not be left alone. He may also need to be roused should his breathing become too slow.' He closed his bag and picked up the unused splints. 'I shall return this time tomorrow, but someone sensible needs to remain with him until then.'

'Of course. Thank you.' Tom shook his hand. 'I shall see you out.'

They departed, leaving Cecily alone with the Earl. Well, since he was incapacitated, she supposed there was no impropriety in it. Returning to his bedside, she saw beads of sweat were gathering on his brow, and he was moving his head around, as if troubled by a nightmare. What could she do to ease his discomfort? Reaching for the pitcher, she poured clean water into an empty bowl, and dipped a clean cloth in it.

All was darkness, but darkness without peace. Images, sounds, ideas fluttered through Jack's mind like drops of fiery rain, each indistinguishable from the next, yet each hitting him with a drop of pain. Papa, a stern expression on his face. Tom, falling from a horse. A paper, listing shipping routes. Mama, crying. Cecily, crying.

No! Please!

He had no idea who he was or where he was. Only his responses gave him some clue. He knew these people. They mattered to him.

My knight! Where is it?

He was seven, and Mama was dead, and he was coming home from boarding school for Christmas. He had not lost his precious knight figure at school and was proudly preparing to show it to Tilly. *Tilly!* There she was, her face alight with love and kindness. Somehow the image was faint, much fainter than the others.

'Hush now, my lord. You are safe, and all is well.' A gentle voice, nearby. He was not alone. He tried to open his eyes, but they were too heavy.

Who...?

Something was pressed into his right hand. His fingers knew the shape and closed round it instantly.

My knight!

A cool damp cloth was placed on his forehead. It was the most beautiful sensation he had ever experienced.

'Thank you, Tilly,' he murmured. 'Don't leave me.'

Oblivion slipped over him again.

Tilly!

Cecily's heart wrenched. Somehow, in the throes of laudanum, Jack was reliving Tilly's departure yet again. As she mopped his brow, he seemed to settle again, into something that looked much more like a natural sleep. He had asked for his knight, and she had been glad to give it to him instantly. Her mind went wandering, wondering again why Tilly had gone so abruptly all those years ago. It did not seem to fit with what she had heard about the woman. Perhaps Molly could enlighten her. She had been with the family back then.

I should—

'Cecily! How are you?' It was Nell, tiptoeing in, and speaking in an exaggerated whisper.

'I am well, thank you,' she replied prosaically. 'The Earl is resting, but we are to ensure he is not alone until tomorrow.'

'Yes, Tom has just told me. He intends to sit with him all night, and so is having a quick meal before resting for a few hours. He says we are to entertain the guests at dinner and arrange for Jack's valet to sit with him this evening.'

'His valet? The chap who turned green when anything difficult was to be done for Jack? I think not.'

Nell frowned. 'Then you think we should remain with him instead?'

'For tonight, yes—because of the laudanum. From tomorrow the valet can take on his care.' She glanced at Jack, noting that he was sweating again. Dipping the cloth in the tepid water, she reapplied it to his forehead. 'You may do whatever you believe to be right, Nell, but I intend to stay here until Tom takes over.'

'All evening? But—'

'The Earl remains seriously ill. I cannot have it on my conscience to leave him. Why, anything might occur!'

Nell bit her lip. 'You are right, of course. I shall stay with you. But who then will accompany Mr Harting and Mr Carmichael at dinner?'

Cecily thought it through. 'Tom is right, you must go to dinner. As hostess, you cannot abandon your duties.'

'Mr Harting and Mr Carmichael have already offered to leave on the morrow, as the household will likely be all disorder until Jack is better. So it is only tonight that we must plan for.'

'Can you stay here for ten minutes while I wash and change?'

'I must speak to Cook first but then, yes, I can replace you. But…' her brow creased in puzzlement '…why should you do this? Jack is nothing to you, after all. Surely it is *my* responsibility as…' Her voice tailed away and her eyes widened.

Cecily eyed her evenly.

'Cecily!' Nell's jaw dropped. 'You—'

'Hush!' There was a possibility that the Earl could hear

them. Drawing Nell to the door, she hissed, 'Please, do not say anything!'

'But I must!' Nell took both her hands. 'You…have an affection for Jack?'

'Affection? I suppose you could call it that.'

'And what would you call it?'

'A conflagration. An explosion. A multitude of fireworks. A sickness. A miracle. An obsession. A desire to shield him from all harm. A need to ensure his happiness.'

'Oh, Cecily! You love him!'

Cecily nodded grimly. Hearing it said aloud reminded her how hopeless it was to love a man such as Jack, who denied he even needed to love and be loved. 'I do. He does not, however, love me in return—or at least he has not said so. Now, please send Molly to my room and tell her I shall be there in a few minutes. There is something I should like to ask her.'

'Even if he does not love you yet, dear Cecily, he must come to do so in time.' Nell hugged her fiercely, then departed.

Three days after his accident, the Earl declared himself bored with the surgeon's advice and rose from his bed. He was relieved to discover that Harting and Carmichael had indeed departed, for he knew himself to be irritable and frustrated by his injuries, and in no fit state for company. Tom and his valet had fussed over him as though he were a hatchling, and he had not seen the ladies since the night of the accident. Cecily had sat with him until midnight, he had been informed, refusing to give way to Nell, and had waited steadfastly until Tom had taken over for the nightwatch.

He owed them all a debt of gratitude, and his newly-found insight did not prevent him from being guiltily grumpy. Could he read anything into Cecily's devoted care of him? Probably not, for she was so good that she would likely have done just the same for Harting or Carmichael. Jealousy flared as he briefly imagined her leaning over Harting, pressing cool cloths to his brow and speaking in a soft voice to him.

Well, Harting was gone and he, Jack, remained. Tom and the ladies had postponed their plans for London, giving Jack an extra week in which to woo Lady Cecily.

How does one woo?

He had no idea. He could not imagine himself smiling giddily at her or writing poetry. All of the actions he associated with men wooing women seemed stupid, foolish, pointless. Yet he *wished* to woo her, wished to ask her if perhaps, someday, there might be a chance that she might consider…

Lord, here is a fix!

Instead, on his first morning downstairs he chose a moment when Tom and Nell were engaged in private conversation and offered her the opportunity to review Carmichael's business proposal. It was all he could think to do.

'Then—you have not yet decided whether to invest in this project?' She was looking remarkably pretty today, he noted, her pale green dress displaying her perfect figure, while the spring sunshine through the casement lit up her blonde hair and her sparkling amber eyes.

'Not at all, for Carmichael wrote down the details only that morning. I have not yet studied his information.' He rose to fetch Carmichael's workings from the side table, ignoring the jarring pain in his shoulder. He was in shirt and breeches, with his jacket hung awkwardly over his shoulders and his left arm still in its sling. He felt underdressed and unsure of himself.

Scanning his friend's scrawl with narrowed eyes, he

commented, 'Lady Cecily, I will surely need your assistance. While I can see most things, I confess Carmichael's penmanship is challenging my vision.' Indeed his eyesight was not yet fully returned to normal, with a faint blurring around the edges of his vision and a definite tiredness when he tried to read.

She took the paper, their fingers touching. Had that been deliberate? He could not know. What was beyond doubt, however, was the sparkle in the glance she threw him before dropping her eyes to Carmichael's proposal.

Despite being decidedly unromantic, his approach may have been the right one for he and Cecily spent the next several hours poring over Carmichael's figures and reviewing the arguments for and against.

'I am so glad that you have shared this with me,' was her pointed comment, but he took it as a good sign that her eyes shone, and that she gave him *such* a look.

I must not make assumptions, he reminded himself.

Tom, naturally, had joined in the business debate, while Nell watched them all, fascinated. In the end they decided collectively that Carmichael was to be disappointed, for the plan, on closer inspection, did not look viable. Having the ladies involved also smoothed over any remaining awkwardness between Tom and himself. It was good to be in charity with his brother again.

There were limitations in the aftermath of his foolish accident, too. Nell and Tom seemed always to be there, hovering over him as though he were on his deathbed, so he had no opportunity to speak privately with Cecily.

Of course, he had no idea if Cecily even wished to be alone with him. If anything, she was more reserved now than she had been, and he had difficulty in reading how she was feeling most of the time. She had taken to venturing out walking in the mornings, with only Molly the housemaid for company, and he could never rest until he saw her back again. How quickly she had become the centre of his world! He shook his head slowly. The entire situation was slowly driving him to madness.

Chapter Twenty-Eight

Two more days passed, and still Jack had not declared himself. Indeed, he had no notion how he might do so. Confidence that she might return his feelings had slowly leeched out of him, and he was also now half-convinced she deserved better than a broken soul such as he, regardless. So it was with mixed feelings that he agreed to Nell's suggestion of a walk through the village.

'We might even reach the top of Thursley Hill, if you are well enough, brother, for the day is clear and mild.' Tom joined in immediately, arousing his suspicions that they had made this plan when he had not been present.

'An excellent idea!' Cecily's reply was rather more enthusiastic than the topic warranted.

Do they think me slow to recover? I was never invalidish!

The notion stung, so naturally he declared himself as fit as a fiddle, with only the mildest twinges in his various wounds.

In fact, he knew himself to be healing well. The head wound had suffered no infection, his eyesight had fully returned, the shoulder pain decreased by the day and his injuries, according to the surgeon, were likely to continue to mend well, as long as he maintained his sling and did not do anything foolish.

They set off after nuncheon, and before long Tom and Nell had walked ahead. This was entirely predictable, and it also gave Jack and Cecily the chance for a degree of privacy for the first time since his accident. She was wearing an elegant pelisse in a warm red and a poke bonnet tied with a red ribbon under one ear. It framed her beautiful face to perfection—to the extent that Jack found himself forced to *not* look at her lest he betray himself with spontaneous poetic compliments. The very notion was mortifying.

He himself had donned a warm cloak over his shirt and waistcoat. At least he *looked* whole to any passer-by. He was pleased to find himself fit enough for the walk, with only the ache in his left shoulder to remind him of his self-induced injuries. He and Cecily chatted idly and easily as they approached the village.

Ahead, Tom and Nell paused, and a quick glance confirmed them to be embracing. This time Jack's reaction had more envy than irritation in it.

Cecily was quick to note his glance. 'They really do love each other, you know. I admit I had concerns that their marriage was too hasty, but I have been reassured during my time here.'

He grunted, unwilling at that moment to admit how wrong he had been. Naturally, she did not let him get away with it.

'Well?' She stopped walking and turned to face him, hand on hip and her tone of voice decidedly challenging.

'What is it you wish me to say?'

'I wish you to admit what you already know!'

That I love you? That I am unworthy of you? That I am

envious of the love my brother shares with his Nell? That my heart will break when you leave Hazledene?

The thoughts tumbled through his mind. Ignoring them, he said only, 'Very well, I accept that they are a reasonable match.'

She made a strangled sound of frustration. 'Sometimes, my lord, I believe you delight in vexing me. They are not simply a "reasonable match". They *love* each other. I should like to hear you admit it.'

Love? His every thought in her presence centred on it, yet his tongue struggled to speak it. Old fears rose within him again, yet he forced himself to speak. He could give her this, at least.

'Love is not something that comes easily to me. I love my brother, naturally, but love between a man and a woman has always evaded my understanding.' There. That sounded rational. It also had the benefit of being the truth.

'But why?' Her voice was low, but it was clear she was not prepared to change the topic.

'Because,' he shot back, looking dead ahead, 'women leave.' As his words landed in both their hearts, his face crumpled. He took a deep breath, then sighed with a strange sense of relief. Finally he had spoken, sharing the deepest secret of his heart. Now, seeing his brokenness, would she leave him?

His words reverberated through Cecily like thunder. 'Women leave,' he repeated, this time quietly. He turned to eye her directly, the sorrow of twenty years clearly visible in his expression. 'Mama died. Tilly left. I needed them, and they went away.'

Cecily could hardly bear it. There in front of her was the seven-year-old child still living inside the man. She could see him in Jack's stricken expression. The hurt, lonely boy he had been had shaped the man before her now. 'Jack,' she said softly. 'Your mama did not *wish* to leave you. And your nurse did not want to leave you either.'

His lip curled. 'You are determined to see the best in people, are you not? But on this occasion you are mistaken. My rational mind understands that my mama did not wish to die, but my nurse was quite another matter. As I have already told you, she had a good position with our family, but she left because she was offered a more lucrative post elsewhere. She departed from Hazledene, in fact, as the family were in residence here at the time. It is partly why my attachment to this place is so complicated.' He shook his head. 'I was away at school when she left, so it was something of a shock to arrive at Hazledene and find her gone.' His tone hardened. 'I shall own that I now understand much better the considerations of money, and how more is always better. Always. At the time I had a childish view of such things, and could not see beyond my need of her. A hard lesson learned, but never forgotten.'

Cecily bit her lip. This conversation was not proceeding as she had hoped. Reminders of Tilly might harden his resistance to love, rather than open his heart. Still, if there was to be any healing of this inner wound, it had to be exposed to the light, and cleaned. And she had one card yet to play. She took a breath. 'Yes, I remember you spoke to me before of Tilly, your old nurse. Miss Tillot was her full name, was it not?'

He paused, his jaw slackening briefly. 'Yes. How did you discover her surname?' His tone was clipped. 'Regardless, I do not wish to speak of her.'

'I understand, but I must ask you to indulge me today. After this conversation, I promise not to mention her again if you wish it.' She must tread carefully. He was showing her his wounds and might withdraw at any time.

He sighed. 'Very well.'

'After our previous conversations, I was curious about her. I took the liberty of discussing her with some of the Hazledene servants.'

'You did *what*?' He looked furious, so she pressed on hastily.

'I know that it was impertinent of me, and forward, and that your old nurse is none of my concern, but I discovered some interesting information about the time when she went away.'

They were now in the only street in the village. The cobbles were dusty following almost a week of dry weather, the shops had shut, and the villagers were all likely preparing for their evening meal. The street was empty, so they continued untroubled past the haberdasher's, the butcher's and the general store, before climbing the slight incline past the fifteenth-century church where they had attended Sunday service not so long ago.

With a silent nod to the church, and a plea for help in her task, Cecily and Jack took the left fork after the church, where the road climbed towards Thursley Hill. Cecily was now much more familiar with local geography, due to her recent walks with Molly. While she had yet to climb to the hilltop, she had walked this way on a number of occasions.

Once Nell and Tom had again passed out of sight in front of them, Cecily returned to the subject of Tilly. 'I discovered that your nurse, Miss Tillot, did indeed leave your father's employ that Christmas. I am told, indeed, that she left on the very day you were expected home from school.'

'I know this already, Lady Cecily. Why are you persisting in bringing up painful memories? Is it your intention to punish me in some way?' His tone was flat, emotionless, but his message was clear.

'Oh, no! Please, believe me, I could never knowingly cause you distress. Indeed, it is because of my—my regard for you that I wished to discover the circumstances of Miss Tillot's departure.'

'Your *regard* for me?' He raised a quizzical eyebrow. 'Do tell me more of this regard.'

She sniffed. 'You do not deserve to hear of it,' she declared, her chin lifted defiantly. 'But suffice to say that, despite your arrogance, your boorishness, your pride—'

'And *this* is regard?' he murmured. 'Remind me, Lady Cecily, never to ask you to outline my faults.'

'*Despite* your faults,' she continued ruthlessly, 'of which there are many, I continue to foolishly hold some liking for you. No.—' She held up a gloved hand. 'I refuse to elaborate. I wish to continue to speak of Miss Tillot.'

'Very well,' he conceded, a welcome glint of humour in his eye. 'But we shall return to this conversation very soon. Pray continue.'

She nodded graciously. 'At first, I was given the same tale that you were told—that Miss Tillot had left to take up a more lucrative position elsewhere. But I noticed something strange about the reactions of the various people I spoke to.'

'Which was?' He still looked disinterested, she noted, but she had no doubt that the boy inside was desperately gripped by their discourse. Reaching for her reticule, she closed her hand around the little figure inside, as if it would give her strength. She had gently retrieved it from the sleeping Earl's hand the night of his accident, just before ceding her place to Tom for his night vigil.

'None of them could say where exactly she had gone.

There was no mention of London, or Tonbridge, or Sevenoaks. Yet, if the servants had been telling the truth, surely one of them would have remembered where this lucrative posting was, or who her new employers were?'

'You believe they were lying?' His eyes had narrowed, and there was a decided crease between his brows.

'I do. And so I determined to persist with my questions until I uncovered the truth.' The gaps between the houses were widening as the road climbed, the spaces around them punctuated by gorse, heather and spring wildflowers, their colours unnaturally bright in the twilight glow. 'It was Molly who finally admitted that you were lied to.'

He stopped, looking thunderstruck. 'Tell me.'

She took a breath and nodded, then walked on, keeping half an eye on the various cottages they were passing. He walked with her, eyeing her curiously.

'Miss Tillot did not *choose* to leave.'

She waited, watching him closely. He frowned, then his eyes widened briefly as he worked it out. 'Damnation! My father turned her off?'

She nodded, laying a sympathetic hand on his arm. 'I am sorry to say that he did. Miss Tillot was reportedly distraught and attempted to appeal with him on the basis that you and Tom had need of her.'

His face had turned noticeably pale. 'We did.' He paused, considering, then his eyes widened. 'Which is exactly why my father wanted her gone.'

Tears sprang to her eyes. 'I am so, so sorry, Jack. The servants were horrified but did not wish to drive further distance between your father and you two boys. They agreed together to repeat the lies that your father put about. They told you that she had left of her own volition, for the sake of a higher wage. In later years, they did not think it of importance that you should know, for neither you nor Tom ever mentioned her.'

'But that was because—'

She laid her hand over his. 'I know. It hurt to remember her, did it not?'

He nodded grimly, then rage spread across his face. 'That man! I had known his cruelty, but this!' They continued walking, but now his right hand was fisted by his side, his entire frame had stiffened, and he was staring off into the middle distance.

Moved beyond measure, she stopped, until he did, too. Moving close to him, she gently touched his face, wishing her hand was gloveless. 'Jack, my lord, do you wish me to stop?'

He looked directly at her, and the pain she saw in his expression was almost her undoing. 'There is more?' he croaked.

She nodded, and they walked on again. 'Miss Tillot was given only a week's wage when your father turned her off, and she had—she had nowhere to go.'

He blinked slowly, swallowing hard, and she could see his jaw was tightly clenched. Out of the corner of her eye she could see that the next cottage on the right had a single, smoking chimney, and that the front door had been painted a fading pale blue. At this point, she knew it well.

She stopped walking again and turned to him. 'She apparently travelled to Tonbridge, where she tried unsuccessfully to find work. Within a month she was destitute, and was forced to seek a place in the workhouse. There she lived for the next five years, and it is reported that she became dangerously thin and that her health failed.'

'Did she die there? Tell me the truth, Cecily. If so then he murdered her! It was nothing less than murder!' His voice cracked. 'She, who should have been cared for by our family after all she had done for us! She should have been allowed to remain as our nurse until we were grown, then given a generous pension and a secure cottage as she aged. She was not old when she disappeared, as I recall.'

'Indeed. I am told she was not yet fifty when she left Hazledene.'

'So what happened to her? Do you know?' His right hand was on her arm, and she could tell from its grip that he was overcome by strong emotion.

'I do. Someone from Hazledene village had occasion to visit the workhouse and recognised her. Word was brought back, and there was, apparently, outrage among the villagers and the house servants about her plight. However, they all feared your father, so were frightened to openly aid her.'

'My father, the tyrant.' He nodded grimly. 'I understand that.'

'The vicar co-ordinated a charitable collection, and they were able to rescue her from her dire situation. Each person pledged to pay a shilling each month to support her, and with the money they were able to provide her with food, and clothes, and a small rented home.'

'I am shamed by the good people of Hazledene, who have showed more goodness than I ever have.'

'No! That is not the lesson you must take from this! How could you have known of her situation? You are also a good person!'

He shook his head slowly. 'I am not. I have been consumed by anger, and bitterness, and fear. I am, at heart, a selfish tyrant. Just like my papa before me!'

'But no!' This conversation was not proceeding in the way she had hoped. 'You—'

'Tell me,' he interrupted her, his tone harsh. 'Was Miss Tillot still alive when my father died?'

'Yes. In fact—'

'So why did they not come to me? Why did they not tell me the truth then and ask me to care for her? Why did they maintain the lies? *Why*, Cecily?'

Her gaze dropped. 'I do not know. I—'

'We both know. It is because they know me to be cut from the same cloth as my father. Harsh, selfish, unfeeling, ruthless. I could not be trusted with the truth.'

She eyed him directly. 'That is how you like to be seen, yes. But that is not who you truly are.'

He snorted. 'Oh, spare me the false compliments. I do not judge the villagers, or my servants. I have spent my life focused on building the family wealth. All else was secondary. Why should they think I even had a heart?'

'And yet I know that you do. You have a strong heart, a heart capable of generosity, of pain, of love.'

Now was the time to tell him the final part of the story she had unearthed. 'Jack,' she began softly, 'the woman who dwells in this cottage has not seen you for many years.' She indicated the small stone house to her right. 'Perhaps it is time you saw her again.'

His head turned swiftly, then turned back towards her, shock and incredulity apparent in his expression. 'Tilly?'

She nodded, unable to speak. Taking the knight from her reticule, she offered it to him. His hand closed around it and he squeezed his eyes tightly shut for a moment. He slipped it into his watch pocket then stepped towards the gate, pausing for Cecily to catch up. With a gesture she indicated he should go ahead.

He knocked on the door then after a moment cautiously opened it to call inside. An answering voice came, barely audible to Cecily. After a brief exchange of conversation he stepped inside. A moment later Cecily heard a crash, as of china breaking on a stone floor, followed by exclamations of delight. She smiled, her heart singing, then waited.

After a few moments she approached the door and gave a cautious knock.

'Come in, come in, Lady Cecily!'

She did so, her eyes adjusting to the dim interior. They were seated close together on Tilly's small settle. Shards from a broken plate littered the floor. The old lady's face was beaming, and wet with tears. Jack had also had to make use of his handkerchief. Wordlessly, he held out his right hand to Cecily. Tears misting her vision, she stepped forward and took it.

'Tilly, how do you?'

'Ah, Lady Cecily, I shall never be able to thank you! Just to see my Jack again! I shall die happy now.' Tilly's smile was bigger than the universe, and just as beautiful.

'You will do no such thing, for I expect you to live happily for many, many years first!' Jack smiled at Tilly, and Cecily's heart ached to see the love shining between the two of them. 'You shall have a well-appointed cottage, as large as you like, and a good pension, and all the luxuries you desire! Or you may come to live at Springfield, if it suits you better.'

Tilly's jaw dropped. 'My lord! I had not sought any such thing! I—'

'Of course I know that, Tilly. Nevertheless, you shall have whatever you desire. And in the meantime, would you do me the great honour of joining us for dinner at Hazledene tomorrow night?'

Anxiety creased her kind face. 'Oh, but I could not, my lord. I—'

'Please, call me Jack.'

Jack.

His name on her own tongue, Cecily recognised the

power of him giving Tilly this honour. Unlike the Earl, however, she understood Tilly's reluctance.

'Tilly,' she began, 'there will be only Jack and Tom, along with me and Tom's wife, Nell, at dinner. And you will love Nell!'

Tilly dabbed her eyes again. 'To see my Tomkin again! But I cannot possibly...'

'I believe,' offered Cecily, 'that the haberdasher has a good stock of silks and bombazines, and his wife is said to be a skilled dressmaker. And with a sizeable pension— which is, of course, yours by right—you can afford to dress again in the manner that befits your true station.'

'My true station?' She looked bewildered. Jack and Cecily exchanged a glance, and the emotion in his gaze burned through her.

'Yes,' he affirmed, then cleared his throat. 'I remember well how my mama valued you. Had she lived, I have no doubt you would have remained a highly valued member of our household. You would have eaten well, slept easy and worn good clothing every day of your life. I expect you would have been promoted to her lady's companion, for I think you had already occupied that place in her heart.' His brow furrowed. 'I must again apologise, Tilly. I am so, so sorry. I did not know—'

'Hush now, child.' She patted his hand. 'Lady Cecily has told me the whole, and there is to be no blame on your part. All of this is your father's work. What was done is done.'

'You are too good,' he croaked. 'Both of you.'

The sorrow in his gaze made her heart turn over.

'I do not know what I have done to earn such good fortune, particularly after all my coldness these many years.'

'Stop, now, Jack. I shall hear no more of this.' Tilly spoke firmly, and a sudden grin broke across Jack's face.

'Yes, Tilly.'

'Now, I need some time to consider what I must do. If I can get a suitable dress, I shall gladly join you for dinner one of these evenings. As to whether I live in a cottage or at Springfield itself, I do not know.' She tilted her head to one side. 'Do Tom and his wife have children?'

'They only married at the start of the year.'

She nodded, then glanced speculatively at Cecily. 'And what of you, Jack? I hope you are not so lost to common sense that you cannot see what is in front of your nose!'

He stood, a slight flush along his cheekbones. 'May I return tomorrow, with Tom?'

'You may.' She inclined her head graciously. Despite the poverty of her simple surroundings, at that moment Tilly held more quiet dignity than the grandest duchess.

He kissed her cheek then embraced her, holding her gently with his one good arm. Cecily glanced away, unwilling to intrude on their renewed tears. She knew what they were made of, those tears. Sadness for the lost years. Happiness for the reunion. Relief for the opportunity to heal a deep wound.

She, too, hugged Tilly. They had come to a good understanding since she had started visiting with Molly, almost a week ago. 'Thank you,' Tilly whispered in her ear. Cecily gently squeezed her hand, then straightened and looked at Jack.

He held out his arm and she slipped her hand under his elbow. She looked up at him, and he looked down at her, and everything she wished to see was shining in his eyes.

Outside it was surprisingly bright, causing Jack to blink in confusion. The scene looked just the same as when they had gone inside, yet the whole world had shifted.

There was, naturally, no sign of Nell and Tom, and so

by unspoken agreement Jack and Cecily took the uphill path, walking briskly in an attempt to catch up with the other couple.

Both were silent. Cecily seemed to be concentrating furiously on her own thoughts. Jack's mind, too, was racing.

As well it might, for I have just sustained something of a shock.

A good shock, but a shock nevertheless.

Tilly lives! Tilly did not leave me! Cecily brought her back to me.

His mind was reeling, struggling to understand it all.

A few moments later they reached the top. Tom and Nell were there, to their left, but Jack, after waving to his brother, led Cecily to another part of the hilltop. 'This is my favourite view,' he murmured, 'especially at this time of day.'

She eyed him in puzzlement. 'Should we not tell Tom about—?'

'We can tell him later. I want to—to *know* it myself first. To believe it, and feel it, and let the *knowing* settle into my bones. Does that make sense?'

She nodded. 'It makes perfect sense.'

They quietened, standing together and breathing in the spectacular scenery. Now that his eyesight had fully returned, he found himself glorying in hitherto unnoticed visual beauty. Like Cecily's face. Like this sky. The sun was slowly sinking, sending golden sunset tones glowing upwards into pale blue. It was now only an hour till sunset, and the light was taking on a mystical quality.

His heart swelled with fullness. Standing here with Cecily, the beautiful colours of a spring sunset spreading around her like a halo, he knew he could never have a more perfect moment. Yet the shadows within him could not be denied. The armour that had kept him safe for so long was being ripped apart, and all he could do was survive it, open and exposed.

He reached for her hand and she gave it, steadying him in a world that seemed to rock alarmingly.

Cecily!

Reaching for one another, they embraced—the most natural, inevitable, *required* kiss in his entire life. It was a kiss full of everything he was feeling and yet could not yet say. His eyes closed, he tasted the warmth of her, felt the glow of the setting sun envelop them, knew his heart was painfully, tentatively opening.

After a few moments they separated to open their eyes and gaze at one another. As the glow of their embrace began to settle gently, Cecily took a breath, then eyed him directly. 'You said that women leave.'

'I did.' His gut was twisting, as old beliefs and new knowledge warred within him.

'You rejected the notion of loving women. Of trusting women. Because of Tilly and your mama.'

He nodded, his stomach twisting with anxiety, yet he knew he must endure this conversation. Beyond the pain, there was the possibility of happiness as golden as the sunset.

Bracing himself, he focused on her every word.

It is time.

Cecily, her heart still pounding from the most beautiful kiss she had ever known, knew that it was the right time. Time for her to press him, to force him into saying what she knew to be true. She knew she still had work to do. The door to his heart was ajar, and she had to prise it open before it shut again.

Still keeping hold of his right hand, she looked directly at him. Daringly, she continued to repeat some of his earlier words. 'You rejected the notion of loving women. Of trusting women. Because of Tilly and your mama.'

He nodded then simply gazed at her, seemingly stunned into silence. Emboldened, she continued. 'You do love Tom. I have seen it. Seen the evidence of it in so many ways. Even when you were behaving atrociously towards me when first we met, it was because you were trying to protect him. You admitted earlier that you love him.'

He could not deny it. She pressed on. 'But you also loved your mama. You will, I think, love Nell before long. And you love Tilly. You always have. And Tilly never stopped loving you.'

He cleared his throat. 'I know that now, but for most of my life I thought otherwise.'

'But you acknowledge that you love her? You have found that love still residing within you.'

'Yes.' It was almost a whisper.

She took a breath. *Say it.*

'And you love me.' He looked at her helplessly, seemingly lost in her gaze and her words. 'I feel it, and I sense your reluctance to admit to it. You do not like it. You may think yourself unworthy. You fear love.' She laid her hand on his arm again. 'You fear that if you surrender to your love for me, I might leave you.'

'Yes.' The word was the merest whisper, yet her heart leapt. 'Yes.' His voice was stronger. 'Hearing the words spoken aloud, it seems foolish that I should feel this. Everything I know of you tells me of your goodness, your endurance, your loyalty.'

'So…?' This was the final line of the riddle. Could he decipher it?

'So… I need to trust you.'

'Yes.'

'Yes.'

He reached for her with his one good arm, and they shared the gentlest of kisses. Opening her eyes, Cecily allowed a slow smile to grow on her face. His smile, radiant with love, matched it and more.

'Will you marry me, Cecily?' His voice was a little ragged. 'You already know that I am unworthy of you, but—'

'Hush!' She stopped his lips with a finger. 'Yes, I shall marry you. If Mama and my guardian agree, naturally.'

'They will agree.' He kissed her again, before pulling back to stare deeply into her eyes. 'Then you truly love me?'

'I do.'

'That seems incredible to me.' He kissed her again. 'And I love you. I intend to tell you so a hundred times a day, until you believe it.'

She laughed happily, relief and joy coursing through her. 'Oh, I already suspected that you loved me! I worked it out these past days since your accident—or, at least, I believed I had. Until you confirmed it just now, it might have simply been my own imaginings running away with me.' She grinned, happiness flooding through her like sunlight. They kissed again, more deeply, a kiss where unspoken feelings were exchanged, promises made, and passion shared.

Breathing heavily, they paused, his chin resting on the top of her head. After a moment she leaned back to see him properly. Once again, they smiled at each other.

A loud cough from over to the left made them both turn. Tom and Nell were approaching, both grinning.

'Tom, you may wish me happy!'

'Ah, Jack, finally you have come to your senses!' Tom punched his brother's right arm playfully, and they both grinned, while Cecily and Nell embraced, laughing together in happy excitement.

As the sun slipped even lower in the sky, they set off for home, Jack and Cecily leading the way. As they passed Tilly's cottage they grinned at each other, knowing they would have yet more good news to share with Tom later.

They stopped to kiss three times between the hilltop and the village, ignoring the teasing comments from the others.

'We must appear as besotted as Tom and Nell.' Cecily twinkled at Jack. Would the comparison make him regret his proposal, even fleetingly? She rather thought not.

He laughed. 'It is true. I have just calculated that it is a little over a month since I was so rude to you on Lady Jersey's terrace. I berated Tom for falling in love so quickly, yet now that it has happened to me, I understand completely. I care not what the world thinks. I love you, I shall always love you, and we shall be married just as soon as it can be arranged.' He bent his head to kiss her. 'I could not be more happy, Cecily, for I am surely the luckiest man who ever lived.'

Cecily murmured an appropriate reply, inwardly committing this day to her memory.

The sunset, the kisses, his words, the knowledge of the future they would share.

There was no other word to describe it.

It was perfect.

* * * * *